PENGUIN BOOKS

Play to Kill

Play to Kill

P. J. TRACY

PENGUIN BOOKS

PENGUIN BOOKS

Published by the Penguin Group
Penguin Books Ltd, 80 Strand, London WC2R ORL, England
Penguin Group (USA) Inc., 375 Hudson Street, New York, New York 10014, USA
Penguin Group (Canada), 90 Eglinton Avenue East, Suite 700, Toronto, Ontario, Canada M4P 2Y3
(a division of Pearson Penguin Canada Inc.)
Penguin Ireland, 25 St Stephen's Green, Dublin 2, Ireland (a division of Penguin Books Ltd)
Penguin Group (Australia), 250 Camberwell Road, Camberwell, Victoria 3124, Australia
(a division of Pearson Australia Group Pty Ltd)
Penguin Books India Pvt Ltd, 11 Community Centre, Panchsheel Park, New Delhi – 110 017, India
Penguin Group (NZ), 67 Apollo Drive, Rosedale, Auckland 0632, New Zealand
(a division of Pearson New Zealand Ltd)
Penguin Books (South Africa) (Pty) Ltd, 24 Sturdee Avenue, Rosebank,
Johannesburg 2196, South Africa

Penguin Books Ltd, Registered Offices: 80 Strand, London WC2R ORL, England

www.penguin.com

First published as *Shoot to Thrill* in the USA by G. P. Putnam's Sons 2010
First published as *Play to Kill* in Great Britain by Michael Joseph 2010
Published in Penguin Books 2011
001

Printed in England by Clays Ltd, St Ives plc

ISBN: 978-1-405-91044-6

www.greenpenguin.co.uk

ALWAYS LEARNING   **PEARSON**

Prologue

From top to bottom and everywhere in between, Minnesota was a bleak and frigid place in January, whether you were shivering on a blizzard-swept western prairie or paralyzed under a foot of snow smack in the middle of Minneapolis. But there was no greater sense of winter desolation than on the north shore of Lake Superior, where the big water that looked like an ocean was forever pushing enormous blocks of sharded ice against one shore or another.

The past two weeks had been particularly cruel to the lake. A parade of low-pressure systems had stalled, battling each other for command of the winds, freezing the great body of water almost to the horizon line. It was profoundly disturbing to see something so powerful completely subdued, like King Kong in chains on a Broadway stage.

Randy Coulter had a lot of empathy for the lake, because he knew what it felt like to be the helpless victim of a greater force, trapped by circumstances he was powerless to change. But that was the old Randy – the new, improved Randy finally had the power to make things happen. And if he could muster the guts, he'd make something happen today.

The trail on the edge of the cliff provided spectacular winterscape views for the snowshoers and cross-country skiers who frequented the winter resorts along the shore, and their numbers were legion in the week between Christmas and New Year's. City dwellers accustomed to the protective environment of crosswalks and guardrails flocked to the north in a foolish fit of adventure, where you actually had to rely on your own good sense instead of the nanny state to keep you safe.

Randy slipped out of his snowshoes and off the groomed trail, testing each step toward the edge of the cliff with a pole to make sure there was frozen earth beneath the wind-swept snow. The closer he got to the lip of eternity, the colder the wind that blew on his face. He began to despair, thinking that no would-be athlete would venture out on such a day, when the barometer rose and the temperatures plummeted. They were all inside their cozy cabins and resort rooms, frolicking in hot tubs or drinking in front of a fire, and Randy would be the only soul to see this cliff today.

He had to drop to the snow on his stomach to safely examine the magnificent sight over fifty feet below him. The shoreline bristled with stalagmites of frozen water that vaulted upward from the shore like monstrous icy teeth, just waiting for something substantial to gnaw on. 'Beautiful,' he whispered.

'Hey. You okay?'

Randy nearly tumbled over the edge at the sound of a male voice behind him, and then looked over his shoulder and saw everything he would never be. From the logo on the Gore-Tex suit he knew immediately that the man drove a foreign sports car and had left a probably augmented blonde woman back in his cabin, and for a moment he felt himself shrink away, curl inside himself, until he remembered the power. 'Thank God,' he said, and the man's waxed brows moved into a frown.

'Are you hurt, buddy? How can I help?'

Randy closed his eyes. 'I think there's a body down there,' he whispered, rising to his feet. 'I didn't know what to do . . .'

'You're kidding.'

'No, really.'

'Jesus Christ.'

'Do you have a cell phone?'

'Sure. Let me get a look first.'

'Okay, but be careful. It's a little slick out here near the edge.'

The man removed his snowshoes, moved cautiously toward the edge and peered over. 'I don't see anything.'

'You have to come further this way. Those ice spikes block the view . . . oh, man, this is horrible, I've never seen anything like this . . .' Randy felt the man's hand come down firmly on his shoulder. Oddly, he found the touch comforting.

'Take it easy, buddy. Just relax, take a breath. It's down there?'

Randy didn't have to fake the tears. They came on their own, and he couldn't imagine why. 'Right . . . down . . . there . . .' he pointed, and when the man leaned forward to follow his finger, Randy locked his knees and braced his legs and pushed against the man's back with all the strength he had.

The wind carried away the prolonged scream as Randy just stood there, looking out toward the horizon, his face expressionless. It might have been seconds or hours when he finally fell to his stomach again and peered over the edge.

It looked like Mr. Gore-Tex was humping one of the ice stalagmites, and Randy thought that was pretty funny.

'I told you there was a body down there,' he whispered, then pulled a tiny video camera out of his parka pocket and hit the zoom button.

Chapter One

Alan squinted hard at his three faces in the Tiara's bathroom mirror, trying without any real success to bring a single reflection into focus. But even with his vision swimming and pixilated by vodka, he could see enough to know he looked like a Picasso portrait of Liza Minnelli. His false eyelashes were drooping like tired spiders, spinning crazy webs of mascara down his cheeks, and his smeared lips looked slightly askew, a scarlet counterbalance for his cockeyed wig that was tipping to the opposite side.

His billowy white dress had also suffered the indignity of his twelve-hour party day, and it was shedding pearls like a vomiting oyster.

He cringed as he tried to tease out snippets of the evening from his memory, but there were a lot of black spots in the matrix. Sweet Jesus Lord Almighty, he was drunk. How many martinis had he had? Two at home, another four or five at Camilla's place for sure, and then there had been an unrelenting succession of those disgusting, tragically pink cocktails here at the club, pushed on him by the new Dominican bartender who'd been so guileless in sharing the various intimate locations of his body piercings.

The thought of needles being poked into certain sensitive areas of a male's anatomy sent his stomach into turmoil, and he leaned over the sink and splashed cold water on his face until the nausea subsided.

When he finally felt sturdy enough, he pushed himself into an upright position and aimed his compass for the nearest exit. The night was young, there were still some A-list parties he was planning to attend, and he needed to sober up before he did, especially if he was going to perform. Fortunately, Camilla had given him the key to her condo, which was just a few blocks away if he went as the crow flies and took the riverside walking path. He'd take a shower, drink some juice, and he'd be up and running again just in time for the drag show.

It was never easy negotiating the path along the Mississippi in four-inch stilettos, even with your sense of equilibrium intact; and it was harder still when you were wearing a fabulous pair of Dolce & Gabbanas you just *had* to have because they were fifty percent off at Neiman's, even though they were a size too big. He'd stuffed the toes with cotton balls and had doubled up some duct tape and put it in the heels, because dancing to 'It's Raining Men' wasn't exactly a minuet, and he needed the extra security. But he was still slipping in and out of them as he half-careened, half-bulldozed down the path, and at one point he stumbled, fell, and came to lying in a nest of damp, putrid-smelling weeds so close to the river, he could hear the hiss of water in his ears.

He could also hear Wild Jim's psychotic, drunken rants echoing in the darkness: 'Crazy faggot! Crazy faggot, crazy queen, fell down and broke his crown!'

Wild Jim was a fixture along this stretch of the Mississippi, and the locals who lived around here knew him every bit as well as the cops did. He was clearly on a superior bender of unknown origin tonight, like almost every other night, and in that regard, the two of them had a lot in common. In fact, Alan felt strangely comforted by the familiar presence, as annoying as it was.

'Yoo-hoo! Jimmy!' he called in his best soprano lilt. 'Where are you? Come here and help Mama up!'

Wild Jim answered with a grunting salvo of unintelligible expletives from somewhere above him on the embankment.

'Puh-leeze, Jimmy,' Alan needled. 'Come help your mama.'

'Stop talking shit. You crazy faggots are messing up my river and always talking shit.'

Alan giggled and stared up at the stars, wondering if he'd ever be able to muster the strength to pull himself up. And in truth, he wasn't sure he wanted to, at least not yet. It did smell down here, and the ground was damp, but it was surprisingly peaceful in this little hollow where the riverbanks absorbed the urban cacophony of the streets above. If Wild Jim would only shut up, he might actually consider taking a little nap right here.

He had no idea how much time had passed before he finally struggled to his feet, and as he did, he heard the rustle of grass coming from somewhere behind him, drawing closer. He hadn't ever expected that Wild Jim would actually show himself – he had a big mouth, but he usually stayed out of sight.

It was a delicious, naughty surprise to feel two powerful

arms scoop him up like a bride. Not a common scenario for gay men meeting by the river for a one-time, anonymous assignation, which was the saddest thing about being a queen. Normally there were no real kings in the circle; no take-you-down-and-have-their-way-with-you romantic heroes, and Alan's girlish heart had always pined for that. How lovely that at last he was the romantic heroine of his imagination. Too bad he was so wasted he'd probably never remember any of this.

He heard the splash when his hero first stepped into the river, but didn't process the implications until he felt himself being lowered into the water. His first thought was for his shoes; his second for his dress; but both of those major tragedies were blasted from the ruins of his mind when the man pushed him to the bottom and pinned him there. Alan held his breath dutifully, looking up through the water, waiting to see what came next in this kinkiest of all encounters.

It wasn't very deep this close to the shore; maybe five inches over his face. Less than half a foot of water between Alan and oxygen. Suddenly that became very important, but by the time he realized that nothing came next, that this was the grand finale, it was too late for his tortured lungs. He struggled mightily, but only for a few seconds before his body told him to gasp, gasp now, and he had no choice but to open his mouth wide and take in his first drink of the Mississippi River. He didn't struggle much after that.

Chapter Two

The auditorium was dimly lit, and very cold. Outside the temperature was reaching for the mid-eighties; in here the air conditioning was set to keep an audience of a thousand comfortable. No one had told the maintenance staff that there would be less than fifty attending this seminar, and now all of them were huddled in the front two rows, freezing whatever body parts were exposed, which, in some cases, were considerable.

Special Agent John Smith was gathering his thoughts just offstage. In his thirty years with the Bureau he'd never given a single speech; never taught a class; never spoken at a press conference; never dealt with the public in multiples. He was a behind-the-scenes workhorse. Most agents were, walking through entire careers without leaving a ripple. He'd interviewed a lot of suspects, of course, but most of them were handcuffed in a locked room – a literal captive audience. And yet here he was, six months out from mandatory retirement, finally facing the prospect of being the sole focus of a crowd's attention, really nervous for the first time in his career.

John Smith's life had always been about as ordinary as his name. His parents loved, but did not spoil, the one and only child they would ever have. And they loved each other, even now, as they grew old and stayed happy in

Florida, where all elderly parents should be sent for their dotage.

He'd been a good kid, smart to a degree, but no genius by anyone's estimation; raised with the strong values that were common back when people had to be civilized enough to deal face-to-face. He was sent on to adulthood with a college education and a middle-class sensibility that would see him through life with only a few potholes along the way.

He'd been in second grade, eight years old, when he'd first learned how to fold a flag; how important it was that it never touched the ground or was left flying after dark or in the rain. These were lessons written into school curriculums then; a learning assignment as important as multiplication tables, although no second-grader could imagine why, or think to question it. They only knew that if they did it properly, they might be chosen to exit the stifling classroom without supervision to lower the flag from its pole at the end of the school day.

Every time he passed a car dealership or a Perkins restaurant that flew those monstrous flags from towering poles, he thought of those second-grade respites from times tables and spelling bees when he and two others who had earned the privilege had been excused from the class to perform the duties of tradition and pomp. The funny thing was that they found something else on that empty playground, where they fled for freedom from the teacher and the confining classroom; something almost spiritual that seeped into your memory without you ever knowing it was there. He still felt the red and white stripes and the stars on the blue field under his fingers all these years later, and that memory had shaped his life.

He did not become the superhero he wanted to be in comic-book kindergarten, not the super agent he'd hoped to be when he first went down the FBI path, but not a failure, either. Just a man in the middle, as most men were. He believed in God, family, his country, and the Constitution, and still, none of that had prepared him for the audience he faced now.

He took his place at the podium and looked out over the motley collection of humanity that was probably the world's only hope of solving this particular case, and a direct reflection of the Bureau's desperation.

There was a cluster of normalcy on one side of the aisle – ten FBI agents dressed in the customary suit and tie, all sitting together in one section. Paul Shafer, the Minneapolis special agent in charge, sat on the aisle seat of that group, looking self-righteously indignant to be present at a seminar where the law and law-breakers shared the same space. Smith had to hold back the nasty smile. Shafer was still young enough and gung-ho enough to believe he'd be part of this exclusive, frighteningly powerful club of suits forever. Wait until he found out the FBI's sell-by date crept up a whole lot faster than he'd thought it would.

Then again, because a little gung-ho of his own still gasped for breath every now and then, Smith could almost sympathize with Shafer's discomfort when he looked on the other side of the aisle. There were young and old, body piercings and tattoos, a few beardless boys who looked like they'd just walked off the set of *Revenge of the Nerds*, and a lot of people who sported tank tops and hairy armpits – men and women both. And these were the normal ones. Monkeewrench was in the back, isolated from the rest, which was fine with him. He'd deal with them tomorrow. They'd agreed to host a panel in one of the smaller, closed rooms, but Grace MacBride had flatly refused to get up on a lit stage.

'Most of you have an understandable reluctance to work with the FBI,' he began, looking over the audience with a very slight smile. 'Probably because most of you break several Federal laws on a regular basis.' Nervous laughter from the audience. 'Oddly enough, this is why you were asked here today. Your hacking ventures have brought you to our attention, won you an FBI file of your own, and, legality aside, your skills have impressed us. Now we need your help tracing an anonymous, extremely sophisticated network operating through several foreign proxy servers in countries that will not grant the United States access to their servers, which is why our own Cyber Crimes Unit has not been able to trace the users of this network.'

'Dude. Are you seriously asking us to hack into servers in hostile countries so you can catch one of our own? First off, we don't kiss and tell. Second, we could go down for years on something like that.'

John looked at the man who had actually had the guts to stand up and speak. It surprised him that it was one of the nerds, probably 120 pounds soaking wet with a chest that looked like a safe had fallen on it. 'Certainly not. The FBI would never suggest or condone such a violation of international law. We ask only that you use your own unique skills to track this network and find the origination sites of the users.'

'Come on. You know damn well our "own unique skills" happen to be hacking illegally into closed sites. Personally, I already did one-to-three for that, and I'm not about to risk it again.'

A lot of murmuring from the group then, and John couldn't blame them. He had to measure every word, say everything exactly right.

He leaned his arms on the podium and let his eyes travel over every face. 'We trust you all,' he said, and everyone laughed. 'For that reason, we are absolutely certain that we will never have reason to suspect that any of you would violate federal or international law. It would be pointless to waste Bureau time investigating such a possibility. Is that perfectly clear?'

For a moment, everyone went silent. Nobody knew double-speak as well as a really good hacker. Special Agent in Charge Paul Shafer looked like he'd swallowed a toad, which, for some reason, pleased Smith mightily.

'Furthermore,' John continued, 'your efforts will not be expended on catching "one of your own." These people are not identity thieves, spammers, or virus disseminators. These people are cold-blooded killers. They film their murders and post them on the Web for the world to see.'

The lights in the auditorium dimmed further and the screen behind the speaker became illuminated with the introduction to a PowerPoint presentation. The caption read: 'Cleveland, Ohio.'

'What I'm about to show you is a series of five videos

that were pulled from various websites over the past several months. Some of you may have stumbled across these videos before they were pulled from the Web, and even though you now know that these are authentic, please be warned – the images you are about to see are extremely graphic and disturbing. Before we begin, I want to give anybody here who doesn't feel comfortable with viewing such content the opportunity to leave the auditorium now.'

No one in the room moved a muscle.

'The reason we are showing you these films is to highlight the critical importance of tracing the murderers who posted these films. They are still out there, probably still killing, or planning to kill, and we have absolutely no idea who they might be. They are extremely computer proficient. For this reason, I warn you not to discuss this case with fellow hackers who have not been invited to this seminar. If you do, you may unwittingly be talking to one of the killers. All of you here have been thoroughly vetted to the very limits of our resources. Still, we realize that the vetting process is not perfect, and that some of the murderers may be in this room at this very moment.' He paused for effect, pleased to see a few attendees cast sidelong glances at their seatmates.

'Now. The films you're about to see have already been seen by hundreds of thousands of people on the Web, but very few of those people realize that what they were watching was actually real. Nor do they understand that these may not be anomalies, but perhaps the very grim beginning of an unimaginable new cyber crime.'

He tapped some keys on his laptop to roll the first film

but didn't turn around to watch the images. He didn't have to. He knew exactly what was happening on the large screen by the involuntary gasps from his audience.

You had to see a body close-up, touch it with your own hands, to connect with the deadly real loss of a single human from the entire race. Everyone in this room saw murders almost every day. On television, in movies, video games, on computer screens that showed that which was real, and that which was staged. The average person never connected a depiction of death with a human being, and that was more than a problem; it was a moral catastrophe.

'These are real people,' he said in the break between one film and another. 'People who were here one moment, and cruelly torn from the world the next. Please remember that.'

In the very back row, in the darkness under a balcony, Grace MacBride watched the next film and felt her heart take a double beat, because if this couldn't be stopped, it could change everything.

Chapter Three

The thermometer on the sleek black Cadillac read eighty-five degrees when Detectives Leo Magozzi and Gino Rolseth pulled into a slot in the underground garage.

It was a new car, relatively speaking, confiscated from a dealer who'd been smart enough to finance a bells-and-whistles model and too stupid to latch the trunk. A couple of kilos of coke started blowing out behind him on the freeway, leaving a Hansel and Gretel trail right to his front door. Magozzi and Gino had the Caddy on loan from Narcotics for a week until their new bare-bones sedan was delivered.

Gino had pretended disdain when Narcotics made the offer. 'Oh, yeah, sure. Every major dealer in Minneapolis tools around in a Beemer or a Mercedes, and the only one you guys can catch is some low-level incompetent with a stinking Cadillac. Thanks a million. Does this piece of crap have a GPS?'

The guy from Narcotics shrugged. 'If you hadn't beaten your old sedan to a pulp you'd still have a nice ride.'

'The damn thing was three years old and the only thing that worked in it was us.'

'Whatever. Is Angela cooking for Thursday-night poker?'

'Maybe. We'll see how I like the car.'

As it turned out, Gino liked the car just fine. It had GPS,

a working air conditioner, a tricked-out engine, and electric seats with more positions than the *Kama Sutra*. Angela had cooked for Thursday-night poker, and they had the Cadillac for another week.

Magozzi turned off the engine and opened his door. The garage was stifling already, and it was barely eight o'clock. The imposing red block building that was Minneapolis City Hall squatted on top of the garage like a stone comforter, holding the heat and humidity its ventilation system never handled very well on days like this. Gino started mopping his brow immediately.

'This sucks. Let's get back in the car, push the seats on full recline, crank up the air, and plug in some tunes. They'll never find us.'

'Nice talk for a crime fighter.'

'It's too hot to fight crime. You know what I've been thinking? About shifting from homicide over to Water Rescue, just for the summer.'

Magozzi glanced over at his partner's generous paunch. 'What?'

'I just had a really scary visual flash of you in a wet suit.'

Gino gave his protruding belly a fond pat. 'Some women find this profile irresistible.'

'What women?'

'Some women. Somewhere.'

Amazingly, Detective Johnny McLaren had beat them to work and was trolling City Hall like he usually did at least a few times during any given day, looking for scraps of conversation like a dog at a barbeque. It's wasn't that the skinny Irishman had a shortage of friends in the department, but with no life to speak of outside the job, he was chronically lonely. And without the companionship and human contact he craved, he tended to drink a lot off duty, and sometimes he gambled too much. Still, he was one of the sharpest detectives on the force.

He didn't look hungover, but his wardrobe choice made Magozzi think twice about the condition Johnny had been in when he'd dressed himself this morning – he was wearing a terrible blue seersucker suit that had surely been pulled out of the throw-away bin at the Goodwill. With his blue suit, flame-red Irish hair, and Pillsbury Dough Boy complexion, he sort of looked like an American flag. Not that Magozzi was on the *GQ* style radar by any stretch, but Johnny had found a niche for himself in the annals of bad taste.

Next to him, Gino snorted, his train of thought obviously tracking Magozzi's own. 'Jeez, Johnny, there must be a naked homeless guy out there somewhere.'

McLaren gave him an indignant look and brushed an imaginary speck of lint from his puckered sleeve. 'This is the height of sartorial genius, Rolseth. You're looking at a five-foot-four walking chick magnet. See, women are threatened by men who dress better than they do, so you have to look like you don't care.'

'Mission accomplished. I sure as hell hope you aren't wearing that thing in your on-line dating profile or you're never gonna see any action.'

Johnny scowled, looking a little sheepish.

'How's that going, by the way?'

'Sucks. Everybody's looking for Brad Pitt. I signed up for a new one, though. JDate.'

Magozzi lifted his brows. 'You do realize that's a Jewish dating service, don't you?'

'Yeah, I know.'

'And you're Catholic.'

'Well, I'm not having any luck with my tribe, so I figured maybe I could find a nice Jewish girl and convert.'

'Seems like sound reasoning,' Gino said. 'Hey, aren't you supposed to be in Colorado this week?'

'Yeah. But my brother blew his knee doing some weekend-warrior bullshit and had to have surgery, so I canceled my trip.'

'Bummer.'

'Yeah, bummer, but he's a dumbass. Still thinks he's eighteen, and that rock climbing is a good idea. Anyhow, I figure no way I'm going to spend seven days' vacation time listening to him whine. So instead, I'm an even bigger dumbass and decide to take the holiday fund and hit every casino in Minnesota.'

'How'd that work out for you?'

'I'm back here, three days into my vacation, how do you think it worked?'

'Probably better than if you'd put that money into your retirement account.'

'Ain't that the sad truth.'

They heard heavy footfalls echoing in the hall long before they turned a corner and saw Joe Gebeke jogging toward them, all dolled up in his Bomb Squad gear.

McLaren raised a hand in greeting as he approached. 'Hey, buddy. Got an exercise today?'

Joe Gebeke was a big man, and the gear he was wearing

added another fifty pounds, at least. He was already red-faced and sweating, and had yet to step out into the blast furnace outside. Magozzi felt sorry for him.

He paused, gave them all a nod in greeting, then took a second to catch his breath. 'Ninety-nine percent of this job has been an exercise lately. Right now, we got an anonymous tip on a suspicious package in the food court at Maplewood Mall. Last week it was Rosedale Mall.'

'What's going on?' Gino asked.

'Snot-nosed delinquents messing around, thinking they're cute and sucking up tax dollars. They're driving us crazy – last month we had four call-outs at four different high schools during finals week. Now that the school year's over, the little bastards are terrorizing the malls.'

'Did you catch them all?'

'Sure we did. No-brainer. The only good thing about delinquents is they're stupid, thank God. But it's like there's a union or something. Somebody gets busted, another one comes off the bench to take their place. They're just like the pyros who start fires and get their jollies watching fifty thousand acres burn up on the news, thinking they'll never get caught. Look, I gotta run, guys. May be a false alarm, but we have to respond like it was the real deal.'

'Be safe,' McLaren called after him as Joe jogged toward the door.

Magozzi and Gino parted company with McLaren and stopped at Tommy Espinoza's office on the way to Homicide, primarily because Gino had heard the crackle of a bag that sang to him like sirens on a sea cliff.

'Gino, it's eight o'clock in the morning.'

'What's your point? I hear the sound of salt and fat and I obey.'

'Could be a bag of raisins.'

Gino snorted and pushed past him into Espinoza's office, central command for the department's computer division. Tommy looked up from his monitor, his dark Hispanic coloring making his blue eyes strangely intense. Gino always thought they were about the same color as the blue stuff people put in toilet bowls.

'Hey, guys.' He automatically handed Gino a bag of Cheetos.

'Not those. I can never get all that orange stuff off. Angela will find a speck and I'll be busted. Got anything white?'

'Sure. Popcorn, potato chips . . .' Tommy spread his arms expansively toward a metal table that looked like the snack aisle at Cub Foods. 'Rummage away, my friend. *Mi casa, su casa.*'

While Gino went on a cholesterol hunt, Magozzi looked at the monitor Tommy was working on. 'You're on YouTube?'

'Sad, but true. We who serve the public must sometimes walk the sewers. Take a look at this.' He tapped the screen where a streaming video showed five girls beating the crap out of another girl trying to crawl away.

'Jeez. Is that for real?'

'This one is. A lot of the ugly stuff that gets posted is staged – Spielberg wannabes trying to outdo each other – but some of them are the real McCoy.'

Gino walked over to look, his hand deep in a package of potato chips. 'Hey. I saw that on the news. High school girls from someplace advertising stupid. They put that girl in the hospital, then they posted it with all their faces showing. How dumb is that?'

'Thank God for the dumb ones. The Brits are having a ball monitoring these sites, ID'ing the idiot perps then heading right for their digs like they had a written invitation. But every now and then, a smart one surfaces, and that's when it gets really scary. Take a look at this. This is Cleveland, four months ago.' He fiddled with the mouse until a new video appeared, this one showing a man from the back, beating another one on the ground.

'Jesus,' Gino said. 'Why the hell do the servers let this kind of shit on the Web, and why the hell aren't we shutting them down? My kids could see this, for God's sake.'

'Take it easy, buddy,' Tommy passed him a Butterfinger as if that would cure everything. 'Don't kill the messenger. YouTube and all the rest of them screen like crazy; they've even got software in place with certain words and symbols, like the swastika, tagged so a screener can do an eyes-on assessment. Trouble is, no bad words or symbols, no alarm for an eyes-on, and that's how stuff like the Cleveland film slips through. They only caught it because it had so many hits, which is another alarm tag, but by that time over a hundred thousand had seen it.'

Gino was not comforted. 'Then why aren't they looking at every single post before they let it on site?'

'Because they get millions of them. The volume is crippling. No way they can look at them all.'

'Arrest a couple of CEOs and I bet they'll find a way to look at them all.'

Tommy shook his head. 'You can't lock up the mailman for delivering kiddie porn, Gino. He doesn't know what's in the package.'

Gino put down the potato chip bag, a measure of his distress. 'Damnit, Leo, I told you we should have stayed in the car. This is really depressing. How bad did he hurt that guy, Tommy?'

'Pretty bad. He died on camera.' He clicked the mouse to run the video to the end.

Magozzi didn't want to watch. In Homicide you saw a lot of aftermaths, but few murders in progress – yet in a weird way, he felt he owed it to the guy on the ground. Bearing witness, he thought, pulling a phrase from a childhood of religious training, shifting it over to a cop's version of respect for the victim. He closed his eyes when the film ended, and listened to Tommy talk.

'YouTube pulled it the minute they saw it and turned it over to the Feds. The guy on the ground was gay, which makes it a hate crime, and he was dead long before the end of the film. That's a metal pipe he's swinging, no question he was out to kill, and there isn't a chance in hell of ID'ing him. Not from this film, anyway. He didn't talk, he didn't show his face, and from the back he could be anybody. Cleveland Homicide worked every angle they could think of, including gay-bashing incident history, and came up empty. The Feds aren't doing much better nailing down the origin of the post, which is why they called in outside help.'

'They called you in?' Gino asked.

'Me and about fifty others. Invitation only to the big

seminar last Saturday. I met gurus from all over the Midwest, cyber crimes guys from St. Paul and a lot of other departments, some teenage hackers they pulled off their summer jobs at McDonald's – kind of a geek fest hosted by suits with really bad ties. How come you don't know about this? I figured Grace must have told you. Monkeewrench was the major panel.'

'Yeah?'

'Oh, man, yeah, and let me tell you, that was a trip. You got all these Brooks Brothers types lined up at a table and then in comes Fat Annie in sequins, knock-'em-dead Grace, biker Harley, and Mr. Lycra. It wasn't a Star Trek-convention high, but it was damn close.'

Gino frowned. 'They're pulling in that many outsiders for a case that's four months old?'

Tommy grimaced. 'That's the thing. They found some more videos the sites pulled before they made it to the Web, and they've got bodies to match the film. Five cities across the country so far. They think Cleveland might be just the tip of the iceberg.'

Gino was uncharacteristically silent as they walked back to their office from Tommy's, a sure sign that he was processing some sort of philosophical revelation. Magozzi, being an expert in the varying degrees of his partner's rare verbal lapses, drew the quick conclusion that this particular soul-searching session was less cognitive and much more reflective than usual. Too bad Magozzi couldn't transfer the same intuition to his relationship with the woman he loved.

'That was the worst goddamned thing I've ever seen,' Gino finally said.

'It was bad.'

'I mean, I've had a car accident vic bleed to death in my arms on scene; I was holding my grandpa's hand when he made his final exit; and you know exactly how many corpses I've helped you clean up over the years. Me and death are on a first-name basis. But, Jesus. We just watched some guy's final nightmare minute of life – *on the Web. On the goddamned Web.* People are filming this shit. Posting it. Other people are watching it. I don't get it. I just don't get it.'

'Can't argue with you there, buddy.'

Gino shook his head irritably. 'It's like the Roman Colosseum. Call me a dreamer, but I thought the human race got over that after two thousand years.'

'We never got over it. Think about it – the Inquisition. Public executions. Genocide every day, somewhere in the world. Terrorists. People can really suck.'

Gino rolled his eyes. 'Thanks for that uplifting message of hope. Should I just kill myself now?'

'I don't think that's the solution.'

'Okay, how about I go kill all the assholes?'

'Better.'

They arrived at their desks, and sank into their chairs. Gino immediately withdrew a purloined packet of beef jerky from his suit-coat pocket and began gnawing. 'You know what? I blame this on Hollywood. And the Web. We've got a bunch of kids calling in bomb scares for their fifteen minutes, and now we've got psycho killers posting their carnage on the Web so *they* can get their fifteen minutes. Celebrity culture gone wild. Everybody wants to be a star. And they don't care how they do it. Can't make the *American*

Idol cut? Hell, kill somebody and make a movie of it. Jesus. I never thought I'd say this, but, man, just give me a plain old straightforward homicide to solve, because those always make sense in the end.'

Out of the corner of his eye, Magozzi caught the blinking red light on his phone. 'Gino, I wish you hadn't said that.'

Chapter Four

Gino was running the electric seat buttons in time to the bass throb of the sound system in the car next to them, and it was driving Magozzi nuts.

'Do you have to do that?'

Gino was looking down at his belly. 'I do. This lumbar support thing is amazing. You know it actually pushes your stomach out?'

'How can you tell?'

'Gee, thanks, Leo.'

Magozzi braked at the fourth red light he'd hit on Washington and glared past Gino at the do-ragged dumbo in the car next door. 'Sorry. I don't like river calls. And that kid's radio is driving me nuts.'

Gino took a look at the jacked car bouncing to the beat next to them, opened his window and waved his badge. 'Sound ordinance, buddy. You're way over. Shut it down now.'

Magozzi took a breath when the throbbing stopped. 'Thanks.'

'Not a problem. The little bastard looked like a skinny Eminem, and I hate Eminem. I caught Helen listening to one of his piece-of-shit songs when she was eleven – you ever hear that guy's lyrics?'

'Not on purpose. They got him out of the hood, though.'

'Bullshit. He brought the hood out with him, and now the rest of us have to worry about our kids listening to it. Man, when I was growing up all my mom had to do was worry about me running in front of a car. Now you gotta screen the radio, check out every album, every game, every TV show, and this morning I find out we got snuff films on the computer. Christ. Makes you want to uninvent electricity.'

The light finally changed. Within minutes they were in sight of the Hennepin Avenue suspension bridge. Gino still took Angela and the kids down here three or four times a year to watch the fireworks from the bridge; Magozzi hadn't liked bridges much since the night he'd gone into the Mississippi after two babies whose mother had just tossed them over the rail. The babies had drowned, but not before Magozzi had heard the noises they made. The mother took a dive in a halfhearted suicide attempt, but came through the swim golden, which was more of a miracle than anyone knew, considering that every man in the river that night wanted to push her under and hold her there instead of dragging her out. Sometimes Magozzi still dreamed about killing her, and woke up in a sweat, wondering if he was the only one that close to the edge.

'Light's green.' Gino rapped a knuckle on the dashboard. 'You know what we ought to do? Drag this out until noon and do a little lunch at St. Anthony on Main. There's a place here that deep-fries cauliflower so even I can eat it.'

'Jesus, Gino, we're going to look at a body.'

'It's three hours to lunch. We'll get over it by then.'

The Mississippi moved like a lady through this part of

downtown, taking in the city sights, lapping at the feet of the new Guthrie on one side and the aged bricks of the old flour mills on the other. Until this morning, it had always been Gino's favorite part of Minneapolis.

'Why do the floaters always wash up in Minneapolis? Can't St. Paul get one for a change?'

He and Magozzi were standing at the crest of a shallow, wooded embankment that led down to the river. The Parks Department took great care with the green areas down here, frequented primarily by good Minnesotans who took their families on picnics and probably ate grass; but there were a few spots where nature foiled their efforts at judicious pruning and brush clearing, and this was one of them. After dark, a different stratum of society sought out such places, well hidden from the eyes that admired the river views from their million-dollar condos.

Both men moved slowly down the slope on a path a lot of feet had worn through the tangled trees and brush. Nobody hurried to a death scene. The officers stringing tape behind them said it was a woman, and, in their words, fresh. Yeah, it was totally sexist, but there was a different feeling when the body was female. Magozzi beat himself up more for those, trapped in the macho mind-set that men were supposed to protect women, and dead ones were a personal failure.

'You know what the worst thing is?' Gino grumbled on the way down. 'That there's probably no homicide here; no villain; just another stupid, useless accidental drowning that didn't have to happen.'

'No homicide ever had to happen, either.'

'Yeah, I get that, but at least with homicide you get somebody you can blame, somebody you can hate. Accidental death? You get to blame the victim, or you get to blame God. That's it. You ask me, that isn't much of a choice.'

Magozzi squeezed the bridge of his nose, trying to push back one of the headaches Gino always gave him at a crime scene. Twenty hours out of every twenty-four, the man thought of family and food, in that order. But show him a body and all of a sudden he started beating a philosophical drum that boomed in Magozzi's head like a pile driver.

There was a uniform at the water's edge, standing watch, preserving the scene, trying not to look at the thing that didn't belong in the water.

The body was face down in the shallows, wearing a white formal gown that moved gracefully in the current as if the body inside were dancing. The scene sent creepy-crawlies up Gino's spine as he tried to quell images of his wife, Angela, walking down a church aisle toward him all those years ago. 'Oh man,' he said quietly. 'Is that a wedding dress?'

'That's what it looked like to me,' the uniform said, 'but you have to think someone would miss a bride.'

Not if the groom is somewhere else in this river, Magozzi thought. 'You found her?'

'Yes sir. Officer Tomlinson. The river walk is on my regular patrol.'

The kid was doing a pretty good job of putting on the tough cop face, but that face was unlined and the troubled blue eyes didn't have the flat look of a seasoned patrol yet. Magozzi figured he was about three days out of the academy. 'You're a little off the walk here.'

'The white caught my eye through the trees, so I came down. Thought maybe it was a heron, something like that . . .' He stopped and swallowed, then took a breath. 'Anyway, the ME's on his way; my sergeant took six other officers to start the canvass, but if this is where she went in, the cover's pretty dense.'

Magozzi nodded. 'We could use some more tape up top, Tomlinson, and wider on both sides. The lunch walkers are going to be out soon. Can you handle that?'

'Yes sir, thank you, sir.' He made double-time up the slope.

Gino shoved his hands in his pockets and tipped his head at Magozzi. 'That was uncommonly kind of you.'

'He's just a kid. He's been here alone for a while.'

The hand on Magozzi's shoulder was gentle. He felt himself take a deep, cleansing breath before he turned around and smiled at the medical examiner. It didn't surprise him that Dr. Anantanand Rambachan had simply appeared behind him without sound, without disruption of the environment. The man moved through the world like silk on water, disturbing nothing, taking his place like sunlight.

'Good morning, Detectives,' he greeted them with a warm smile and handshakes. Anant still loved the Western handshake. Even after all his years in this country, the ritual never failed to tickle him. *Touch is everything, Detective Magozzi,* he'd said once. *The Americans understand this, when many cultures do not. Touch is connection.* 'You are both looking

31

very well indeed. It's as if no time has passed since our last meeting.'

'Same with you, Doc,' Gino said. 'You still playing hoops?'

'Hoops?'

'Basketball.'

'Ah, yes, of course, basketball. I find I am enjoying the sport a great deal, especially now that my boys are old enough to join me. Perhaps I might have a second career after all.' His mouth didn't smile, but his dark eyes certainly did.

'Well, you just let us know if you ever want to pick up a game with our department squad – we could use the height.'

'That is a kind offer, and I thank you. And I am hoping that both of you and your loved ones are quite well?'

And so it went for a few minutes – the small talk before attending to the unpleasant business at hand was a ritual Magozzi figured all doctors learned their first year of med school. *Hello, Mr. Jones. How are you today? How's the family? You're looking good, have you been working out? Remember those tests we ran last week? Well, they didn't turn out so well.*

Finally, Dr. Rambachan stood on one leg while he removed a shoe and pulled on a rubber wading boot. Gino watched in amazement as he repeated the process with the second boot. 'Jeez, Doc, how the hell did you do that? You looked like a flamingo standing there, didn't even wobble. I gotta sit down to put on my socks or I keel over like a bowling pin.'

'Balance in all things,' Anant smiled, then turned sad eyes to the body in the water. 'So this is our lady friend. I can see she has not traveled far to meet us here.' The man never saw corpses; he merely saw complete human beings that didn't exist any longer in this particular place and time. 'Has anyone touched her?'

Gino made a face. 'No reason to start messing with a possible crime scene when the victim is obviously dead.'

'But we must always confirm the obvious.' He went into the water without creating a ripple, then bent to his task. After a moment his hands went still in the water. 'Ah. Here we have a little surprise.'

When Magozzi and Gino finally walked up from the river to the staging area, the sergeant who'd been running the canvass was back on site, leaning against his car and draining a can of Red Bull. Dark stains made Rorschach patterns on his uniform shirt, and his face was a particularly vivid shade of ripe tomato.

'Hot one today, Detectives,' he said, giving them the customary weather-related Minnesota greeting as he raised his can in their direction. If it had been winter, the greeting would have been, 'Cold one today, Detectives.'

'Are you gonna be okay?' Gino asked, mopping at his own brow. 'You look like you're already in full meltdown.'

The sergeant grunted. 'I grew up on the Iron Range. If the temp rises above sixty, I go into full meltdown. So what's the news on that poor gal? I'm telling you, never in my life have I seen such a sad and sorry sight.'

'Well, we got a newsflash for you – our bride down there? She's sporting a package.'

'What kind of package?'

'The kind of package you can only get with a Y chromosome.'

The sergeant's brows jumped up his forehead. 'No way.'

'Yes, way.'

The sarge thought about that for a minute while he chucked his empty can into the car. 'I guess there's no surprise there, come to think of it. We get all kinds down here after hours, especially the creative dressers – the Tiara's just a few blocks up, you know, and they've got that big drag show that runs every night.'

Magozzi nodded. 'We know.'

'Any idea whether it's a homicide or an accident?'

'No real signs of foul play that the ME could see. And Crime Scene didn't have a whole lot of luck with trace. If there is any, most of it's probably on the way to the Gulf of Mexico by now.'

'Probably an accident.'

'Probably. But we're going to have to wait for the autopsy before we know for sure.'

'Well, I can tell you from experience that there's a lot of booze and a lot of drugs down here. I'm surprised we don't get more tooted-up riffraff falling into the drink.'

'How did the canvass go?' Magozzi asked, trying to find a patch of shade in the one spot along the river that didn't have much tree coverage.

'All the respectable citizens we talked to didn't see a damn thing. But then we stumbled across Wild Jim, drunk as a skunk, taking a nap under some bushes.'

'Who's Wild Jim?'

The sergeant gave them a wry smile. 'Oh, you guys have

been off the street way too long. Wild Jim is a regular down here, and a frequent flyer at the station.'

Magozzi got interested. 'For what?'

'Public drunkenness, disturbing the peace. Every now and then he brings one of his guns down by the river and fires off a clip and wakes the neighbors, but mostly he's harmless; just a real pain in the butt. We've pulled his guns a half a dozen times, but he just gets clean and another judge gives them back. Some of those bastards really stick together. Anyhow, he was ranting about some "crazy faggot" raising hell down here last night, but who knows? He hasn't been able to see straight since he got kicked off the bench, and I'm guessing his blood alcohol is around point-three right now.'

Magozzi and Gino shared a look. 'You're not talking about Judge Bukowski.'

'Oh, yeah, the very same.'

If you were in law enforcement, you knew who Judge James Bukowski was, even if you didn't know him as Wild Jim. He'd always been a little left of the dial, but after six DUIs and a narc charge, he'd decided to take his Wild West show elsewhere three years ago; obviously down by the river. 'Does he live around here?'

'Sure. In one of those seven-figure lofts by the Mill City Museum. But he likes camping better, I guess.'

'I'll be damned,' Gino said, shaking his head.

'Like I told you, we get all kinds down here. We've got him in the tank if you want to talk to him later.'

Chapter Five

It had been a year since someone had tried to kill Grace MacBride. In the span of her thirty-some years, this was quite an impressive hiatus, but it hadn't been long enough. She still carried the Sig and the derringer every time she left her house; she still wore the knee-high riding boots that would make it difficult for someone to slash the arteries in her legs; and she was still constantly, painfully aware of every detail of her surroundings. Every time she abandoned one of these defenses in a pathetic shot at normalcy, something bad happened. This particular pair of boots was getting worn; a little soft at the ankle, a little run down at the heel. She would have to replace them soon.

Get over it, Grace. She said that to herself every morning when she woke up, because, truthfully, she was living such a wonderfully ordinary life now. Get up, dress, feed the dog, eat breakfast, go to work. This was the routine of hundreds of thousands who lived in this city, and even if some of them were carrying, she'd never seen one other in a pair of riding boots they were afraid to take off.

'I'm pathetic, Charlie, you know that?'

The dog at her side wagged his whole body at the sound of her voice. Apparently the stub that was left of his tail wasn't expressive enough.

Whatever had taken Charlie's tail and his courage had

done so long before Grace had rescued him from an alley, and if anything, his paranoia exceeded hers. No matter how urgent the need or how intense the excitement, he usually went out of any door slowly, cautiously, sniffing the air for imaginary danger. The woman and the dog were incredibly alike. The single exception was the back door of Grace's house, which opened onto a small rectangle of yard enclosed by an eight-foot fence of solid wood. This was a secure place, populated by a single magnolia tree that Grace babied with a hose, and Charlie babied with a hose of his own.

In the mornings, they went out the front door, over to the garage, into the Range Rover, then off to the Monkeewrench offices on the third floor of Harley Davidson's Summit Avenue mansion, the dog's favorite place in the world.

It was only the third week in June, barely the first kiss of summer in an average year, and already Minnesota had racked up a record number of blistering dry days that had lowered the rivers and left burgeoning crops wilting in dusty fields. Every farmer in the state knew that the cycle of drought and flood was a problematic yet normal course of events that those who lived off the land had learned to expect over the centuries; but the media lived in the cities, and such extremes spelled ratings, turning every anchor desk into a doomsayer machine. Suburbanites were quick to jump on the bandwagon when watering restrictions turned their Kentucky bluegrass brown, and no-wake zones on the lakes and rivers kept them from the thrill of high-throttle boating.

Normally there was no weather condition that kept

Minnesotans inside. They stood in the streets, videoing tornadoes that bore down on their houses; they broke the ice to swim in frozen lakes; they stripped to the furthest point that Lutheran decency would allow and jogged around the city lakes in summer. But not this year. This year the jogging and biking trails were almost always empty, there had been no tornadoes, no violent summer shows of thunder and lightning, and the city hummed with the constant under-current of air conditioners like a giant monster breathing.

Charlie started whining in the backseat of Grace Mac-Bride's Range Rover when she made the turn onto Summit Avenue.

'Soon,' she told him, going a little faster than the speed limit, the Gothic turrets of Harley Davidson's red stone manse already visible, two blocks away. By the time she pulled through the gate and under the portico, the black Town Car had already deposited the precious cargo of Annie Belinsky at the enormous wooden doors.

Annie always traveled by Town Car, particularly in the summer, when the drivers tended to be muscular, tanned college boys. She could have seduced them all, but didn't. She just liked to look at them.

This morning Annie was an overly voluptuous Fitzgerald heroine in ankle-length linen and lace. A wide-brimmed sunhat, balanced on her dark bob, and T-strap pumps clicked nicely on the slate walk.

If anyone had ever doubted that Charlie was a brilliant dog, all they had to do was watch the great restraint he always exercised when greeting Annie. His emotions wiggled all over him as he went within two inches of her and then stopped, eyes on her raised finger. 'Respect the outfit,' she reminded him, then bent and willingly offered her cheek to the big sloppy tongue. No one had ever told him to respect the face.

Grace smiled at her. 'Very Gatsby. I like it.'

'You know me, Fat Annie was just born for croquet and champagne, although you're not about to get me out on a lawn in this heat. Come on, let's get ourselves inside before I start to render.'

Annie had always thought Gothic to be a particularly uncivilized and slightly distasteful architecture, which therefore suited Harley perfectly. The baroque furnishings he favored were as massive as his frame and his personality, but as far as she was concerned, they were just plain Frankenstein.

They found Harley at the eight-burner stove in the kitchen, dumping canned chili in a pot with one hand, holding a beer with the other. Charlie was already next to him, nose up to a skillet of warming breakfast sausage. 'Just for you, buddy.' He tossed a link into the air and Charlie rose on his hind legs to catch it.

Grace leaned an elbow on a counter, chin in her hand, and watched the pair of them. The really amazing thing about this vagabond dog was what he taught you about the people he interacted with. Harley, for instance, oblivious to his own great value, bought affection shamelessly. Charlie was the easiest mark. One sausage, and he was yours for life. 'Where's Roadrunner?' she asked.

'In the shower. He made a new land speed record biking over here this morning, and I had to wring him out before I'd let him in the house.'

Annie peered into the mess in the pot and punched her hands into her pillowy hips. 'Nobody's going to eat that crap. And why are you drinking at eight o'clock in the morning?'

'Technically, since I didn't sleep last night, it isn't really morning. It's just a continuation of the dark time, only with light.'

Grace smiled at him. 'You're really shook up about this, aren't you?'

'You're goddamned right I'm shook up about it. We're going to have a Fed in this house for God knows how long, watching over our shoulders, looking at every move we make.'

'So?'

'So? *So?* Are you kidding me? We break about a hundred Federal laws every day when we work. We bust into secured sites – hell, we hack into the FBI like it was our own e-mail. They're going to wait until they get the software program they want from us, then they're going to throw us in the pen for about four hundred years. Christ. We beat these guys black and blue for ten years. They hate our guts, so what do they do? They ask permission to send this Trojan horse asshole right into our office and we open the door.'

'Are you talking about John Smith?' Roadrunner ducked through one of the kitchen doorways in his perpetual uniform of bicyclist Lycra. Even though the entire house was built on a grand scale, at six-foot-seven his head nearly brushed the lintel. 'Hi, Grace, Annie. Sounds like you're getting the four-hundred-years-in-prison lecture.'

Harley scowled at him. 'Very funny, dipshit. And that damn well better not be the same suit you were wearing when you got here, because I just got the chairs reupholstered to match the koi.'

'I'm not an animal. I put the sweaty one under your bed. And all your koi are dead, anyhow.'

Annie's bow lips turned down in a troubled pout as she focused on the disturbing possibility of wearing a prison-orange jumpsuit for any length of time. 'They wouldn't do that, would they, Grace?'

'Do what?'

'Throw us in jail for a teeny-weeny bit of computer mischief.'

'No, of course not. Harley's just being paranoid. The Feds know all about us working under the table every now and then . . .'

'Right,' Harley grumbled. 'They just haven't been able to prove it.'

Grace rolled her eyes. 'They asked for our help, and they're going to cut us some slack. Besides, Smith is the new FBI, not the Hoover archetypes we were dealing with back in Atlanta.'

'Are you kidding me? Did we meet the same guy? He had the suit, he looked like a Feeb, he talked that stupid Feeb talk, shit. The only thing that wasn't Hoover archetype about Smith was that he wasn't wearing a dress.'

Grace shook her head. 'They're desperate, Harley. They tried tracing this network and they can't do it. Not legally, anyway. So they bring in us and a bunch of hackers so we can do what the law keeps the Feds from doing themselves. You can't stick religiously to every letter of the law when lives are at stake, and maybe they're starting to get that. Sometimes you have to bend some rules. Hack into private phone records and save a life, or respect privacy laws and let somebody die. There's no choice if you're a human being.'

Harley nodded. 'Exactly my point. Who ever said the Feds were human beings?'

Grace shrugged. 'We had a choice. An office of our own in D.C., or D.C. came to us.'

'Yeah, well, I agreed to that before they told us they were sending a full-time spy.'

'Liaison,' Grace corrected him. 'He's here to help us.'

Harley snorted. 'That's what they say to the mental patients when the guy comes in to give them electric-shock therapy. Christ, Grace, you're talking about the same agency that set you up to bait a serial killer, and now all of a sudden you think they've got scruples?'

'Harley.' Grace took in a breath and exhaled noisily; one of those secret signals that told people who knew her they should pay attention. 'There are creeps out there filming fake murders to get their fifteen minutes on the Web; but there are other creeps filming real murders for the same kind of celebrity. The FBI wants them all shut down, and the first warrant step is a software program that can tell the difference between something staged and something real. They're doing the right thing, Harley, trying to nail the real killers fast, and scaring the creep idiots straight. And it's simple for us. Software 101.'

Harley snorted. 'I'm glad you're so optimistic. Even if we use one of our existing software platforms, we're talking a week, minimum, just to get an idea if this is doable. It's going to be a ton of extra work, and my point is, we've got a lot on our plate right now. We're staring down deadlines on security software for three of the biggest corporations in the world, which, incidentally, is going to make us filthy, stinking rich . . .'

Annie cocked a brow at him. 'We're already filthy, stinking rich. Half the computers in the world run at least one of our software apps or games.'

'Besides, the security software is already in beta version,' Grace reminded him. 'We'll be finished by the end of the month, easy.'

'Okay, but we still have to finish the updates for all the educational software . . .'

Roadrunner lifted his hand and waved. 'I finished those this morning.'

Harley folded his big arms across his chest and grunted. 'All right, all right, so maybe we can squeeze this in. Big whoop. The bottom line is, I do not trust the guy, I do not want to work with him looking over my shoulder, I do not want him in my house.'

Roadrunner shrugged. 'I kind of liked him.'

'Yeah, but you're a dipshit.'

'Besides, we've got more bad-guy radar in this room than all of MPD, and if he is one, we'll know it after the first hour.'

Harley blew a raspberry. 'Oh yeah? It took us ten years to figure out who was trying to kill us. Our record for reading people isn't exactly sterling.'

Grace didn't exactly make a face. The one she already had just went very still and stayed that way. For a woman who had spent her entire life anticipating and preparing for danger, she didn't like reminders that she had locked out the world and locked in the most dangerous people of all. It had almost cost all of them their lives, and it was her fault, no one else's. 'When's he coming?'

'In an hour.' Harley grabbed a manila folder off the counter by the stove and slid it over to Annie. 'In the meantime, Roadrunner and I did a little surfing on some of the websites the Feebs red-flagged for us at the seminar. This came off one of them this morning.'

Annie opened the folder and pulled out a photo. 'Oh Lord, is this a real dead person?'

Roadrunner shrugged. 'No way to tell. We scanned it for Photoshop-type alterations and couldn't find any, but that doesn't mean it wasn't staged and posed. Heck, we did that for the Serial Killer Detective game and even the cops thought it was the real thing. We called Smith to have the thing pulled and passed to Cyber Crimes and the recruited geeks, but it doesn't look good. The ISPs are shifting too fast to trace.'

'Just like the posts of the five city murders,' Roadrunner said.

Grace shrugged. 'That doesn't make this one real. The fetish and porn sites get better at hiding every day. Some of those networks are so sophisticated they make the military's system look bad.'

Annie passed the photo to Grace as if it were a poison mushroom. 'Real or not, this is sick. Somebody has to stop this.'

Grace nodded. 'That would be us.'

Chapter Six

When the doorbell rang at 9:05 a.m., Harley Davidson was out of his chair like an ICBM, cruising fast to intercept the Federal bogeyman at his front door.

'For God's sake, Harley, settle down,' Annie sniped behind him. 'You're as jittery as a long-tailed cat under a rocking chair. He's going to think you're on meth.'

Harley shot her a nasty look over his shoulder. 'Don't mention drugs,' he whispered.

'You have unequivocally lost your mind. There isn't even a bottle of aspirin in your medicine cabinet, you idiot, and, last time I checked, possessing multivitamins wasn't a felony.'

Harley made a face, then pulled open the big double doors. John Smith was wearing the standard-issue blue suit and an all-business countenance. He had a craggy face that hadn't aged well, making him look a little scary and a lot older than the mandatory retirement age of fifty-seven. 'Good morning, Mr. Davidson.' His eyes drifted down to the empty beer bottle in Harley's hand, but he didn't comment. Harley hated that about cops and Feds – their eyes were always too damn busy.

Harley jerked his thumb down the broad hall. 'We're in the breakfast room, looking at some of the crap we pulled off those red-flagged sites you turned us on to.'

Smith stepped inside and followed what looked like a mountain of leather to a room where the others waited around a table. 'Good morning, Ms. MacBride, Ms. Belinsky, Mr. Roadrunner.'

The two women nodded from their chairs, but the man in the body stocking jumped up, smiled, and actually shook Smith's hand. It was like stepping into a circle of reserved adults who just happened to own a cocker spaniel puppy. 'Just Roadrunner,' he said, grinning. '*Mr. Roadrunner*. Jeez, that's funny. You want some coffee?'

'Thank you, no, I've had breakfast. Once again, on behalf of the Bureau, I'd like to thank you for your generous offer of help.'

Grace had to concentrate to keep from rolling her eyes. Everything Feds said sounded like it came off a script. She nodded an acknowledgment. 'Shall we go up to the office and get started?'

'There are a few ground rules to cover before we do that . . .'

'You got that right,' Harley interrupted. 'So let's get it all on the table. We break more laws in one day than any hacker at that seminar breaks in a year. Developing the software you want is no problem; but if we're going to try to trace these guys, we're going to have to break a ton more just to get started, and I'm not about to do that with you looking over our shoulders so somewhere down the road you can testify against us.'

Smith nodded. 'Understood.'

'I don't think you get how fast we could rack up a few hundred years on our sentences for – ' Harley stopped and blinked. 'What do you mean, *understood*?'

'I am not here to interfere with your work. My role here is primarily to liaise between you, Washington, and other law enforcement agencies, to keep you briefed on new developments, and to make suggestions as to the direction of your work as I see fit. I am also required to stay with these files at all times' – he patted his briefcase – 'and when I leave for the day, I will take them with me. There is sensitive, classified information about Cyber Crimes' procedures that under no circumstances are you to copy to your hard drives.'

'We work strange hours, Agent Smith,' Grace said. 'Sometimes around the clock.'

'I'm prepared to be on duty twenty-four hours a day, if necessary. I will be as unobtrusive as possible, but I will be present.'

Annie smiled at him sweetly. 'How computer savvy are you?'

'Fairly.'

'Well, then you know that any one of us could copy these files right under your nose.'

He nodded. 'I know that. I'm asking you not to. Those files contain detailed records of the tracking formulas we've developed over the last several months . . .'

'Did any of them work?' Grace asked.

'Uh . . . no . . .'

'Then why on earth would we want to download them?'

A muscle in Smith's jaw tightened. 'For one thing, to give you a template of things that have already been tried so you don't waste time. More importantly, having this information on another computer system just increases the odds of a breach.'

'No one hacks into our stuff,' Harley grumbled.

'That may be, but if we limit the computers this information is on, any breach will be easier to trace.'

Annie gave him the kind of sweet smile you gave to the mentally deficient. 'So, the criminals you tapped at the seminar to do your dirty work for you aren't getting a look-see at this stuff?'

Smith's spine straightened imperceptibly. Apparently the Feds didn't mind encouraging law-breaking when it suited their purpose; they just didn't like to hear it spoken aloud.

'Oh, come on. Let's cut to the chase here. You've got posts of real live murders the FBI can't track, at least not legally, because the servers are registered in countries where U.S. access is denied. So what do you do? You call in a bunch of salivating hackers and tell them that if they try to access these foreign server accounts they will be in violation of international law. Good grief. Talk about dragging a slab of bacon in front of a bunch of wild dogs.'

'I can assure you that was not the Bureau's intention.'

'Yeah, right. And these eyelashes are real. The point is, we don't give a gnat's ass about your text files. Don't even have to look them over. But if you want us to write software that differentiates real murders from staged ones, we need to download the videos of those bodies in the five cities.'

'I am not authorized to give you permission to do that.'

Harley moved the mass of his body a step closer to Smith. To his credit, the smaller man held his ground. 'We're going to download the videos. Are you going to fink us out?'

It took Smith a minute to remember what *fink* meant. He

had to go back several decades. 'I do not believe you will do that.'

'I just told you we're going to do that.'

'Yes you did. But in my opinion, that was bravado. I do not think it was sincere; therefore I will not report it.'

Annie tucked her hands into her hips and tapped a toe on the marble floor. Agent Smith watched the toe moving up and down, mesmerized. 'I can't decide if your instructions are to handle us just like those other poor fools at the seminar, or if you might actually be a good guy.'

'I have never been accused of being a good guy.'

'Uh-huh. You want some chili before we get to work, darlin'?'

'No, thank you very much for the offer.'

'How about a beer?' Harley raised his own bottle.

'FBI agents do not drink alchololic beverages on duty, sir.'

'Yeah, yeah, and FBI agents are always on duty, right?'

'Precisely.'

'Well, I guess that makes my goals pretty clear here. Before you leave I'm going to see you totally snockered with three belly dancers sitting on your chest and a really great Cuban cigar stuck between your teeth. Let's get up to the office.'

For the first time in his career, John Smith was conflicted. When you boiled it all down, this whole assignment required that he consort with the kind of criminals he'd spent his life trying to convict. Who knows how many laws these people had broken. Besides, they looked weird. And they all carried concealed weapons. On the other hand, they were totally up-front about who they were and what they did, which was more than he could say for the Bureau, and they helped law enforcement across the country free of charge. Hell, they were starting to look better than most of the agents coming up the ladder from some Shangri-la place where an Ivy League education counted for more than ground law enforcement and a cop's brain.

What the hell do you think you're going to get from the Feds?

That had been his dad, a D.C. beat cop for thirty years, totally psyched on instinct and puzzle-solving, totally down on a bunch of suits who thought academia trumped people skills.

You got the Feds, who think those of us in the trenches are pretty much part of the trash they're trying to sweep under the rug, and then you got the cops, who know the people on the streets and do the hard work separating the bad guys from the good guys. And here you are, choosing the high road that doesn't know shit about what's real.

His dad hadn't come to his graduation; hadn't even sent a card when he'd made agent, but he'd read his future in a bottle of Pabst when John had come home for his uncle's funeral.

They'll eat you up for your first ten years, use you up for the next ten, then turn their back when you start to show gray. I'm telling you, Son, and I sure wish you would listen . . .

'Agent Smith?'

He came back from his reverie instantly. They were all sitting at a round table in the third-floor office, and now the skinny guy was shoving a mug of coffee under his nose.

'Well. Thank you very much. Do you happen to have any sugar?'

Roadrunner took a step backward. 'Are you kidding me? That's Jamaican Blue. Taste it first.'

Agent Smith had no idea what Jamaican Blue was, but he complied, set his mug on the table, and looked down into the brew. 'My goodness.' He felt Harley's massive hand clap him on the shoulder.

'Okay, Agent Smith. You've got a palate. You just went up a couple of notches. Now, we pulled something interesting off the Web this morning.'

'Another murder scene?'

'Maybe. You show us yours, we'll show you ours. So what have you got for us?'

Smith started emptying his briefcase. 'These are the video films of the five murders. Cleveland, Seattle, Austin, Chicago, and Los Angeles.' He dug deeper into the leather case and pulled out a bound folder of untold pages. 'This is a detailed record of our Cyber Crimes Division's failed attempts to trace the posts involving those murders. And these are the fringe sites we'd like you to monitor.' He slapped down a folder stuffed with printed pages.

Annie pulled the folder toward her and started shuffling through them. 'My God. There must be hundreds of them.'

Smith nodded. 'We narrowed it down as much as we could. The fringe sites we've listed are limited to those dedicated exclusively to murder scenarios. Some of them are distinctly amateurish and clearly staged events; others are questionable. We need a program that spots the real crimes instantly so we can get law enforcement on the ground right away, before critical evidence and possible witnesses are lost. Now tell me what you pulled off the Internet this morning.'

Roadrunner showed him a couple of print frames from the site. Smith looked at them without expression. The Feds were good at that. 'Did you get anything from this? Did you try a trace?'

'No joy,' Harley said. 'We already passed it on to Agent Shafer so he can put your people on it, but they're not going to get anywhere. That post was flying around the world at the speed of light. Right now we're running some enhancement programs on the film to see if we've got a real murder or Memorex.'

'Which won't do a lot of good without a location, and you can't get location without a trace.'

Annie tipped her head and gave him a little smile that gave him a little funny feeling in the pit of his stomach. 'A picture's worth a thousand words, darlin'. Or is it ten thousand?' She scooped up the folder containing fringe sites and stood. 'Are you okay there, or do you want us to set up a desk for you?'

'Well, I think this will work for the time being.' He sat quietly for a moment, watching and listening to the others as they scattered to their respective workstations, then opened his laptop to begin his daily report. He looked up from his screen when he heard a timid clicking, and stared in amazement as a sorry-looking dog with no tail climbed up onto the chair across the table and sat down facing him.

Chapter Seven

Magozzi had never been one for self-examination, although the department shrink suggested it every time he shot someone. Well. The two times he had shot someone. It hadn't told him much then – killers had taken a shot at him, and he shot back, what was to introspect? – and it wasn't going to tell him much now.

He'd had this silly idea as a young man that he'd make his way in the world, marry and have kids and a house and whatever the hell it was people called a normal life. That was the plan. That was what you grew up expecting when you were raised Italian Catholic with a family bigger than the population of Rhode Island and were stupid enough to believe that things would be the same for you as they had been for your parents. No one ever suggested that it might be otherwise; that your marriage would go south and you'd end up with a recliner and a twelve-inch TV and a blasted remnant of what your life was supposed to have been. And for sure no one ever told you that after the first marriage was erased like a mistake on a blackboard, you'd end up falling for a woman who would probably never say the word *love* out loud because it was a concept that eluded her. There would be no second marriage in his future; certainly no children, no shared house, no normal life. Not until he could manage to convince himself that he had to learn to live without Grace MacBride. He wasn't there yet. He wasn't even close, for all of Gino's prompting. But maybe he was stepping back, just a little; or maybe she was pushing him.

She opened the door when he knocked, and there was the thin smile reticence made, the swinging black hair, the face that always made his breath stop in his throat. And as if that weren't enough, there was Charlie's tongue licking his palm, and he was so goddamned stupid he thought all of this was the welcome home he'd been waiting for his whole life.

'Hey, Magozzi.'

'Hey, Grace.'

She stepped aside, reset the alarm when the door closed behind him, and just assumed he would follow her down the hall into the kitchen. When he didn't, she turned to look at him, puzzled. 'What's wrong?'

'You're working with the Feds. You were center stage at the seminar last weekend.'

Grace frowned at him. She didn't do facial expressions often, which made them strangely precious. 'It's just work, Magozzi.'

'Tommy told us a little about what was going on. It's not your everyday average security-system setup. It's big. You never mentioned it.'

Her frown deepened, almost making a line between her brows, but not quite. 'You want to know what I'm doing every minute, every day?'

Oh yeah. That was exactly what he wanted. 'Of course not. It just pissed me off to hear the FBI's sitting on some new kind of Internet-connected homicide without sharing info with the cops. We're the guys on the ground. If this stuff is really happening all over the country, we ought to get some sort of heads-up.'

'Only five confirmed so far.'

'Oh, good. I feel better. So they're bringing in outside geeks because their geeks couldn't trace the posts, right? And they brought us in on absolutely nothing. Every decent-size department in the country works the Internet, and yet Tommy gets a private invitation instead of through protocol channels. Is there a gag order on this thing?'

Grace blew out breath. 'Not that I know of. They're just trying to get something in place the locals can use before they bring everybody on board, which is where Monkee-wrench comes in. And if you want to know anything more, you can come back to the kitchen instead of standing out here being a puke. I've got things on the stove.'

Magozzi blinked as she stomped away down the hall. *Puke?*

He walked into the kitchen and was immediately assaulted by food aromas that mellowed his mind. He'd read some-where that the most sexually stimulating aroma for a man was cinnamon, but all he could smell was garlic, which probably was a good indicator of the way the night was going to go. 'You have something to drink?'

'Wine? Beer?'

'Something stronger.'

She set a whiskey, straight up, at the wooden table and sat down next to him. 'Bad day?'

Magozzi sipped at the whiskey before he spoke again. 'We had a floater.'

Grace winced. 'I hate that term.'

'Makes it easier. Less personal.'

'Homicide?'

'No. Anant called just before I left the office. No bruising, hyoid bone intact, blood alcohol through the roof. It's off our desk, just not out of our minds yet. Plus, Tommy gave us a look at the Cleveland homicide video, which didn't do a whole lot to make the day brighter.'

'Shall I try to cheer you up?'

'Go for it.'

'Harley's got a Fed in his house.'

Magozzi actually smiled. 'Dead?'

'Not yet. He's going to work with us on the software the Bureau wants us to create.'

'Which is?'

'They want a program to separate staged death scenes on the Web from the real thing.'

'Sounds impossible.'

Grace shrugged. 'We've got some ideas. The agent brought us the classified films and files, and a huge stack of fringe sites that pop in and out on the Net we have to look at. It's creepy stuff, Magozzi, especially the fetish sites.'

He nodded. 'We saw a few of those at the Cyber Crimes happy golf weekend last spring. Sex stuff, sadomasochism, like that.'

'It's a lot worse than that. People are acting out murders on instant messaging, taking turns being the victim and the killer . . .'

'How do you act out a murder on instant messaging?'

Grace made a sour-pickle face. 'It's really depraved. They

text this crap. One writes something like, "I'm plunging the knife into your stomach", then the other one writes back, "Oh my God, oh my God, I feel it going in, the blade is cold, my blood is hot . . ." '

'Jesus.'

'Yeah. And as disgusting as the texting is, the photos are worse, especially on the specific fetish sites. There's one totally dedicated to drowning, by the way.'

Magozzi reached for his whiskey to get the bad taste of sick people out of his mouth. 'Yeah, well, let me know if you run across film of someone holding a bride underwater.'

Charlie pushed his nose under Magozzi's arm, demanding attention, shifting the focus from all the weirdness in the world to more important things, like getting your ears scratched. 'Good old Charlie,' Magozzi bent to give him a doggy massage, and then realized that Grace hadn't said anything for a while. He looked up to see her staring at him. 'What?'

She reached for his glass and took a sip, which was frightening. Grace hated whiskey. 'Nothing, really. Probably just a coincidence. We pulled a staged drowning off one of the fetish sites this morning, with a victim in a wedding dress. But it wasn't real.'

'How do you know?'

'We did some tinkering with the resolution. Turns out it wasn't a bride at all. Just some guy in a wedding dress and a wig.'

Magozzi closed his eyes.

Gino had a belly full of Angela's lasagna, a glass of terrific Chianti at his side, the Twins game on the big screen, and the massage cushion on shiatsu mode. Maybe there was some guy in the world who had it better than he did at the moment, but he couldn't imagine who it would be.

'Daddy?'

Such a gentle whisper from the doorway, somehow attached to the corners of the mouth so he smiled every time he heard it. 'Hey, kiddo. Have a seat. Top of the ninth and a tie ball game.'

'Whoopee.' Helen sat in the chair next to him. She was almost sixteen, and scary beautiful. This year she'd go to her first prom with some sweaty-palmed, hormone-heavy scuzzball teenager who had pimples on his face and probably a condom in his wallet, and Gino was pretty sure he'd never survive the experience.

'Okay, Daddy. Why did you try to put a block on YouTube?'

Gino closed his eyes. 'Not just YouTube. I blocked MySpace, MyPage, a bunch of others. Took me hours.'

'Yeah, I know. You kind of suck at it, though.'

'Excuse me?'

'Your blocks were lame, Daddy. You want me to show you how to do it?'

'What do you mean my blocks were lame? I followed the instructions to the letter.'

Helen actually patted his head. He loved it when she did that, and he hated it. It was affection and patronization, all at the same time. 'A toddler could have busted through those blocks. You have to work on your computer skills.'

Gino jabbed the mute button and wished he'd been born a hundred years before that jerk had gone into his garage and decided that personal computers were the future. Some fucking future. Sex and snuff films in every kid's bedroom. Christ. 'Computers are evil. Spawn of Satan. The downfall of civilization, and I don't want you online ever again.'

Helen giggled, which was humiliating.

'Seriously, Helen. There are things popping on those sites I blocked—'

'Tried to block.'

'Whatever. There are things on those sites I don't want you to see.'

'Okay.'

'Okay, what?'

'You don't have to block the sites, Daddy. Just tell me to stay off them and I will.'

'Really?'

She smiled and bent to kiss his forehead, which was what her mother did when she thought he was being endearingly stupid. 'Really. Nite-nite.'

The phone rang before her slippered feet hit the top step.

'Rolseth.'

'Film of our waterlogged boy bride was posted to the Web last night.'

'No way.'

'I'm looking at it on Grace's computer right now.'

'Who is this?'

'We've got a homicide, Gino. This shows the guy being held underwater, struggling, and then the bubbles stop.'

'Oh, man.'

'And if Anant's time of death was even close, this film

was posted either from the river, or real close. The scene is still hot enough to give us a chance, so pray the bad boy's on camera somewhere with his arm around our bride while you put on your dancing shoes. We'll start with the Tiara Club.'

Gino shifted longing eyes to his glass of Chianti. 'Thanks for the invite, Leo, but I've had a bit of wine. Can't drive. You take it.'

'I'll pick you up in twenty minutes.'

Gino hung up the phone and sighed. Lord. He hadn't been to the Tiara Club since he'd dogged dealers when he was still a beat cop. He hated drag queens. They always hit on him.

Chapter Eight

Gino was standing on the sidewalk with a glass of wine when Magozzi pulled up to the curb. 'There's a city ordinance against drinking on the streets, you know.'

Gino drained the glass and set it under a bush. 'I wasn't on the street. I was on my own front walk which I laid with my own two hands on my own property, drinking my own Chianti. Damn stuff cost thirty bucks a bottle, and I wasn't about to toss it down the sink.' He got into the car and took a breath. 'Maybe the film you saw wasn't our guy. Maybe we're jumping the gun here, because Tommy was showing us all that crap and it was in your head, so . . .'

Magozzi shoved a photo under Gino's nose and turned on the map light.

'Oh shit. That's our scene.'

'That's just a few frames from the film.'

'Jeez, Leo, what's going on here?'

Magozzi raised a brow. Gino never asked that question. He looked at a homicide and laid out the whole murder scenario within seconds. He was always wrong, of course, but at least he was sorting through the reasons that were always behind a killing. Except maybe this time there weren't any reasons that made sense.

Gino was quiet for a long spell, which was scary, and then he started talking a mile a minute. 'So we've got Cleveland, but that was a beating, and probably a hate crime. That leaves us with four other murders on the Web, and now Minneapolis. What did Grace say? A stabbing, two shootings, and a strangulation, right? And then our drowning here. I've got it. I know what's going on.'

Magozzi sighed. 'What?' he finally asked against his better judgment.

'We've got ourselves a traveling serial killer. Like maybe a truck driver, crossing the country. Or a traveling salesman. He goes from city to city, does his thing, and takes pictures. He gets his jollies by posting his dirty deeds on the Web, leaves town, and that's it. Kind of like Willy Loman, except he kills people.'

'A Willy Loman serial killer.'

'Sure, why not? He'd be damn near impossible to track – he's moving, practically undocumented, and he doesn't stay in any one place for long, so he's opportunistic. The victims are all different, and so are the MOs, out of sheer necessity. Like the Railroad Killer back in '97, remember? Hopped the freights, offed any convenient victim at a stop, hopped on the next freight, and away he went.'

Magozzi sighed. 'That guy was an anomaly.'

'Or a maybe a forecast of things to come.'

'Serial killers aren't usually equal-opportunity types.'

'That one was. Killed men, women, young, old, doctors, college kids, whoever was there, using whatever weapon was handy.'

'The profilers said he was one in a million. The exception to the rule.'

'Profile-schmofile. The world is changing. Maybe the

killers are, too. So maybe our guy's not your classic bed-wetting, fire-starting sociopath who kills prostitutes because he can't kill his mother, but that doesn't mean he's not a psycho with serious bloodlust who found a great gig. We have to take a closer look at those other murders. Hell, we play our cards right, we could have this thing sewn up by noon tomorrow.'

'Okay,' Magozzi humored his partner.

'You're not buying my theory, are you?'

'It's a fine theory.'

Gino lifted his chin, out of pride or indignation, Magozzi wasn't sure. 'Yes, it *is* a fine theory. And it totally explains why the Feds are jumping this like hyenas on a crippled water buffalo. You've got interstate crime, cyber crime, and a serial killer all balled up into one.'

Crippled water buffalo? 'You've been watching the National Geographic Channel during Food Network commercial breaks, haven't you?'

'Scoff if you will, but this time I've got it nailed down. Go ahead. Try to poke a hole in it.'

'Some of the murder films were posted to different sites.'

Gino blew a raspberry. 'So what? The guy's a brainiac. He knows damn well the more he posts to one site, the more vulnerable he'll be to tracking. He's crossing all the t's.'

'Okay. Serial killers generally stick to the same MO because they get particular satisfaction from it. The method is important to them.'

'Wasn't important to the Railroad Killer.' Gino smiled, basking in the glory of his breakthrough. It wasn't often that he could point to a precedent to support his silly theories. 'Damn, I should drink Chianti more often when I'm trying to work this stuff out. It's like liquid muse.'

'There's a couple other possibilities.'

'Oh yeah? Dazzle me.'

'People post crap on the Web every day. Everybody wants their fifteen minutes. Why not murderers? Which means none of these killings are necessarily related.'

'Goddamnit, Leo, you're raining on my parade, 'cause that kind of makes sense. The Paris Hiltons of homicide.'

'On the other hand . . .'

'You like the serial theory better.'

'No. I was thinking of something else. Remember the I-94 drownings? Forty-some, mostly college kids on a toot falling into whatever river was handy.'

Gino squirmed in his seat. 'You think you gotta remind me of that nightmare? We got the only one that finally went off the accidental list.'

'So you also remember the NYPD dicks spending their retirement investigating all those drownings . . .'

'Don't even bring that shit up, Leo.'

'Can't help it. Those cops, who probably know a lot of things the rest of us don't, made a pretty good case for a nationwide network of killers, instead of one.'

Gino folded his hands and rubbed his thumbs together. His grandfather had done that with an almost obsessive regularity, whenever he sat idle in the rocking chair that squeaked while he looked around at the progeny who had come for the annual awkward visit. 'You don't want to go there, Leo. *I* don't want to go there.'

'You're right about that. But we have to consider it. I asked Grace to take a look at the timeline on those murders the Feds pulled off the Web.'

'Excellent move. Unless any of them happened on the same day, my theory is still golden.'

'Then you better start praying your theory sucks. If this guy's a traveler, he's gone. If he's local, we've got a shot.'

'Yeah. There is that,' Gino sighed, watching out the window as the shiny city on the prairie deteriorated block by block.

The Tiara was in a crusty fringe neighborhood that clung to the hem of downtown's posh skirt, existing mostly below the radar, unless you were a hipster or a drag queen. For years, the city council had been trying to sanitize this river-adjacent chunk of turf with future revenue in mind, but for some reason the gentrification spitballs never quite stuck.

'Look at this shit-box neighborhood, Leo. When I was a kid we used to walk this street on the way to the Saturday-night horror flicks at the Majestic. Worst thing you ever saw was winos drinking Mad Dog in doorways. Now look at it. You can practically spit to the Mississippi from here, and what do you have? Chop shops, heroin balloons, busted streetlights . . . If the city council had half a brain between the bunch of them, they'd steamroll this place and put up about fifty Starbucks.'

Magozzi turned onto a dark, sketchy backstreet that terminated at the club. 'Then you'd have fifty Starbucks filled with drug dealers doing business over double mocha lattes.'

'Ain't that the truth.' He squinted out the window against the glare of a flashing neon crown that lit up an old, brick building. A colorful parade of characters dressed in elaborate costumes and gowns were lined up on the street, waiting to get in. 'Are you sure these are all men?'

Magozzi shrugged. 'I don't know. I guess. What difference does it make?'

'Because if that she in the green dress is actually a he, then you could have fooled me and I'm not sure how I feel about that.'

'It's theater, Gino. Try to stay focused.'

'Yeah, right. I'm kinda out of my element here. Let's hit a side door. I don't want to walk that gauntlet. We're already getting weird looks and we haven't even gotten out of the car yet.'

On the north side of the building, they found a bent-up metal fire door manned by a monolith of a security guard whose day job was probably chewing glass at carnival side-shows. 'Out front, like everybody else!' he barked at them.

Gino was quick to pull out his badge and shove it toward the man's face. 'MPD Homicide, pal.'

The bouncer looked skeptical until his eyes landed on Gino's holster. 'Oh.' He pulled open the door for them and a throbbing wall of high-decibel dance music blasted them like a sirocco.

'Hang on,' Magozzi said, gesturing for him to close the door, then pulling out the photo of their river body that Grace had printed out. 'You ever see this guy here?'

He took the photo, examined it for a second, then his eyes got huge. 'Jesus. He's dead.'

'Hence, the homicide part of our introduction,' Gino grumbled.

'Hell, I'm only here two nights a week, and I see about a thousand faces each time.'

'He was wearing a wedding dress.'

The bouncer shook his head. 'Working a place like this, you just stop noticing the craziness after a while. You should talk to one of the bartenders. Or better yet, talk to Camilla – she runs this place, she's always here, and she knows everybody. Go inside and head up the back staircase. Her office is at the end of the hall. God. I can't believe you showed me a picture of a dead guy.'

The inside of the Tiara was sheer mayhem. Hundreds of people swarmed on an enormous dance floor in a riot of color, feathers, and sequins. Lights strobed in time to the screaming sound system. Magozzi and Gino didn't even try to talk – they just shoved their way through the crowd toward the staircase, badges clearing a path for them.

It was no small blessing that Camilla's office was soundproofed. You could still hear the din of the music, and the throbbing of the bass was turning Magozzi's guts to Cream of Wheat, but conversation was possible without shouting.

Camilla *looked* like a she – a really pretty she, in a demure, well-cut skirt suit – but the booming voice told another story. 'Homicide?' His/her hands fluttered at his/her throat like distressed moths. 'Good grief, Detectives, tell me what's happened.' She gestured to two empty chairs that flanked her desk. 'Please, please, do sit.'

Magozzi pulled out the photo again and slid it toward Camilla. 'Do you recognize this man?'

Camilla answered the question with a deluge of tears, and there was no question that the grief was genuine, and not just manufactured melodrama. 'That's Sweet Cheeks,' she finally choked out. 'Oh my God . . . she was just here last night . . . oh God, what happened?'

Gino had a good heart and a fairly open mind, but a man in a wedding dress carrying around a handle like Sweet Cheeks messed with his head. He squirmed a little in his chair, trying to pick a pronoun. It was hopeless. 'The body was found in the river this morning. We believe it was homicide.' This brought on another round of tears, which made him feel bad for not saying right up front what he was supposed to say, what he always said and always meant. 'We're very sorry for your loss. You two were obviously close.'

Camilla nodded, blotting at her eyes with a tissue. 'Thank you. We were very close,' she sniffed. 'Not in the way you're probably thinking, of course, not as partners. We were just dear friends.'

'You mentioned that he . . . uh, she' – Gino corrected his pronoun – 'was in here last night. Do you remember what time you last saw her?'

'I think probably around ten-thirty. She was extremely . . . compromised.'

'Compromised?' Gino asked.

'Drunk. Poor Sweet Cheeks. She lost someone very close to her years ago, and never got over it. She was almost always drunk. Oh, good lord, I can't believe she's dead.'

'I take it Sweet Cheeks was not a legal name.'

Camilla shook her head. 'No, just a stage name. Her legal name is . . . was . . . Alan Sommers.'

Gino scrawled on his notebook. 'Is that Sommers with an *o*?' 'Yes.'

He pulled out his cell. 'I'll get an address from DMV.'

'No need for that. She has a couple of rooms over the Stop-and-Go Market on Colfax. That was her day job. I have a key if it will help.'

Magozzi said, 'We appreciate that. Were you aware of any plans she might have had after leaving here last night?'

'Her only plan was to go to my condo to sober up before the big drag show last night so she could perform. I often give her my key on nights when she's had too much to drink. Sometimes she just passes out until the next morning, but often she'll sleep a few hours and come back to the club, or go elsewhere – you never know with Sweet Cheeks. I didn't get home until 3:30 a.m. last night, and she wasn't there. I didn't think anything of it, of course. She's always been unpredictable in that regard.'

'Was there any indication that she ever made it to your condo last night?'

Camilla frowned and tapped a long cherry-pink fingernail on her cherry-pink lips. 'Come to think of it, not really. The bed she normally uses wasn't mussed, there were no dishes in the sink . . . but that doesn't mean she didn't straighten the bed, although that would have been out of character.'

A sad portrait of Alan Sommers was filling in fast for Magozzi – an obviously troubled man living a high-risk lifestyle, drunk out of his gourd, stumbling along the river at night. Homicide would normally have been the last conclusion in this case, but for the film Grace had pulled from the Web. A perfect victim. And maybe, a perfect crime. The thought sent chills down his spine. 'Do you have any idea if she left with anyone?'

'None. But we have security cameras at every door. I have the tapes if you think they might help.'

Chapter Nine

It had taken Camilla less than half an hour to isolate the security footage that showed Alan Sommers in full bridal regalia entering and leaving the Tiara Club the night of his murder – alone both times – which eliminated all hope of an easy conclusion with a slam-dunk suspect.

'Why don't we ever pull a case where our perp is so stupid he gets caught in the act on surveillance tape wearing his work uniform with the name tag in plain view?' Gino complained as Magozzi pulled the Cadillac away from the Tiara Club's flashing neon and headed north toward Alan Sommers' apartment. 'You read about that stuff all the time, but it never happens to us.'

'That's because the really stupid felons are almost always bank robbers.'

Gino sighed. 'We should move over to Robbery, then.'

'I thought you were angling for Water Rescue.'

'A mere pipe dream. I can't swim.'

'Seriously?'

'Yeah.'

'Why don't I know that about you?'

'Why would you? It's not like you ever asked me to go surfing or anything. Shit. It's late. I better call Angela.'

While Gino checked on his hearth and home, Magozzi watched the neighborhoods deteriorate with each city block.

This part of Minneapolis had never exactly been mink and pearls, but when the gangs moved in during the eighties and nineties, they left a lot of carnage in their wake. The MPD Gang Task Force had worked hard to sanitize things over the years, and they'd done an impressive job, but the lingering hangover of too much violence for too long was still evident. Half the houses were still unoccupied, and the few viable businesses that remained were girded in the graffiti-scarred armor of steel gates and chain-link fencing.

Gino clicked off his cell phone just as Magozzi pulled into the parking lot of the Stop-and-Go. 'How's the homestead rolling without you?'

'It all went to hell in a handbasket. The little guy has a fever and Helen has a sore throat. Angela told me to take vitamin C.'

'What's that do, and where are you going to get it?'

'Are you kidding? She tucks shit like that in my pants pockets every day, and it does absolutely nothing except keep my marriage intact.' Gino craned his neck and looked out the windshield at the darkened Stop-and-Go sign. 'When I was on the beat, the guys used to call this place "the Stop-and-Die." Doesn't look much better than it did back in the day. And it's closed, damnit. Don't tell me we have to come back here tomorrow for interviews.'

Magozzi shrugged. 'My gut tells me Alan Sommers wasn't killed by anybody he knew or worked with. Camilla said everybody loved him – and we didn't see any Norman Bates-type stalkers on the vid.'

'That was a bummer, wasn't it? So Alan Sommers was

probably just a great victim of opportunity for some sick asshole who wanted a little exposure on the Web.'

'That's what I'm thinking. Let's see what turns up in his apartment and we can go from there.'

Gino nodded, then unsnapped his holster and drew his gun. 'I'm going in armed and dangerous. This place still gives me the creeps.'

It took them a few minutes to find the battered metal access door behind the Stop-and-Go that led up a flight of stairs to a squalid, dark hallway of doors. The place was a true dump, crawling with cockroaches and rodents that didn't seem the least bit put out by the presence of humans. If there were any other squatters utilizing the space, they were either dead, very quiet, or out for the night, because the place was as silent as an anechoic chamber. It was the kind of silence that was inherently and deeply menacing – and, oddly, the same kind of silence that kept you dead quiet. If you didn't make any noise, the bad things might not find you.

They found Alan's place at the end of the hall and let themselves in with the key Camilla had given them. Magozzi flipped on a light, which cast a harsh, bare-bulb glare on a surprisingly tidy, freshly painted room that bore no resemblance to the scary hallway they'd taken to get here. There was a twin mattress on the floor, made up with a clean bedspread that Magozzi had recently seen in one of the IKEA catalogs he mysteriously received every couple months in the mail, even though he'd never shopped there. The tiny kitchen and bathroom were both spotlessly clean – not a speck of dirt or a roach or rat in sight – and there was the pervasive smell of patchouli incense that battled with the funk of mold that was probably emanating from the walls in highly toxic quantities. Alan Sommers had lived in a hellhole, but he'd obviously put forth some effort to make it livable.

Gino ventured into the second room, which was little more than a big closet, filled with an astounding array of wigs, makeup cases, shoes, and gowns wrapped in plastic, hanging from a sagging dowel. And in shocking contrast, amidst all the finery, were two brown-and-yellow-polyester Stop-and-Go uniforms, neatly hung and ready for service. 'Christ, look at this,' he said. 'It's like Cinderella's closet. Char girl by day, princess by night. This guy was leading a double life. And he had more wigs than Cher.'

'It gets weirder,' Magozzi said from the living room as he stared up at a framed diploma that hung on the wall. 'Alan Sommers graduated cum laude from Billy Mitchell Law back in 1989. How the hell do you get from there to here?'

Gino joined Magozzi in the living room. 'Huh. That's a damn big fall. But remember what Camilla said? That he lost somebody close? She kind of implied that that was what sent him over the edge.'

He started rummaging in the apartment's few drawers and cabinets but didn't turn up anything except the mundane scraps of day-to-day life. 'Man, this is the sorriest place I've ever tossed. There's nothing here, not even a can of Coke in the fridge. It's like Alan Sommers wasn't even a real person, just a cardboard mock-up.'

'I think the real Alan Sommers is in that closet.'

'Christ, you're going to have to put me on suicide watch if I stay here much longer. I hate poking through dead people's stuff. Reminds me of having to clean out my grandpa's house after he died.'

Magozzi nodded. 'There's nothing here. Let's get to the jail and bribe a boy in blue to let us see Wild Jim before they let him out in the morning.'

'I got nothing to bribe a jailer with.'

'Give him some vitamin C.'

'You get that I have had no sleep, right, Leo? Zero, nada, not even a Salvador Dali nap.'

'I get it. Join the club.'

Magozzi pulled in at an angle in front of the Hennepin County Jail.

'And you also understand that it's three o'clock in the morning.'

'I do.'

'So here's the thing. My eyes are fried eggs, my brain cells are crisp around the edges, and at the moment I'm about three levels down from any drunk coming off a high toot, let alone an ex-judge.'

Magozzi put the car in park and rubbed his eyes. 'No choice. The golden time is wearing off on Alan Sommers. We already lost a day thinking he was an accidental, more time finding out he left the club alone, and Wild Jim is the last lead. We've gotta milk it.'

During visiting hours, Hennepin County Jail kept at full ballast with a cross section of society that would never mingle in the real world. There was always the predictable, en masse scum, coming to chitchat with significant-other scums; then there was the regular meat-and-potatoes crowd, always a little shell-shocked by having to visit an errant friend or family member in lockup; and, less frequently, the dressed-to-kill cocktail crowd, sporting major attitude and pissed as hell that their lover or spouse had gotten a DUI after drinking too much champagne at an important charity event. It made for excellent sport if you were into people-watching, but as a cop, you got over that brand of voyeurism your first or second day on the job.

At this hour the lobby was calm, the sign-in deputy was bored, and Magozzi and Gino were relieved. Efficiency was at its peak, and Wild Jim was escorted immediately to the standard, Plexiglas booth that was blurry with scratches and fog from the breath of loved ones declaring their heart's desire through a quarter-inch of plastic.

The judge looked perfectly lucid, eyes as sharp as they always had been on the bench, blood alcohol notwithstanding. He plunked down on the steel chair across from Magozzi and Gino with a gracious thanks to the jailor who'd escorted him, then lasered in on the both of them without prelude.

'I remember you, Magozzi. You were in front of me twice. As I recall, you were trying to lock up a couple craven sociopaths that your wife at the time wanted desperately to put back on the streets, for some incomprehensible reason.'

'She was a public defender.'

That elicited a snort from Wild Jim. 'Bad bedmates, cops and public defenders. But I guess you figured that out.'

The comment really pissed Magozzi off. It was incredibly bad form to bring up his ugly divorce that had been so painfully public in the law enforcement community, but he had no choice but to humor him. Drunks coming off jags could change like the wind if you pushed the wrong buttons.

'Come on, where's your sense of humor, Magozzi? I've had five divorces, so that makes you four times smarter than me. Hey, do you know what the difference is between a criminal and a public defender?'

'No, Judge, I don't,' Magozzi said flatly.

'Neither do I!' He busted a gut laughing at his own tired joke, then his eyes honed in on Gino. 'And I remember you, too, Rolseth. Only saw you once, but we made a good team. We exterminated some vermin that day, yes indeed. So, Detectives, assuming this isn't a social call, what can I do for you?'

'A body was found in the river this morning,' Gino said.

'Ah. *That's* why there were so damn many cops in my front yard. So what happened to the poor schmuck?'

'Drowned.'

'And I'm talking to two homicide detectives. Isn't that interesting.'

Magozzi ignored the comment. 'We understand you may have seen something last night.'

'You wouldn't believe the depraved shit I see down by the river, every goddamned night. People having sex, shooting up, smoking crack . . . I don't know what happened to this city.'

'Last night specifically,' Magozzi said, trying to get him back on track. 'The sergeant running the canvass said you mentioned a commotion.'

The judge smiled. 'Very delicate phrasing, Magozzi. Yes, I told a cop this morning that there was some crazy faggot raising hell down by my river, like usual. Sorry, but I'm not politically correct.'

'Raising hell? What does that mean?'

'He was crashing through the brush, yodeling like a coloratura soprano on helium.'

'Calling for help?' Gino asked.

Wild Jim leaned back in his chair and rubbed his bloodshot eyes. 'You know what the problem with this line of questioning is, Detectives? I'm a bourbon aficionado. And when you like Kentucky horse piss as much as I do, memories and recollections are hard to come by. If I saw something, I don't remember it. All I can tell you is I heard yodeling, then I heard a cop shouting at me to wake up this morning. There's nothing in between.'

Magozzi sighed audibly.

'Don't look so dejected, my friend. I may be a dissolute drunk, but just because I don't remember last night right now doesn't mean I won't think of something later. So, are you expecting your perp to get into more monkey business down there, maybe return to the scene, or is this a one-off murder?'

Magozzi and Gino just shrugged noncommitally.

'Well, there's my answer. Tell you what – I'm down there every night anyhow. I'll be your eyes and ears. And I know where to find you.'

'We wouldn't recommend night walks by the river for a while.'

The judge smiled. 'I'm sure I'll have plenty of company.

You cops always blanket an area after a homicide, at least for a week or two. By the way, am I a suspect?'

'Should you be?'

'Absolutely. Anybody down by that river last night should be a suspect, but I don't have to tell you that. Anything else you need to know?'

Magozzi looked straight at him. 'Yeah. What happened to the respected judge who sat on the bench, handing out justice for twenty years?'

The judge looked surprised. 'Nothing happened to that respected judge. You're looking at him. I sat on the bench handing out justice for twenty years, and for every one of them I was drunk out of my mind. Kind of puts a wrinkle in the robe, doesn't it?'

Chapter Ten

Clint ran his red pen down the list next to his computer, crossing off the items he'd completed one by one. Feed Ruffian. Eat supper. Wash dishes. Code post.

If you're too stupid to remember your chores, write them down, Clinton.

The only valuable advice from the dead bitch who claimed to have borne him, although the thought of such a thing still made him sick to his stomach. To have lived in the sagging, bloating belly of such a creature was more than he could imagine.

He put a gold star on the last of the one-page essays the dear children had written in class today, then crossed 'grade papers' off his list. Perhaps the gold star hadn't been earned in this case – certainly not grammatically – but this particular boy always tried so hard, and needed a pat on the back every now and then.

He put down his pen, leaned back in his chair, rubbed his hands together, then keyed in the magic that would send away the post he had coded earlier. The anticipation began the moment he pushed the last key. It filled him with energy, and made him jump up from his chair. Two more items on the list: Walk Ruffian; Chesterfield's. He could hardly wait to cross off the last one.

'Ready for your walk, boy?'

The golden retriever rose heavily from his bed next to

the desk, but he wagged his tail as he walked to where his leash hung on the hook by the door. He was old for his breed, and his beloved nightly walk took longer as the arthritis got worse. Clint didn't mind the extra time. It was still too early, and he had a few hours to kill.

Marian put away her mop and bucket, took a last swipe at the bar with her rag, checked the final load of glasses, and started turning out the lights. On nights like this, when she was especially anxious to get home, there seemed to be a million switches: one hooked to the mirror lights that reflected the polished bottles; another for the window lights; then the interior neon signs. 'This is ridiculous, Bert. Get an electrician in here and put these all on one circuit. I spend ten minutes every night shutting them off.'

'Can't.' Bert was already at the door, receipt wallet under his arm, hand on the knob. 'All these lights on one circuit and this place would blow like a two-dollar whore. The electric's way below code.'

'They're going to nail you on that one of these days and shut this place down, and there goes Alissa's college fund.'

Bert snorted. 'They're not going to nail us on any damn thing. Cheetah Bacheeta did some lip service to our noble inspector in the can one night, and I got it on film.'

Marian rolled her head to release the tension in her neck. She didn't understand the world anymore. All men were pigs, and the system sucked. 'Jeez, Bert, you are the slimiest of slimes.'

'Maybe. But Alissa's going to college, and I'm all over that. Any acceptance letters yet?'

Marian smiled. 'A couple. She's waiting for Barnard.'

'What's Barnard?'

'The grand prize.'

Bert chuckled and reached deep into his pocket and pulled out a wad of bills. Big bills, even for a weekend night. 'Tips, baby, for Alissa's tuition.'

Marian thumbed through a few of them and made her mouth hard. She could take all the crap the guys dished out here every night without blinking, but kindness always brought her up short. 'Christ. I didn't even blow any of the guys here tonight.'

'Yeah, well, there you go.'

'Bert?'

'Yeah?'

'How many times have I got to tell you not to walk out of here with that receipt wallet? You're going to get mugged one of these nights. Everyone in town knows you take the cash home.'

'Everyone in this town loves me, doll baby. Kiss the kid going to college for me. Tell her the boys all want to see her down here before she shakes the dust of this town off her shoes. You gonna lock up?'

'Don't I always?'

Marian wiped at her cheek as the fat slimiest of all men walked out the door. She was dead tired. Six days a week for fifteen years she'd worked two shifts at the diner; then the night shift here at the bar, and most of the time she felt like she was being pulled through a knothole backwards. But Alissa was going to college, by God, and that was the brass ring.

By the time she locked up and the worn heels of her

cowboy boots clicked across the empty parking lot, the stars were out, shining on who she was and what she'd done, and the moon looked surprised. Maybe, she thought, it didn't matter so much what you did as what you made happen for somebody else. Like your kid.

She knew Alissa was already asleep. She also knew that there would be a freshly baked, beautifully decorated chocolate almond cake on the scarred, shabby kitchen counter, because the kid baked a birthday cake for her mother every year. There was some guilt wrapped up in that, because Marian had always had three jobs to support them, and no time to be Betty Crocker. Alissa had jumped into the role. There would be forty candles on the top of the cake, and some sloppy sentiment written on the brown icing, and wrapped presents around it with curlicue ribbons.

Marian's face had weathered and hardened into a mask that no man would want; her knees were bad and her hips were shot, and most of the time she couldn't feel her fingers from all those years carrying the heavy trays; and still she figured she was the luckiest woman in the world.

Dew sparkled on the windshield of the old Ford Tempo, lighting her way, and made Christmas in July on the spruce that towered around the slab of tar cut into the forest. 'How lucky are you?' she whispered to herself, key out to unlock the door, heart open to the blessings of her life, and even when she saw the tripod with its mounted camera, and felt the hand on her shoulder and the cold knife on her throat, she couldn't imagine that this could be anything bad.

Chapter Eleven

Gino had the passenger seat of the Cadillac on full recline, but his eyes were wide open. Magozzi kept glancing over to make sure he blinked.

'Close your eyes, for God's sake. You look like you're dead.'

'I am dead, or might as well be, and I am never going out with you after dark again. First you take me to a drag club, then to some poor dead sap's apartment so I can see the sorry remains of his sorry life, then to the county jail. Christ. I had a better time at my vasectomy. What time did you drop me off?'

'Four a.m.'

'And what time did you pick me up?'

'Seven-thirty, just like always. Jeez, Gino, you got three hours. What are you complaining about?'

'No, I did not get three hours, because the little man toddled into our bedroom at a quarter after five and hurled all over me. Why do little kids get the flu all the time? It's not even flu season. It pisses me off. And why do we have to get up and work our regular shift when we worked all night? They don't let pilots do that. So many hours in the air, you gotta take so many hours off. Shit. Even truck drivers have rules like that. But cops? Nah. No sleep? No problem. Load your weapon and get out there. I'm an armed man with a brain you could stir with a straw. Now, that's just plain stupid.'

Magozzi yawned. 'Tell you what. I got three hours' sleep. Ask me before you shoot somebody.'

'Okay.'

Magozzi pulled onto Summit Avenue, and a few blocks later through the open wrought-iron gate of Harley's driveway. 'Up and at 'em, partner. Time for our play date with the Feeb.'

'You're not going to go off on this guy and get us thrown in the pen, are you?'

'You want me to make nice with a Fed? Your onions fall off in the shower or what?'

'This is a little Fed. A hapless soldier. He didn't make the decision not to pull cops in earlier. Besides, I'm too weak to referee one of your pissing matches.' He got out of the car and stretched, looking around. 'Man, I keep forgetting to get the name of Harley's gardener. Look at those peonies. They're just about enough to break your heart. You know what I think of when I see peonies? Cheerleaders. Don't ask me why.'

'I will not. I promise.'

Gino veered to the right of the walk and tromped across Harley's perfect lawn to the koi pond, his favorite feature of the house. He pulled a bag of miniature marshmallows out of his pocket and tossed a few in the water, then started humming the *Jaws* theme music while he waited for the feeding frenzy. After a few seconds he called over his shoulder. 'Hey, Leo. These guys aren't moving today.'

Magozzi sighed and joined him at the pond's edge. 'Of

course they're not moving. They're dead. That's why they're floating on their sides.'

'Aw, shit. I loved those big guys. What do you suppose killed them?'

'Marshmallows.'

'Now that was just plain mean.'

As far as Gino was concerned, the really cool thing about coming to Harley's mansion in the morning was that it always smelled like his grandmother's house. Which meant that it smelled like animal fat. This was not permissible breakfast food in the home he loved so much, because Angela wanted him to live forever instead of letting him die young, fat, and happy. Bacon, sausage, the occasional flat steak, sometimes pork – these were the aromas that filled his memory, reminding him of Grandma's oak table and tin sink and the cast-iron pan spitting grease on an old wood-burning stove. Every time he showed up here in the morning he half-expected Harley to show up in an apron with yellow sunflowers and crinkly gray hair pulled back into a bun.

Grace was waiting for them in the breakfast room, her eyes fixed on the cup of coffee that was cradled between her hands. Gino wanted desperately to hate this woman, because she messed with the mind of the best friend he would ever have in this life; but there was something about her that tugged at him.

'You had food of the gods for breakfast,' he said with a smile, and Grace nodded.

'Harley cooked cholesterol. He knew you were coming. By the way, we checked the dates on the murders confirmed so far, including your river bride. Lots of time between all of them, so your traveler theory is still alive, Gino.' She looked back at Magozzi. 'Any breaks with the river body?'

'Nope. We got an ID on the guy, a timeline that shows him leaving a club alone, and the last person who saw him alive is a pickled judge who can't remember his own name half the time. How about you? Any luck tracing the film?'

She shook her head. 'Nobody's been able to trace it. We think that tactic is a dead end – whoever did this is too good to leave tracks.

'Did you bring our films?'

Magozzi patted his sports-coat pocket. 'Ten bodies, some fresh, some not so fresh, just like you asked. It was a pretty weird request, Grace.'

'If Roadrunner's idea works, these disks are going to teach our software program how to tell if a murder is real or staged. He can explain it better than I can. How long can we keep them?'

'No real hurry, all the cases are cleared. But I signed for them, and they have to go back to the locker eventually, so don't give them to your pet Fed.'

She gifted him with her rarest of expressions – a tiny, one-sided smile. 'You're going to like Agent Smith. He reminds me a lot of you. Now, can I have the disks? We need to get started. Food's still warm in the kitchen if you want to load a plate to bring upstairs.'

Gino did a drill turn toward the kitchen, but Magozzi stopped him.

'Maybe later. We'll meet with Smith first.'

Charlie was waiting for them at the top of the stairs,

floppy ears trying to stand erect, stubby tail trying to make a breeze. He went for Gino first, as he always did, standing on his hind legs so his tongue could reach the man's face. 'This dog really loves me.'

Grace grunted. 'That dog assumes you always have food on your face.'

Roadrunner covered the fifty feet from his workstation to the doorway in about ten strides. 'You got my films, guys?'

Magozzi and Gino just stared at him, speechless for a moment.

'Jesus, Roadrunner,' Gino finally managed to eke out. 'You're wearing jeans.'

The tall man's Adam's apple bobbed in embarrassment.

'Leave him alone,' Harley bellowed across the room. 'I've been trying to get him in real clothes for years and I don't want you messing it up. Damn Lycra's so hot we had to keep the air on arctic for him to survive up here while the rest of us got frostbite.'

'Oh.' But Gino couldn't stop staring.

'You know what, Roadrunner?' Magozzi said. 'That's a really good look for you. Kind of Gary Cooper. Long, tall cowboy.'

'Yeah?'

'Yeah. Here are the films you asked for.'

'Oh, gee, thanks, this is going to get things rolling.' The long, tall cowboy hurried back to his desk, smiling.

Harley gave Magozzi a thumbs-up from across the room, then tipped his black beard toward the table in the far corner by the window. John Smith was sitting alone, tapping away on a laptop. 'Hey, Smith. Meet Minneapolis's finest. Leo Magozzi and Gino Rolseth.'

Smith stopped typing and stood up, and the three men took each other's measure in an instant. Grace looked on in obvious bemusement. Men always measured themselves against each other, which wasn't all that different from women, except that men did it so damn fast. There was an instant of locked eyes that apparently revealed everything they needed to know about each other. Women spent a lot longer with preliminary social chatter, while their real attention was focused on what Magozzi had told her was the superficial.

Women look at clothes and makeup and weight and all sorts of silly shit . . .

What women do that?

Women who aren't you, Grace. They're looking for flaws. But men look for weaknesses first. Kind of an enemy assessment.

Grace had smiled at him. *They're both kind of an enemy assessment, aren't they?*

'Good morning, Detective Magozzi, Detective Rolseth. I'm Special Agent John Smith. I'm afraid we haven't had much success tracing the posted film of your homicide . . .'

'Grace told us.'

'. . . and I understand from your Chief that MPD is also hitting a dead end on the local investigation.'

Gino pulled out a chair and sat down. 'Great. Now we've established that we're all big fat failures.'

'I certainly didn't mean to imply—'

'Yeah, yeah, sorry. I'm operating on really low voltage this morning. But you gotta remember, our investigation just got started late last night. Up until then, our homicide was ruled an accident, so don't count out the MPD just yet.'

'On the contrary. We're counting on MPD. Toward that end, the Bureau would like to offer any assistance you might require. If you need help on the ground in evidence collection, canvassing, forensics, or suspect interviews, Special Agent in Charge Paul Shafer has committed to provide the manpower . . .'

'Thanks, but we've got it covered,' Magozzi interrupted, still standing, taking the high ground. 'We put twenty more officers on site early this morning, blanketing the area between the club our vic left and where he ended up in the river. Any more would be overkill.'

'Still, some extra eyes and hands might be helpful.'

Magozzi finally sat across from Smith and leaned forward, eye to eye. 'Straight up, Smith. I don't feel like dancing this morning. Washington wants the case, right?'

Smith looked right back at him. 'That was the initial recommendation.'

'You have absolutely no jurisdiction here.' Magozzi always spoke very slowly, very softly just before he started to bellow. Gino closed his eyes and waited. 'Wishful thinking is about the only thing you've got connecting our case to your five. There is no way our Chief will voluntarily sign off on passing the ball to the Feds.'

'I'm sure you're right, but— '

'This is MPD's case, and we don't need a parade of suits stomping all over our scene or interviewing potential witnesses or suspects. We've been down that road before, and when you start dividing tasks and information between agencies, a lot of it tends to get lost. Is it like that in D.C., or is Paul Shafer the only asshole in the organization?'

Smith leaned back in his chair. 'Lord, no, he's not the only one.'

Gino snickered.

'And remember, I said that was the initial recommendation. I talked them out of it, at least for now. Just keep me in the loop, and I'll do the same from my end. That's all I ask.'

Damn, Magozzi hated it when people did this to him. You get all prepped for battle and then the jerk you're ready to stab through the heart lays down his sword. 'Fair enough,' he grumbled.

'I got something here,' Harley hollered from across the room, and everybody gathered around his computer. He pointed to some lines of text on a monitor bigger than Gino's TV. 'Check this out. It's an encrypted post I hacked from one of your hot sites, Smith. It says, "City of Lakes. Bride in the water. Or would that be a groom? Near beer." Whatever that means.'

'The film showed the old Grain Belt sign across the river,' Magozzi said.

'Then that's gotta be your case, guys.'

Magozzi shrugged. 'Sure. But this thing is all over the news, which means it's all over the Web.'

'I know. But you said your guy drowned two nights ago, right?'

'Right.'

'Well, this thing was posted the day before the murder.'

The absence of sound in the room was profound, like a

vacuum had sucked the air out of it. 'Are you sure?' Magozzi finally asked.

'Positive. This sick bastard was pre-advertising and then he posted his trophy film to prove he did it.'

Chapter Twelve

Magozzi looked at the sign on the door that read CHELSEA
THOMAS and his mouth turned down. Who named their kid
Chelsea? And if you got saddled with a moniker like that,
you ought to grow up to be an exotic dancer instead of an
FBI profiler. This was going to suck, big time.

Ten minutes later he was in a private office that looked
like every other FBI office he'd been in. Desk, chair, book-
case, Venetian blinds. Robot land.

And, oh Lord, was she ever a Fed, through and through.
Came in from a side room in a shapeless blue suit and one
of those pasted smiles that flashed on and off so fast you
could never be sure you'd seen it at all. She had real blond
hair pulled back in a bun, apologizing for its brightness, the
fair skin and blue eyes that went with it.

'Detective Magozzi.' She held out her hand for a cursory
shake, then sat behind her desk and opened a thin file folder
centered on the blotter. 'Thank you very much for agreeing
to see me.'

'Agent Smith asked nicely.'

'I'm sure he did.'

'But he wasn't real specific about the reason.'

She nodded. 'I've been working these murders since the
Cleveland film, never expecting to have one land on my
home turf. Talking directly to the detective in charge of the
case might help with my profiling.'

Magozzi pointed at the file on her desk. 'You got our case summary, right?'

'Yes.'

'Everything's in there.'

'There might be something else, something you didn't think was significant that could come out in conversation.'

Magozzi tried not to roll his eyes. Man, she sounded like every shrink he'd ever talked to.

'Sit down, Detective, please. Would you like coffee? Tea?'

'It's five o'clock. You have a beer?'

'Sorry.'

'Not as sorry as I am.'

She was already busily writing on her little pad.

'You're taking a lot of notes for a meeting that's lasted less than a minute. You mind telling me what's so interesting?'

She put down her pen – fountain, not ballpoint – and looked up at him. 'I was just prefacing our talk with the observation that you do not trust the Bureau in general, or my specialty of profiling in particular. Correct?'

Magozzi exhaled noisily and fought off the Minnesota impulse to be polite at all costs. 'I put profiling on about the same level as consulting psychics.'

'It's a little more scientific than that.'

'Oh, yeah? Well, the way I see it, you people go through the records cops made, see that a real high percentage of serial killers are male, white, between the ages of twenty-five and thirty-seven, blah, blah, blah, then predict that any serial killer is male, white, and between the ages of twenty-five and thirty-seven, and then when those same cops nab the guy, you say, "See, what did we tell you?" There was a fake gypsy at my high school carnival that did a hell of a lot better than that.'

Dr. Chelsea Thomas put her elbow on the desk and her chin in her hand, and Magozzi tried to analyze the body language. God knew she was analyzing his, and the least he could do was return the favor. Man, he hated shrinks. He folded his arms across his chest and tipped back his head, looking down his nose at her. See that? Defensive arm posture; disdainful head position. Take cover.

Obviously he wasn't having a whole lot of luck intimidating her, because she smiled at him. A really great smile. 'It *is* five o'clock. Past five, in fact, and there's a terrific Irish pub a few blocks over with some great stuff on tap. If you're up for it, it might be an environment a little more conducive to establishing a productive working relationship. What do you say?'

Magozzi frowned at her, sensing a trap. 'Are you asking me out on a date?'

She laughed quietly. It was a nice laugh, but humiliating, all the same. 'Absolutely not. But this isn't analysis, Detective, and it certainly isn't mandatory. I was hoping that we might be able to help each other on this case, but clearly you're uncomfortable here.' She hesitated for a moment. 'And obviously you've had a very bad day.'

That was one of the great come-ons with the mental health crowd. From priests to psychiatrists, the standard opening was something that was supposed to sound sympathetic, but was really a trick to get you to spill your guts. Magozzi ought to know. He'd used the same tactic in interrogation rooms often enough. 'Killers are getting their rocks off posting films of real murders on the Internet, and at least one of them advertised who they were going to kill ahead of time. If you're even close to human and you've read that file you've had a pretty goddamned bad day, too.'

She looked down at the file in the center of her very tidy desk, then pushed her fingers back through her hair, making it stand up and look weird. This was body language Magozzi understood, because it was brutally honest. Women did not muss coiffed hair or rub mascaraed eyes voluntarily; this was impulsive, careless, and real. 'I've read the file. And, yes, I've had a pretty bad day. And I could use a beer. Maybe two, because it looks like all the beasts are coming out to play.'

It was indeed a terrific pub, with a wild Irish band and the smell of hops and sweat and probably twenty criminals who looked a lot like Harley Davidson doing jigs in their motorcycle boots. Whatever the on-tap stuff was, it hit Magozzi's system like great-grandmother's practice quilt, fluttering down over your body and head, blocking the light, making a hidey hole.

'I've never seen anything like this,' Dr. Chelsea Thomas was saying, words running together just a little, because she was on her second beer, as promised, and she wasn't used to it. 'People use the Web to post documentation of their bad behavior all the time.'

'Like those high school girls beating up their classmate.'

'Exactly. But aside from the very rare snuff film that appears on an underground site, we've never seen film of a real murder posted, certainly not on sites like YouTube, and that's what frightens me. Whoever is posting these films is bragging.'

Magozzi stared at her. 'Bragging to whom?'

'The whole world. The point is, the FBI has confirmed five actual homicides with posted videos – six, counting your river killing – all of which have happened within the last four months. This is truly chilling.'

Well, yes, it was, but in spite of that fact, Magozzi had part of a beer inside and a warm environment outside and a pretty woman across from him, and he was starting to get a little too comfortable. He waved over a waitress and ordered hamburgers and onion rings. This was bar food – bad food – and he was salivating like Pavlov's dog waiting for it. He tried to remember the last time he'd stopped at a bar on the way home for a couple of brews and some saturated fat, and couldn't. 'You and my partner think alike.'

'Is that good or bad?'

'Bad. You've just given validity to his theory that it's a traveling serial killer taking advantage of a world-wide audience.'

Dr. Chelsea Thomas shrugged out of her blue suit jacket and showed a white blouse with little frilly ruffles around the collar that interested Magozzi not at all, because Grace wasn't wearing it. 'Let's hope so.'

'Excuse me?'

'Look at it this way. Take your average serial or thrill killer. All that bullshit— ' she stopped abruptly and blinked. 'Oh dear. Sorry about the language.' She pushed her beer mug away. 'Anyway, all that dogma about killers waiting to get caught, wanting to get caught, makes people think they're remorseful and need to expunge their guilt. Pure nonsense. They're looking for the celebrity. Heck, some of them repeat like they were going for the *Guinness Book of Records* title for most hits, or most horrible hits, whatever. Trouble with a career like that is you can't show off how good you are.'

'So this killer is looking for attention.'

'Not attention. Fame. There's a big difference. Attention invites scrutiny, and, like I said, these sickos don't want to be caught. From the conception to the crime, to the fear they create in the public and the frustration they cause the cops, this whole process is all about power. But we're a visual society now. Headlines don't cut it because nobody reads anymore, and cops never show the butchered victims on the nightly news. Enter the Internet. "See what I did? See what I can do to *you*?"'

Magozzi actually felt his face crinkling up, which, for some inexplicable reason, made her smile again.

'So. If serial killers can show their work on the Net, the power surge intensifies. The film is the new trophy. They don't have to cut off body parts or snatch bloody panties to hide in their walls. They don't have to escalate to garner attention, which is how we've always caught them. They deliver visual evidence to the whole world of what they do like some Hollywood mogul premiering a new movie, and we are never going to catch these people again.'

Magozzi blinked at her. 'That's really negative.'

She leaned back as the waitress slid a plate piled with poison food in front of her. 'Well, that's a shame, because that was the good news. Just what serial killers might do with the Web. Too bad I don't think that's what's happening here, because it's much worse.' She picked up an onion ring, took a bite, and closed her eyes. 'Oh God, that's good. I haven't had one of these in years.'

'Wait just a minute. Put down that onion ring.'

Once she started giggling, she couldn't seem to stop. 'Oh Lord, cops really talk like that, don't they? I feel like I'm in a movie. And I also think I may have had a bit too much to drink.'

'You've had a beer and a half.'

'I know. But I've never actually had a whole entire beer before. Ever.'

'Are you kidding?'

'No, I'm Mormon. At least I used to be.' That made her laugh, too, and she covered her mouth with her hand like a kid with braces. 'Do you think you could order me a glass of milk?'

Magozzi was trying not to smile, because it didn't seem appropriate, seeing that she'd just told him serial killers weren't the worst thing in life. 'Do not drink any more of that beer. Do not get drunk. When I get back, I want to know what's worse than serial killers using the Internet.'

She gave him a silly little smile and picked up her hamburger.

Big surprise. Irish pubs did not serve milk. He had to go to the convenience store at the end of the block and then race back before Miss Psychiatrist FBI agent/profiler passed out in the booth. He slammed down a gallon of skim.

'That's really big.' Her plate was almost empty, and she looked almost normal.

'I wanted one of those little cartons you used to get in grade school. Profiteering money-hungry bastards don't carry them. Don't even carry quarts, or half gallons. You want milk, you lay down your pension.'

'Sorry. I'll buy your dinner. Which is now cold and greasy.'

'Thank you for the review.'

She pushed away her plate with one finger and smiled. 'We're talking about terrible things, and this is very unprofessional, but I want you to know I'm actually having a nice time tonight, which was totally unexpected, and really appreciated.'

Magozzi smiled and took a bite of his burger. It was cold and greasy and fabulous. 'What's in this?' he asked the exasperated waitress as she dodged drunken dancers and passed their table.

'A dead animal. What do you think?'

Chelsea Thomas, should-have-been exotic dancer, watched him dig in. 'Do you have any women friends, Detective?'

He shook his head while he chewed. 'Never have. I have women I love, and women I lust after.'

'Do you lust after the woman you love?'

'I do.'

She picked up her last onion ring and held it up to the light like a jewel. 'That's just about as perfect as it gets, isn't it? Tell me about her.'

Magozzi put his burger down on the plate and stared at it. This was just about the strangest evening he'd ever spent in his life, which was saying something when you were a homicide cop. Maybe it was the beer or the mood or the fact that they were sitting at a table in a bar with a gallon of milk between them, but whatever it was, he opened his mouth and Grace MacBride fell out. He told her everything; things he'd never thought aloud to himself, let alone voiced to anyone else. She listened to every word, drinking it in like it was some kind of magic elixir, and when he was finished, and embarrassed, she did a man thing. She ignored all the intimate feelings he had shared as if they had never happened, and changed the subject.

'This is what I'm really afraid is happening, Detective.'

The room was dark except for the halogen puddles that spilled down onto the worktable, illuminating two pairs of gloved hands that cast eerie, mesmerizing shadows on the wall as they carefully poured viscous liquid into the containers and lined them up in the center of the table – none of them touching, all of them far from the edge. Such a simple task, but the first part had taken over an hour.

All the practice runs had been helpful, but essentially worthless. This time it was the real thing, and nerves crept into the equation, making hands shake and hearts beat faster.

When the last container was sealed, they both stepped back from the table a few steps and just breathed, letting the nerves settle before part two.

They'd prepared the outer packagings first, and those were all waiting on the floor with their tops open like hungry baby birds. The interior shields were secure, meticulously placed and anchored.

Lowering the inner containers was slow, methodical, and nerve-wracking. A drop of sweat loaded with DNA fell and spread on one of the packages. It would leave a telltale watermark, and that package was immediately discarded and replaced with a spare. They'd thought of everything, and it had all been so pathetically simple, as most acts of genius were. Everything you needed to know was all right there on the Internet.

They had often wondered why no one had done it before, but it was certain that a lot of others would do it soon, because it wouldn't be long before the whole world was watching.

Chapter Thirteen

Judge James Bukowski had celebrated his release from the Hennepin County Hilton by re-toxing with an excellent bottle of sour mash that had quelled his shakes and improved his spirits considerably; at least up until the point he'd lost sentience, sometime around noon.

Hours later, when he finally came to in the chilly embrace of his Corbusier chaise, his furry mind surprised him with a singular, revelatory thought that seemed deeply profound to him, primarily because it didn't involve the logistical planning of getting to the bathroom for aspirin and Ativan: he really hated this goddamned fucking uncomfortable overpriced chair. He *really hated it*.

Wife Number Four had managed to convince him, after several years of passive-aggressive torture and craven guilt-tripping, that original Mid-Century Modern was not only chic, not only a shrewd investment opportunity, but also 'outrageously comfortable' – no doubt a paraphrase from some article she'd read, because the woman had never strung a polysyllabic sentence together in her life.

Well, the über-cow had been wrong, so wrong, no doubt brainwashed by *Architectural Digest*, her flaming-faggot designer, and her pathetic, social-climbing friends, just as she'd brainwashed him. The difference was, the hall of famer from the pantheon of idiots had figured that out before he had, obviously – because the chair was about the only thing of value he'd gotten out of that divorce. And if he'd been sober a single day during the five-year marriage, he would have realized this, and probably a lot of other things he'd missed in the black hole of dead brain cells.

Where the hell had that come from? he wondered to himself, and then, for the first time in a long while, the judge smiled a genuine smile. Little nuggets of self-reflection had always raised their ugly, unmanageable heads throughout his life, and they terrified him. Bourbon helped with the whack-a-mole game he played with his deeper thoughts when they inconvenienced him, but tonight, for some reason, things seemed just a little bit different. And as much as he wanted to believe he'd come to this pivotal moment on his own, he had to give Detective Magozzi credit for facing him squarely last night and calling him out. *What happened to the respected judge?*

What happened, indeed! He'd never believed in second chances, not in life and not on the bench, but he was going to make an exception right here and now. It was time for him to stop being such a self-pitying, self-indulgent fuck and get back to the business of doling out justice. He made a mental note to send Magozzi a fruit basket or something.

Feeling more sober than he had in several decades, and with a renewed sense of purpose, he fished his cell phone out of his pocket and dialed Ex-Wife Number Four. She wasn't on speed-dial, but the number lived on vividly, and unpleasantly, in his memory. Of course she didn't answer – she never did – but that didn't really matter.

'Jennifer, this is Jim. No need to call back, I just wanted

to let you know that the Corbusier and I have finally decided to amicably part, due to irreconcilable differences. And instead of consigning it with Christie's, as was my initial thought, I've decided that I want you to have it. I know you love it so much, and who wouldn't, being that it is so outrageously comfortable. I will arrange for a delivery within the next few days, I hope that suits you. That's all.'

He hung up, pulled himself off the chair that had catalyzed his new beginning, and instead of going to the liquor cabinet or the pharmacy that was his bathroom medicine cabinet, he went straight to the gun safe and selected a Remington 870 Express. 'Here comes the judge.'

Chapter Fourteen

The rising sun was just beginning to paint the sky and waken the city, but the Monkeewrench office lights were still burning, as they had been all night. Annie and Grace had finally crashed in guest rooms at five a.m., but Harley and Roadrunner kept working, fueled by a steady intake of overcaffeinated beverages and chocolate.

Harley pushed back from his computer and rubbed his burning eyes. 'Roadrunner, dump the programming work and give me a hand here.'

'What are you doing?'

'Well, I was thinking that if our bride drowning was pre-advertised, maybe there were pre-posts for the other five murders.'

'Not a bad idea, but I can't do it, Harley. We're way behind on programming.'

Harley rolled his chair over to Roadrunner's station and spun his friend around to face him. 'Listen, we can get the new program up and running within a week, and what's the prize for that? Verifying that what look like dead people are really dead people, instead of some asshole teenager's idea of a video prank. But if we find other posts forecasting the murders we know about, then maybe we find a pattern, maybe we find some new posts in time to save some lives.'

Roadrunner tugged at the denim creases bunching around the backs of his knees. 'Well. No contest, then, is there?'

Harley shook his big head. 'Not to my way of thinking.' He jerked a thumb over his shoulder at where Agent Smith was sleeping on a couch. 'Don't know how he's going to feel about it, though.'

Smith rolled his supposedly sleeping head and opened his eyes. 'Go for the posts,' he said, then turned over.

'It might delay the new software.'

'Go for the posts,' Smith repeated.

An hour later Roadrunner entered the last command with a single push of the enter button, and text started scrolling up his screen. 'Holy mackerel, Harley. They just popped up. Every one of them.'

Harley's motorcycle boots pounding across the wooden floor startled Smith awake. 'What's going on?'

Harley was staring at Roadrunner's monitor, rocking on his heels, slab arms folded across his chest, grinning. 'Holy shit. Holy rosy shit. I'll tell you what's going on. My little buddy here found forecast postings for the city murders. Every goddamned one of them. Even our river bride is on the list.' He gave Smith a hearty slap on the shoulder when he came over to read. 'How about that?'

'How the hell did you find them?'

'Oh, man, this was so cool. I kept trying these broad search programs on words and syllables and anything else I could dream up an algorithm for, and all the time I was so pissed at this idiot because he couldn't even type. Kept hitting the shift key in the wrong places, capping letters that shouldn't be capitalized, missing ones that should. And then

I noticed that "city of lakes" was the only part of the header with typos. Every other word was perfect, and that seemed weird. Take a look.' He enlarged the Minneapolis post on the screen.

> CiTy oF laKes. Bride in the water. Or would
> that be a groom? Near beer.

'See? The first, third, sixth, and ninth characters are capped. So I did a search on that specific pattern of caps and lower-case and this one popped: "CiTy oF anGels. No home. Near pier.''

'That's the L.A. murder,' Smith said. 'The victim was a homeless man found under the Santa Monica Pier on June 4th.'

Roadrunner looked up at him. 'This was posted June 2nd.'

Smith pulled up a chair. 'Let me look at the rest of them.'

'It's all right there.' Roadrunner rolled aside to make room for him while Harley hovered behind his shoulder.

'City of Rock?' Smith read.

'Gotta be Cleveland,' Harley said. 'The Rock and Roll Hall of Fame is there. And look at that – City of Longhorns. That's Austin.'

Smith nodded. 'And here's Chicago – City of Broad Shoulders. And City of Starbucks is obviously Seattle. My God. That's all of our five, plus the Minneapolis river murder.'

'Jesus,' Harley muttered. 'What kind of a sick game is this guy playing?'

'It gets worse. Take a look at this.' Roadrunner punched

the page down key and Smith's face went a little gray. 'Page two. This is an old post, from January. "City of Big Water. Hole in one. North Shore." Same typo pattern, same general format, but I don't know if it's a pre-post for a real murder. Any chance your guys in Cyber Crimes missed one?'

Smith closed his eyes briefly. 'That's been a concern since we received the first video. Remember, the only reason we found five was because the sites sent us the murder films when they were posted.'

Harley grumbled. 'If that's a real one, the vic's toast by now. What about the last one?'

'"City of Roses. Bert's barmaid. Near deer."'

'When was it posted?'

'Let me check.' Roadrunner fiddled on his keyboard for a few seconds and pulled up a new screen. 'Okay, here it is. Posted on . . . oh, Jesus.'

'What is it?' Harley leaned closer to the monitor.

'It was posted last night. This one may not have happened yet.'

Chapter Fifteen

Magozzi was sitting at his desk with the morning's fourth mug of coffee, staring out the window at the steady rain and the swarm of colorful umbrellas with legs that were fleeing the streets and disappearing into the downtown office buildings. The downpour had started early, just after dawn, riding in on a massive bank of black clouds that had settled into an indefinite stall over the Twin Cities. At the moment, it was making glacial progress eastward, drenching the center of the state with triple the expected rainfall. Assuming that a storm system of such biblical proportions would be easy to spot on Doppler, it seemed odd to him that the meteorologists hadn't given any advance warning on the news last night. Hell, maybe this *was* an act of God. Or a portent of doom. Or both.

He hadn't slept much after he'd safely delivered a tipsy Chelsea Thomas to her uptown Minneapolis house last night. Probably a combination of too much beer, too much grease, and too much conversation about things that were going on in the world that could drive anyone with a soul to consider suicide. Or perhaps it was the unexpected hug, warm and genuine, that she'd given him in the car before dashing up her front walk and letting herself in with a final, grandiose wave goodbye . . .

'Leo? Hello?'

Gino was suddenly standing next to him, looking wet and bedraggled.

'Oh . . . morning, Gino.'

'Are you even awake?'

'I'm not sure.'

'Good. Me either. What's with this rain bullshit, anyhow?' He shucked off his blazer, exposing a pristine white shirt and intact tie, but the front of his pants were visibly wet, the cuffs still dripping water over his sodden loafers and onto the floor.

'What the hell happened to you?'

'Oh, I was so hoping you'd ask. Angela needed the car today because the Volvo's in the shop – again – so she dropped me off at the corner. And guess what? The storm drains are backed up, there's a foot of standing water in the streets, and I'm the lucky guy who was on the curb when some cowboy in an SUV decided to run a yellow light at thirty-five miles an hour. My toes feel like stewed prunes and I'm not even going to take a stab at describing what cold, wet undershorts are doing to other parts of my anatomy right now.'

'I appreciate that more than you know.'

Gino sank into his chair and ran a hand through the blond hedge of his buzzcut like a squeegee. A mist of water rained down onto his desk blotter. 'So where is everybody?'

'McLaren and Tinker caught a call at a rental on Blaisdell; landlord and tenant got into it and one of them ended up at the bottom of the basement stairs with his head in pieces . . .'

'Man, you're just daisies in the morning, Leo, you know that?'

'. . . almost everybody else is working the "suspicious death" in Little Mogadishu.'

'Ah. I heard about that one on the news on the way in. Seven bullet holes in the kid, and right away someone labels it suspicious.'

'That's the one. And Gloria's at the dentist.'

Gloria handled the phones, the files, and ran roughshod over all the detectives in Homicide. She was almost ebony-black, lived on fast food and flamboyant clothing, and tortured Detective Johnny McLaren's Jack Sprat frame with every single swing of her generous hips. She was also one of the few people in the world who could out-sass Gino, and leave him happy about it, which was a rare and wondrous gift.

'Damn. Gloria was the only bright spot I expected in this day. What was she wearing?'

'That tiger-striped thing she always wears to the dentist. Root canal this time, and she's going to be mean as a wet cat when she gets back.'

Gino grunted. 'Not that anybody'll be able to tell the difference. And what happened to you last night? Tried calling you at ten, you weren't home, and not to put to fine a point on it, but you look like crap. Almost hungover.'

'Bad sleep and not much of it.'

'I get that. I had nonstop nightmares about nuking everything with a circuit board in my house.' His eyes drifted to the huge, cellophane-wrapped wicker basket that monopolized the entirety of Magozzi's desktop. 'Is that a fruit basket?'

'Yeah.'

'What's up with that?'

'It's from Judge Jim.'

Gino frowned. 'You busted the guy's balls last night and he sends you a fruit basket? That doesn't make any sense.'

'Maybe he doesn't get many visitors.'

'Well, shit. Give me a banana. So how was your meeting with the profiler last night?'

'Interesting. Depressing. Scary.' Magozzi ripped open the fruit basket, tossed a banana to Gino, and grabbed an apple for himself.

'Yeah? Did he tell you anything you didn't already know?'

'Kind of. And it's a she, by the way.'

Gino waited patiently for further edification while he peeled his banana, and when it didn't come, he leaned forward on his elbows. 'You're a million miles away, Leo. So who exactly is this "she," and are you going to tell me what she said that has you so doped up, or is it rated X?'

'It's rated G. But she had some insights.'

'Like?'

'Like the Web is normalizing deviant behavior.'

'Is there anybody in the world with a Ph.D. who actually speaks English?'

'She does, and everything she said made a scary kind of sense.'

'Oh, man. She's either one good shrink, or she's a part-time supermodel, if she's got you jumping on the psycho-babble wagon train.'

Magozzi gave him a warning glance. 'Do you want to hear this or not?'

'Sorry. Go for it.'

'There have always been the natural born killers, and there always will be, and of course they're going to use the Web, just like everybody else in the world.'

'Well, yeah, we kind of figured that out already.'

'But, there are also a lot of people on the cusp – disgruntled, twisted, deviant, whatever – who might normally never act on their urges in the real world because there's no catalyst to push them to the next level. And some of these types actually understand that what they're feeling is antisocial and wrong. Enter the Web – a safe, fantasy forum to communicate with like-minded people. "Hey, Joe, you fantasize about raping and killing women? Me too!" Get a blog with fifty or a hundred or a thousand guys like Joe talking to one another, and you've got yourself a whole new culture with its own morals and code of conduct.'

Gino grimaced like he'd just swallowed a bug. 'Christ.'

'It's a support structure. And her assumption is, it can escalate into reality from there. How many of the school shootings in the last few years would have happened if Columbine hadn't happened first?'

'So what we might have is a bunch of amoral whack jobs telling the other amoral whack jobs out there that it's A-okay to murder, and then they all start believing it for real?'

'Yeah. Like that.'

'Sounds like *Lord of the Flies* and a twelve-step program for homicide all rolled into one.'

'That's what she's afraid is happening. That the Web is actually enabling these monsters and the community is getting stronger.'

Gino put down his half-eaten banana and stared at it.

Long ago he'd come to the point in his life where he believed he'd seen it and heard it all, the worst of the worst that humanity had to offer. But if this were really happening, he'd been pretty goddamned wrong about that. 'How can she sleep at night with all that crap running through her head? I mean, I've come up with some pretty crazy scenarios over the years, but even I couldn't dream that shit up. How the hell are we supposed to keep up with something like this?'

Magozzi shook his head. 'I think that's why Cyber Crimes is task-forcing this thing nationally.'

'I should have known this day was gonna suck the minute that asshole in the SUV gave me a shower. So what did she think about my traveling-serial-killer theory?'

Magozzi looked to the side with a pained expression. 'That, believe it or not, would be the best-case scenario, just like you said. Unfortunately, she thinks it's a disconnected group of killers talking to each other on the Web, playing some sick kind of one-upmanship game.'

'Aw, man, Leo, that so sucks. Say it ain't so.' Gino cocked his head and listened. 'On the bright side, do you hear AC/DC?'

Magozzi pulled his cell phone out of his breast pocket. 'New ring tone.'

'"Highway to Hell." How appropriate.'

'Hang on, it's Grace. Hey, Grace.' He was quiet for a long time, his face growing darker the longer he listened. 'Are you sure? Shit. Okay, read it to me and we'll work it.' He grabbed a pen and tablet and started scribbling furiously. 'Got it. I'll get back to you.' He snapped his phone closed and shoved the tablet over to Gino. 'They found pre-posts for all the murders, plus two more. Willy Loman's looking less likely every second. They think this one is in Minnesota, and want us to make some cop-to-cop phone calls and see if we can match it with a body.'

Gino spun the tablet around and read what Magozzi had written. 'Huh. Hello, of course that's Minnesota. Big water, North Shore, hell, that's Lake Superior, the Norwegian Riviera. Let me give old Ole Olssen a call. He's been a Duluth cop for about a hundred years.'

Magozzi looked at him. 'Tell me there's not really an Ole Olssen in Duluth.'

'Tons of them. Where'd you think the Ole-and-Lena jokes came from?'

'And you know him because . . . ?'

'He was down here for that BCA crime-scene deal last year, remember? I went to the stupid lectures and you went to the movies with Grace, thank you very much. Anyway, Ole and I bonded over krumkakke.'

'I don't know what that is.'

'Those hollow cookie things the Swedes make, or maybe the Norwegians or the Dutch, damned if I know. Shit, they were good.' He started punching numbers into the phone.

'You know his number by heart?'

'Yeah, we talk now and then.' He raised his eyes and looked at Magozzi. 'You said they found two more posts. What's the other one?'

'They're working that one with the Feds. They don't think it's happened yet.'

Gino's lips pursed in a silent whistle until he was distracted by the phone. 'Hey, Ole, you son of a bitch, you know that recipe you sent me? It sucked big time. Tasted like dead sheep with the wool still on. And while we're talking about dead things, you have any homicides up there for last January? Well, do a little digging and get back to me ASAP. This is more important than you would believe, and I am not going to tell you what it's about until you deliver the goods.'

Chapter Sixteen

Grace couldn't explain it, not even to herself, and it was embarrassing. She missed her house. They all spent a lot of nights at Harley's when they were working on a pressure deadline – it was a natural, comfortable thing. She had a guest room designated just for her, as they all did, with furniture, a stash of clothes, and everything in the world Harley thought would make her comfortable. But it wasn't her house.

It was too big, for one thing; three nightmare stories of too many points of ingress and egress to watch; too many big open rooms that put you endless yards away from anyplace to hide. She could take a breath in her tiny house with its tiny rooms, steel doors, and barred windows, but here, she never felt really safe. Harley understood that, and occasionally reminded her that he had a gate across his driveway and enough weapons stashed to arm a small country. But he didn't have enough security cameras; didn't have a pressure pad on his front porch; didn't even have a gun on his person at all times, or a wary eye and ear for anything out of order.

Harley couldn't get over the silly idea that most people were basically good. He didn't think the UPS guy was a terrorist, or that the mailman was a psychopath. None of them did. Only Grace.

That difference in perspective had put her at her computer station, searching for the worst this morning, while Harley, Roadrunner, Annie, and Special Agent John Smith frantically scrambled to grab the brass ring that was the victory of good over evil. They had to believe they had a chance. That given just a little time, they could find whoever it was that was Bert's barmaid in a city of roses, near deer, before a killer took that person's life.

'Okay, okay,' Harley filled the room with his voice in boom mode. 'No liquor licenses in Portland with the name of Bert, which may not mean anything. Could be a grandfathered license that goes with the establishment instead of the current owner – Annie, can you check city of Portland ordinances, see how the licensing works?'

'You got it.' Annie clicked at her keyboard with fingers flat, so she didn't chip her nails. They were still polished pearl to match the Gatsby outfit she'd worn yesterday instead of today's maroon silk, a tragic measure of how quickly she'd been forced to make herself presentable when Roadrunner had wakened them in a panic. The jacket was feather-trimmed and cropped, the pants were wide and fluttery, and thank God she'd remembered the T-strap pumps or she would have looked totally undone. She focused on her task and blanked out Harley barking orders to the rest of them.

'So Portland was the City of Roses – maybe too easy. Let's do some free association. Forget the city's nickname or moniker; what other cities bring roses to mind?'

'Pasadena,' Agent John Smith piped in. 'The Rose Parade.'

'Exactly. Check the liquor licenses there, see if you can find a Bert. What else have you got, Roadrunner?'

'Austin, surprisingly. They've got rose growers all over the place.'

'Christ.' Harley slapped his forehead. 'Every rose I ordered for the back gardens came from Jackson and Perkins. Damn. Where the hell are they? Medford, Oregon. That's it. Grace, can you check that out?'

'I'm working another angle,' Grace replied, never taking her eyes from her screen.

'Okay, I'll tackle that one . . .'

And so it went.

Ten minutes later Harley clapped his hands together and shouted, 'Hallelujah! I got a Bert on a liquor license for Medford. Place is named Chesterfield's.'

'You have a number for Medford Police?' John Smith had his cell phone flipped open, and started punching in numbers as Harley rattled them off.

Grace sighed and rolled her chair back from her desk, although she kept her eyes on the monitor. 'Wait. You need to see this first.'

FBI Agent John Smith watched, mystified, as the others rose slowly from their stations and moved toward Grace's desk. No questions, no uncertainty. If Grace MacBride said they needed to see something, they dropped what they were doing and moved. Grace's screen was blacked out, her hand poised over the mouse. She looked up at them one by one. 'Are you ready for this? It isn't pretty.'

Smith said, 'Go.'

The film was remarkably steady and clear; obviously not

produced by some cheap handheld. The camera panned around a thick forest of pine trees surrounding a deserted parking lot, one security light towering on a single pole, spreading a wash of blue-white glow over the night scene. Zoom to door, the darkened neon sign overhead.

'Wait,' Harley stabbed at the screen. 'Does that say Chesterfield's? Looks like a "C," then an "H' . . .'

'We'll check it later,' Grace said. 'Just watch.'

A woman came out of the door, closed and locked it behind her, then walked out into the lot. She paused once to look up at the sky and smile, then walked a few more steps forward and stopped dead.

'She saw the camera,' Annie whispered.

And then in the next split second, almost before they had time to process what they were seeing, a shadow moved into frame from the darkness at the side and the gleam of a knife appeared at the woman's throat. They saw only a masculine arm wrapped around her shoulders, and the metal of the knife.

'Jesus,' Roadrunner whispered.

'Don't,' the woman said, and the camera saw her eyes, and the tears welling. 'Don't hurt me.' And then, bizarrely, 'It's my birthday.'

'This is horrible,' Harley said quietly, and then their eyes flickered as the action on the film stuttered forward. There was a struggle, a short scream, and at the end of the fevered action, the woman was on the asphalt with her knees folded sideways, a massive choke chain around her neck, a leash attached to it. She gagged as the leash was pulled and the collar tightened, then she was dragged out of frame.

'Dear God,' Annie whispered. 'What's he's doing . . . ?'

Grace held up one finger as the film wobbled and then jerked wildly. 'He's repositioning the camera for the next scene.'

And now they saw the woman sitting in front of a small car, her knees tucked up to her chest, her arms spread in a cross, tied to the bumper. The leash was fastened to pull her head backwards, exposing her neck. The man's back came into view as he approached her, the flash of the knife swishing back and forth, threatening her, coming closer and closer while the camera watched, and the woman, God bless her, made no sound. The tears streamed down her cheeks, reflecting in the light of the security lamp overhead, but she was in the moment, watching her assailant, ready to fight, and waiting for her time.

Annie closed her eyes.

'Don't, Annie,' Grace said quietly. 'You'll miss who she is.'

The woman sat curled on the pebbled surface of the parking lot, watching the knife swish back and forth, closer and closer to her neck, but by God she wasn't going to give this bastard the satisfaction of seeing her terror, and when the moment came, her cowboy-booted foot kicked out and connected between her assailant's legs, and with his squeal of pain a triumphant exhalation spilled out of her mouth.

'God DAMN you stupid smelly BITCH!'

And now Grace closed her eyes, because she'd already seen what came next. She'd already seen the flash of the knife at the woman's throat and the spill of blood that flooded her neck, and she didn't want to see it again. Ever.

The screen went black, and no one said anything for a long moment. Finally, Agent Smith turned away from Grace's station and walked back toward the table by the window that had become his place. 'I'll call Medford,' was all he said. He used the landline, and when someone answered, he put it on speaker. 'This is Special Agent Smith of the Federal Bureau of Investigation. I'd like to speak to the officer in charge.'

'You got him,' a gravelly voice replied. 'Chief Frost here, and – mister, I've got my hands full this morning. Can I get back to you?'

'I don't think so, Chief Frost. I'll fill you in on the back story later; for right now, I'm advising you of a homicide committed in your district last night at a place called Chesterfield's.'

There was silence on the other end of the line for a long moment. 'Who did you say you were?'

'Special Agent Smith of the—'

'I'm going to have to verify that with a callback to your office.'

Smith winced. 'I'm not actually in my office at the moment . . .'

'Uh-huh. Well, where are you now, Mr. Smith? Perhaps we could meet and have a little talk in person.'

Smith never lost his temper. You weren't allowed to do that in the Bureau, but this yahoo was wasting precious time . . .

'He thinks you're a nutcase,' Grace said.

'Or the killer,' Annie added.

Grace picked up the receiver on her phone. 'Chief Frost?

This is Grace McBride of Monkeewrench in Minneapolis. We sent you a copy of our software two days ago.'

'Oh, hey. Yeah. It was delivered yesterday. Thanks for that. But I'm a little confused here. First I'm talking to some guy claiming to be a Fed, now somehow you're on the line . . .'

'He is a Fed, Chief. He's in our office and we have you on speaker. We're working with the Bureau on some homicides with a Web connection, and we just finished watching a film of a murder in the parking lot of Chesterfield's.'

'You just watched the film? You mean, like, a movie?'

'It's on the Internet.'

'Okay, sorry, but this is a little hard to believe . . .'

Grace closed her eyes. 'The woman was tied to the front bumper of a Ford Tempo and her throat was slashed.'

'Jesus.'

'Listen, Chief, we'll e-mail you the details as soon as we hang up, but right now you need to get your men out there to contain the murder scene while it's still fresh, and Agent Smith wants the local FBI in on the investigation.'

Chief Frost sighed and cleared his throat. 'I got no problem with the Feds joining in, but there's no murder. There was an attack, but the woman survived, at least so far. She's in ICU, hanging on by a thread – and I want a copy of that film right now.'

Chapter Seventeen

The downpour had finally stopped and the sun was peeking out between the lingering shreds of storm clouds by the time Gino got his return call from Ole Olssen. They started out the conversation by continuing their recipe argument, which didn't sound like it would end anytime soon, so Magozzi took the opportunity to get up and move his body.

He was almost to the front door of City Hall when Chelsea Thomas suddenly hurried in, carrying a laptop. She was wearing her hair down today, and there were streaks of platinum in it that he hadn't noticed yesterday when it had been coiled up in a bun. She caught sight of him and gave him a slight smile, but her eyes were troubled. 'Do you have a moment?' she asked without preamble.

'Of course.'

Her expression turned sheepish. 'First of all, I'm really sorry about last night . . .'

'I'm not.'

'I've never been able to hold my liquor. It's one of my many flaws.'

'Some men might consider that an asset.'

The smile flashed, then disappeared again. She was FBI this morning. 'Is there someplace private we could talk?'

'Would an empty interrogation room work?'

'Perfect.'

Gino was still talking to Ole Olssen as the pair passed through Homicide, and his brows shot up curiously when he saw Chelsea. 'The guy on the phone is my partner, Gino Rolseth.'

Chelsea gave him a little wave, and Gino beamed at her, the way he always did whenever he saw a pretty face. 'He needs to be in on this.'

Magozzi raised his brows, then pointed at Gino and jerked his thumb toward the interrogation room. Gino held up one finger and nodded. As they settled into chairs and waited for Gino, Magozzi said, 'I was actually going to call you. I assume you know that Monkeewrench found pre-posts on all five of your murders, plus our river bride and two more you don't have bodies for yet.'

She folded her lips together and glanced at the doorway. 'Things are changing fast, but I'd like to wait for your partner so we only have to do this once.'

Gino appeared in the doorway, approached Chelsea with his hand extended. 'Gino Rolseth. And you're FBI.'

Chelsea stood up and shook his hand, reminding Gino that he was older than she was, and that once there was a time when standing to greet an elder was a sign of respect. 'How did you know?'

'Gotta tell you, you don't look like a Fed, but the suit's a dead giveaway.'

She tipped her head and gave him a deadpan look. 'I have a python miniskirt at home.'

Gino's brows crept up a notch. 'A Fed with a python miniskirt. That kind of gives me reason to live.'

Magozzi cleared his throat in what he hoped was a very professional manner. He felt a little like he did when Charlie the Stupid Dog forgot he was there and jumped all over Gino to lick his face. It wasn't that he had any lustful intentions toward Chelsea Thomas, except for the kind any man would have unless he was dead; it was just that men, even best friends, were in constant competition, and it always seemed like he was losing.

Chelsea walked to the door and closed it, then started unpacking her laptop. 'I understand both of you saw the Cleveland film.'

Gino slumped into a chair and grunted. 'Yeah, and we're still wishing we hadn't.'

She nodded. 'Agent Smith and I have agreed that you should see the rest of the films.'

'Oh, yippee.'

'We'd like a homicide detective's perspective on the scenes. A fresh eye. Also, Agent Smith said you'd all agreed to share information.'

Gino raised his brows 'Whoa. We thought he was kidding. Well, now that we're all warm and fuzzy and playing nice, here's something for you to take back to Smith. One of the pre-posts Monkeewrench found involved a possible homicide up north . . .'

'City of Big Water. That was the old one from January, right?'

'Right. I don't know if anyone's had a chance to look for posted film on that, but Grace asked us to check with the locals up there, see if we could match a body.' He flipped open his notebook. 'So I just got off the phone with my guy in Duluth and he said there were no homicides in January, just accidentals – a drunk snowmobiler decapitated himself on a barbed wire fence, a skier smacked into a tree, an ice fisherman fell into the drink and froze to death. Standard stuff, he said . . .'

Chelsea made a face. 'Decapitation by barbed wire is "standard stuff"?'

'Happens all the time. I take it you didn't grow up here.'

'Southern California.'

'There you go. Anyhow, nothing happened on any golf course, either, which we figured would fit with the "hole in one" message in the post. But here's something interesting. On February 1st, about thirty miles north of Duluth, they found a snowshoer dead at the bottom of a cliff on the North Shore of Lake Superior.'

Magozzi said, 'Sounds like another accident to me.'

'That's what I thought, but then Ole told me the guy was impaled on one of those ice spikes they get up there when the wind blows into shore.'

Magozzi grimaced. 'Poor bastard.'

'Actually, not really, according to Ole. The guy did time twice for child molestation. A real scumbag, and I hope he suffered. Anyhow, the cop Ole talked to said it looked like somebody had taken a big donut holer to him once they pulled him off the spike. Colorful language, huh?'

Magozzi's face went still. 'Hole in one.'

'Exactly what I was thinking. Of course, there were never any suspects because it was ruled accidental, but given the guy's past, there could actually be a lot of suspects. They're going to beat the bushes for us and do interviews with the guy's friends, family, colleagues, parents of his victims, like that. Maybe something will pop to connect the dots.'

Chelsea was sitting very quietly at the table, looking down at her lap as she listened to two homicide cops talk horror shop.

'Are you okay?'

She glanced up to see Magozzi's look of concern. 'Fine.' She flipped open her computer, then pulled up a list of the pre-posts and spun the screen to face Gino and Magozzi. 'Look at these – exactly as they appeared on the message boards.' She watched their expressions change as they read and reread the list. 'Revealing, isn't it?'

'Hmph,' Gino grunted, squinting at the screen. 'Look at that. They all start with city of something, and they've all got typos in the same places. Like a signature, almost, which is pretty compelling support for my traveling-serial-killer theory.'

Chelsea gave Gino a look he couldn't read, but it felt like he'd been slapped by a kitten. 'You need to see all the films now. Watch them as if you were responding to the crime scene, investigating.'

After fifteen brutal minutes watching human beings kill other human beings, Magozzi felt like somebody had taken a donut-holer to *him*. 'Jesus.'

Gino put his head down and rubbed his eyes, as if to wipe away the unpleasant visuals that were flashing behind them. 'No way all those were done by the same killer.'

Chelsea nodded like a teacher who had heard the correct

answer. 'And the film I'm going to show you next clinches it.'

Magozzi winced. 'Oh, Christ. There's a new one?'

'There were two warning posts without a corresponding video showing up on line, remember?'

'Yeah,' Gino said. 'Our North Shore Popsicle was one of them.'

Chelsea flinched a little at the phrasing. 'Yes. The other was "City of Roses, Bert's barmaid, near deer," posted just last night, so Monkeewrench went after it full bore, thinking there might be a chance to save a potential victim. Unfortunately, they found the film on MySpace this morning.'

Gino rubbed at his eyes again, half-hoping he could blur his vision so he didn't have to see too much. 'So why does this film clinch the multiple-killer angle?'

'For one reason: because the victim is still alive. You'll see the other reasons when you watch the film.' She pushed a key combination and angled the laptop so Gino and Magozzi had a clear view of the screen and she had a clear view of their faces.

Reading people and the acts of people was as much of part of Chelsea's job as it was any cop's. She'd always thought it was pretty funny that her superiors thought she was a genius at it. All you had to do was pay attention. In profiling you looked at what they left behind; with suspects and witnesses you listened to what they said, and watched their faces when they weren't talking. That's all there was to it.

She'd counseled enough agents when things went south for them to recognize the patterns you saw only in law enforcement types and military men. Those were the ones whose jobs mandated a kind of emotional lockdown that made reading their faces a real challenge, and Gino and Magozzi were better than most.

They both had their stone faces on, which was pretty common for homicide cops looking at a scene. Most of the time they looked as dead as the victims, with no giveaway facial-muscle movement, no nervous tics or lip-pursing, none of the blinking-neon-sign clues. But their pupils still dilated or contracted, and their breathing patterns changed, and those things told you a lot.

To the casual observer, Magozzi and Gino looked utterly emotionless, but Chelsea saw the signs of extreme tension when they watched Marian cross the parking lot; the stunned surprise when the attacker grabbed her; the frustration and the rage when they saw her tied to the bumper; and then the transparent jubilation when Marian kicked her attacker between the legs.

'Oh, goddamnit to hell,' Gino groaned at the end, when the blood started to flow. 'Goddamnit, goddamnit. For a minute there I thought she was going to walk away.'

Magozzi was shaking his head. 'I can't believe she survived that.'

'Barely,' Chelsea said. 'She survived the attack, but the doctors aren't optimistic about her surviving the next forty-eight hours. Right now she's comatose.'

'Are they copying you on reports?'

'Yes. The Chief of Police out there' – she consulted a handwritten note – 'Chief Frost, is in contact with Agent Smith, and bending over backwards to cooperate. This was a pretty shocking crime for that area, so he was more than happy to have some Federal help. There was nothing of note in the first-responder report; the bar is about a half mile from the closest residence, so there was no one around to see or hear anything. We have local agents assisting with crime scene, but no reports on that yet. It could take forensics into the night to cover the parking lot and the bar. If anything significant turns up, they'll give us a call; otherwise they'll fax all the reports when they finish up, probably tomorrow.'

Gino blew out a sigh. 'She's the first woman victim that we know of.'

'And the guy talked,' Magozzi added. 'None of the others did that. Not to mention that he didn't hang around long enough to make sure she was dead. This one was a newbie.'

'Totally different from the others,' Gino growled. 'This bastard was into the fear angle. That's what gets him off. None of the others did that.'

Chelsea said, 'They all kill very differently. Take Cleveland, which was fast and obviously fueled by rage; then the Austin stabbing, where the wet work was excessive and slow, suggesting prolonged pleasure; then the Seattle shooting, completely hands-off . . .'

'The Bureau's had these films for a while,' Gino interrupted. 'Didn't they already figure that out? I mean, I'm just a ham-and-eggs homicide cop, but it was pretty damn obvious to me.'

'Look at it from where they started. All they had was a couple of films, then a couple more. There are hundreds of homicides in this country every day. It wasn't unreasonable to assume that certain killers would start showing their home movies on the Web just like everybody else. We didn't know they were connected until Monkeewrench found all the pre-posts written in the same format.'

Magozzi stood and started pacing. 'Okay, so now we're pretty sure we've got multiple killers. And they're all religiously pre-posting details of their up-and-coming murders – location, method, and victim descriptions. Same pattern. So what does that mean? Are they communicating?'

Chelsea nodded. 'Maybe . . . in a way. The formatting of the pre-posts is like their secret code. If you're on these sites they're using and see the pattern, you know you're getting the real thing.'

'So are they an organized group, or are these just a bunch of sickos copycatting each other?' Gino asked.

'Could be either, or a combination.'

Magozzi stopped pacing and scolded his shoes with a head shake. 'All these victims were preselected. The killer knew where they were going to be, what they were wearing in some cases, and how they would die. The pre-posts prove that.'

Gino shrugged. 'So they picked out easy kills, chased them around for a few days, advertised their intentions, and did the deed. Doesn't mean they knew them, or wanted them dead for some particular reason.'

Magozzi looked at his partner. 'Or maybe they were targeted for a reason. We gotta look at that; we gotta pray for a connection between the victims; because if this is just a series of unrelated homicides, we're screwed, and we're never going to catch these people.'

Gino said, 'We could have Tommy plug the vic names into the Monkeewrench software. That program is tailor-made for this kind of thing.'

'What program?' Chelsea asked.

'It sorts through mountains of information and finds patterns. And it works a hell of a lot faster than any cops ever could.' He shrugged. 'It's worth a shot.'

After Chelsea left, Gino and Magozzi went back to their desks to pull together victim names for Tommy.

'Well, that totally sucked,' Gino grumbled, rummaging in his desk for a pen that didn't leave big blobs of ink on the paper. 'But on the bright side, that Chelsea Thomas is a looker.'

Magozzi ignored him.

'You do know she's smitten with you, don't you?'

'Stop it, Gino.'

'I'm serious. And you know how I could tell? Because she was flipping her hair. Women always do that when they're hunting. It's classic body language. I saw it on TV. You got the name of the Cleveland kill? He's the only one I'm missing.'

Magozzi paged through the file Chelsea had given them on her way out, pulled out a piece of paper and frowned. 'You remember that guy up in Ely, ten, fifteen years ago . . . ?'

'I was a mere child fifteen years ago.'

Magozzi snorted. 'He was the prime suspect in that kiddy kidnap and abuse case that turned the state on its ear for months . . .'

Gino slapped a hand to his forehead. 'Jesus, yes I remember. That slimebag perv was guilty as sin, and one stinkin' juror voted to let him walk. After O.J., worst miscarriage of justice on the planet.'

'What was his name?'

Gino scratched his chin. 'Something weird. Elmer? No, Elmore. Elmore Sweet, may he rot in hell.'

Magozzi nodded. 'Elmore Sweet was the Cleveland vic's name. Wonder if it's the same guy.'

Gino's eyebrows lifted to happy-face position. 'Oh, man, if it's true, I'm sending a copy of the Cleveland film to that kid's parents. Tommy'll find out for us.'

Magozzi noticed a neonorange Post-it note on Gino's desk with 'Judge Jim' scrawled in huge letters. 'What's with Judge Jim?'

'Oh, shit! I forgot about that.'

'What?'

'We need to pay him a visit sometime today.'

Magozzi frowned. 'Why?'

'After I hung up with Ole, an Officer Rondestvedt gave me a call. Turns out our friend was drunk down by the river again last night with a gun and a scope.'

'Was it loaded?'

Gino shook his head. 'Nah. But he told Rondestvedt that he was working with us on the river killing, and we sent him down there. We need to tell him to can the name-dropping, and I have a feeling a phone call just ain't gonna cut it with that guy. Hey, you free for dinner?'

Magozzi was hopeful – usually any mention of dinner from Gino meant an invitation to join his family and eat some wickedly delicious concoction from Angela's family recipe stash. 'Absolutely I'm free for dinner. I'd stand up my own mother for Angela's home cooking.'

'Actually, I was thinking more along the lines of a big, fat hunk of cow at that place on Washington.'

Magozzi frowned. 'You're not going home for dinner?'

Gino scowled. 'Hell, no. I'm not going anywhere near my house until ten-oh-five tonight.'

'Why not?'

'Because Angela's throwing a bridal shower for her niece, and it ends at ten. And you know what she's serving? Cucumbers. Cucumbers on little pieces of bread with the crusts cut off. And, worse yet, she got a case of wine and a big bag of "novelty" gifts, and you and I both know what that means.'

'We do?'

'Yeah. It's gonna be ugly. So I figure we go over some of this paper on these cases, punch out for an early steak, then hit the judge on our way home.'

'Okay. But it ain't Angela's lasagna.'

'No, indeed. But a cowboy ribeye and a martini runs a close second in my book.'

Chapter Eighteen

Magozzi and Gino stepped into the impressive lobby of Wild Jim's condo complex and checked in with the receptionist. She maintained her white, Chiclet-toothed smile up until the moment they showed her their shields and stated their business, at which point her lacquered lips closed like a stage curtain over the blinding veneers.

'The judge is up in the penthouse. I'll call and let him know you're on the way up.' She hesitated for a moment, then blurted out, 'He isn't in trouble again, is he?'

'No trouble,' Magozzi reassured her, even though he wasn't in the mood to assuage the anxiety of some drunk's groupie. There was just something so earnest about her concern. In fact, Wild Jim seemed to have groupies everywhere, and a lot of them were apparently on the force, continually cutting him slack that just wasn't acceptable in his opinion. Drunk or not, the guy obviously had charisma.

Once they were inside the posh, mahogany-paneled elevator, Gino crossed his arms over his chest and took in the limited scenery. 'Huh. The penthouse. So, the judge is still doing okay, considering he's been unemployed for a while. From what I hear, an average, one-bedroom schlep unit in this joint goes for almost a mil, and he's living large in the clouds.'

'Maybe he's a financial genius.'

'Yeah. Or maybe he was on the take, and that's really what got him kicked off the bench.'

Magozzi shrugged. 'His rep was always pristine, even drunk as a skunk for all those years. He was a good judge when he had his house in order . . . and even when he didn't.'

'Yeah, I guess you're right. So maybe he is a financial genius.'

The elevator drifted to a gentle, silent halt, and the doors slid open onto a beaming Wild Jim. He had a lowball in one hand and a half-smoked cigar in the other. 'Detectives! Let me welcome you as the first guests ever to my modest riverside aerie. Please, come in.'

They took a few, tentative steps inside and let their eyes wander around the big, mostly empty space. There was no art on the walls, the furniture was sparse and nondescript, and the open gourmet kitchen sparkled as if it had never been used. It was utterly lacking in the owner's personality, with the single exception of a sofa table that served as an easel for a long row of framed pictures. Every one of them featured the judge and a smiling, handsome young man.

'Nice place you got here, Judge, and not so modest,' Gino said politely.

'It's a considerable step down from my former domiciles, and most of the furniture is from IKEA and Target, but it serves me for the moment. Can I interest either of you in a libation? I'm drinking what they call a handcrafted bourbon, which would imply something a toothless hill denizen would concoct in a bathtub in the Ozarks, but it's actually quite smooth.'

'No thanks,' Magozzi said, his eyes still fixed on the table full of photos. 'By the way, thanks for the fruit basket.'

'You're very welcome.' The judge noticed the direction of Magozzi's gaze and gestured to the display with his glass. 'My son. I suppose it's a bit trite, having such a blatant memorial, but when you lose a child, your only child, all your sensibilities, both design-wise and otherwise, cease to matter.'

Magozzi and Gino both cringed inwardly, remembering the relentless media coverage of his son's suicide, and all the speculations surrounding it. He hadn't left much to chance by overdosing or wrist-slashing – he'd gone for the sure thing, which in this case had been a .44 slug with a Magnum load.

'We're really sorry about that, sir,' Gino finally said with the genuine empathy of a fellow father. 'Really sorry.'

'Yes, so am I. There's no getting over such a thing. Obviously.' He gave them a thin, sad smile, then raised his glass with forced bravado and drained it. 'After it happened, people always wanted a reason for why such a kind, intelligent young man with a promising future ahead of him would do such a thing. Hell, I wanted a reason myself, although I don't know why. There just isn't ever a justifiable explanation for such an act, and even if there were, it wouldn't change the impact of the aftermath.'

Magozzi shook his head. 'No, I'm sure it wouldn't.'

The judge refilled his glass. 'You know, I have recently come to realize that people who carry a great burden of guilt ravenously seek saviors anywhere they can, in all shapes, colors, and forms. Intellectually, I find the need for redemption frivolous; but emotionally, I fear I may have succumbed. The difference between me and the delusional masses is that I prefer my personal Jesus to be of the liquid sort, and a warm amber in color.'

'You ever think about going to spin-dry, Judge?' Gino asked him.

He looked amused. 'Not once, Detective Rolseth. You can't drink in rehab.'

'That's kind of the point. It wouldn't be the worst thing in the world, you know. You already lived through that.'

'You're correct about that. However, I don't believe alcoholism is a disease; I believe it is a choice, and I am thrilled with my choice. Not very progressive of me, but it's the truth. At least it's my truth.'

He wandered over to a seating area that faced a stunning vista of the Mississippi. 'I'm going to sit now, and I invite you to do the same.'

Magozzi and Gino followed suit and settled into hard-seated, modern chairs that were so uncomfortable, it almost seemed as if they had been deliberately designed to be that way.

'Can I at least cut some cigars for you gentlemen, since you're not drinking? They're the best Cuba has to offer – utter contraband a diplomat friend smuggles in for me on a biannual basis, but being that such legal transgressions don't fall under your purview, I think you could indulge without ethical conflict.'

Magozzi shook his head. 'We've just got a quick request for you, and then we'll leave you to it.' He noticed a flash of disappointment in the judge's eyes, and perhaps a little desperation, and in that brief moment, he saw the essence of what Judge Jim Bukowski truly was, or at least what he'd become – a hollow man, gutted by tragedy, who didn't want to be alone with his demons at the moment.

'Suit yourselves. You are without a doubt consummate professionals, and I appreciate that, especially given my current disposition as a shamed, previously elected official who will never again have the honor of paying Bar Association dues. So, what's this request?'

'We got a call this morning from a beat cop who covers this area. An Officer Rondestvedt.'

'Ah, yes. The nice young man with that rather unwieldy but regionally appropriate ethnic name. He was kind enough to escort me back to my condo last night.'

'Did you tell him you were working with us on the drowning?'

'Absolutely not. I imagine he merely inferred that from our conversation, but I never actually used the word *work*.'

Gino, who had little patience for subterfuge, just sighed. 'Listen, Judge, you can't be doing that, okay? No more name-dropping or inferences or golden lines of bull to the guys down there, you got it? If you do something illegal, weasel out of it some other way. You use our names out of school, it makes extra work for us, and we've got a full plate already.'

The judge nodded sternly. 'I understand. And I will honor your request because I like and respect you both very much. I'm also sorry for any inconvenience I may have caused you. But in all honesty, justice has defined my entire life, and I don't have skin in the game anymore. So if I can be of service . . .' he let the sentence trail off.

Gino tore his gaze away from the river view that was making him rethink his career choice. 'You could help us out a lot if you could remember anything else from that night.'

'I don't even remember that night anymore.' He narrowed his eyes and looked at both of them. 'I've tried to follow the case in the news, of course. And obviously you know that the story barely made it above the fold in either the St. Paul or Minneapolis papers.' He paused to give them a knowing smile. 'Have we offered the press an edited police report, perhaps?'

Magozzi pretended nonchalance. 'What makes you ask that?'

The judge chuckled, raspy and deep. 'There were no details of any import in either paper or on any local news channel. No photos, except for the body bag going into the bus. Not even a mention of the victim's gender. You did an excellent job blocking the media from the scene, and that's the truly intriguing part. Coupled, of course, with the fact that Homicide is working what appears on the surface to be an accidental drowning.'

Magozzi looked down at his lap and almost wished he'd accepted the offer of a drink. So far the river drowning had been sidebar news. People were always drowning in Minnesota, and the Mississippi had taken more than her share over the past few years. Locals usually assumed it was an immigrant from some place or other who saw any body of water as a free fish shop, and never bothered to learn to swim, so it raised no eyebrows when the story got a sympathetic reading and little else. 'We're obligated to investigate every death until a cause has been determined. You know that.'

'Indeed I do. But I also suspect that the cause of death has already been established by the very efficient Dr. Rambachan, and that your continued interest in my memory of that night indicates that the death was homicide, not accident.'

Gino actually smiled. 'You know what, Judge? You need a hobby. Bowling, maybe. Or bingo.'

The judge smiled. 'Was your victim murdered before he ended up in the water?'

Magozzi and Gino exchanged a long glance that only the two of them could read. 'No,' Magozzi finally said. 'He drowned all right. Somebody held him under the water and watched him die.'

'How do you know that?'

'We saw it.'

'What do you mean, you saw it?'

'Whoever did it took video footage of the murder and posted it on the Web.'

The judge looked skeptical. 'Detectives, I spend a lot of time on the computer for lack of anything better to do, and I've seen some pretty disturbing things. But I doubt that any of them are real.'

'Trust us, it's real,' Gino said.

'How can you be sure?'

Magozzi and Gino shared a look, and the judge chuckled. 'Ah, yes, never share details of an ongoing case with civilians, and especially not with suspects. Officially, I am both, but in actuality, I am neither. I'm also bored, I miss the law, and you have piqued my curiosity. I can assure you that anything you tell me will be kept in the strictest confidence. I wasn't disbarred because I was unethical, I was disbarred because I got one too many DUIs.'

Gino shrugged at Magozzi. 'This stuff is basically all public knowledge anyhow. Hell, it's all over the Web. Doesn't get much more public than that.'

'Come on, Detectives. Give a bored, worthless old drunk a puzzle to work on. It might even bring me back from the dead.'

Magozzi blew out a sigh. 'Well, it turns out our drowning is part of a bigger case.'

The bleary eyes sharpened instantly. 'How very intriguing. And what is this bigger case?'

'Suddenly, murder films are turning up all over the Internet, from all over the country. And the reason we know they're real is because every single murder was advertised in advance, in detail, right in chat room postings for anybody to see, and there's a body to match every post.'

'Including your drowning.'

'That's the first one we found.'

The judge's ruddy, booze-hound complexion turned pale. 'Good Lord. How many?'

'Eight. That we know of.'

'Eight?'

'Well, actually seven dead. The eighth one happened last night in Medford, Oregon, but the woman survived. She's in ICU now.'

The judge shook his head, then looked down into his glass and was quiet for such a long time, Magozzi and Gino started to wonder if he'd passed out sitting up. 'My God. The world has lost its collective mind,' he finally said.

'I'd say so.'

'You've got a true maniac on your hands, Detectives.'

'Actually, we think there's more than one killer.'

He blinked. 'This is simply overwhelming, even to me, and I lost faith in humanity long ago. How on earth did you go from a simple drowning two nights ago to a nationwide murder conspiracy?'

'The Feds are involved, and they brought in Monkeewrench. They're the ones who found the pre-posts that match with the victims – they all follow the same format. They seem harmless out of context, but the pattern suggests these guys are communicating. Showing off their trophies.'

The judge was thinking hard, and he seemed truly present for the first time since they'd met him. He'd even forgotten about his drink. 'But surely, either Cyber Crimes or Monkeewrench will ultimately be able to trace these posts or these films, and then you'll have your perpetrator. Or perpetrators.'

'Whoever's doing this is good. They know how to hide. So far, everything's been untraceable. So there you go, Judge. Is that enough of a puzzle for you?'

The judge cocked a brow. 'I don't know much about computers, but I do know quite a bit about human nature. Our species is reliable in one way and one way only – eventually, we all make mistakes. I would guess your killers are living on borrowed time.'

Magozzi's cell phone started playing AC/DC, and he excused himself and picked up. 'Grace.' He listened for a few moments, then pulled a notebook and pen out of his pocket and started scrawling.

'What is it?' Gino asked when he hung up, not at all liking the expression his partner was wearing.

'Monkeewrench just found a ninth pre-post. "City of Big Cheese, pink polyester, near steer," and they think Wisconsin's a possibility. They want us to call Sheriff Halloran over there and see if he can't help pinpoint a location, because they're running out of time to maybe prevent the murder.'

The judge dropped his glass and it shattered on the floor, spilling amber liquid over white marble. 'I used to have a cabin in Door County,' he said, his voice and expression numb. 'Interstate 94 to Wisconsin Highway 10. There's a diner just before that turnoff called the Little Steer, and thirty miles north of that is the glass semi-trailer that holds what was then the largest block of cheese in the world, exhibited at the World's Fair.'

Chapter Nineteen

Harley was pacing the office like a manic gorilla, pounding a beefy fist into his palm, boots banging the wooden floor. 'Okay. City of Big Cheese. That's in Wisconsin for sure, right?'

'Absolutely positively,' Annie agreed.

Agent John Smith had his elbows braced on the table, his hands pushing through his nowhere FBI haircut. 'California produces more cheese per year than Wisconsin.'

Annie dismissed that silly notion with a fluff of her black bob. 'That is not true. I have been to Wisconsin, that place is practically made of cheese, and they produce more than any other state. I read that on a placemat in a diner over there.'

Smith shrugged. 'Point of pride for the Dairyland. California passed them in tonnage some time ago, but they're still in denial.'

'Crap,' Roadrunner grumbled from his station. 'I have almost three million sites on the search for Big Cheese. Give me some more parameters.'

'Add California and Wisconsin,' Harley said. 'Otherwise all we've got in the post is "pink polyester" and "near steer."'

Annie snapped her fingers. 'What did I tell you, Agent Smith? Near steer. Who has more cows than Wisconsin?'

'California. And Texas. And probably Oklahoma.'

'That is an out-and-out lie.'

'It might be.'

Annie raised her brows. That had sounded suspiciously like a tease, which stunned her. In her experience, teasing a woman was directly related to testosterone, but Agent Smith looked like someone had wrung every bit of that out of him long ago. She opened her mouth to tell him the further edification that in the one Wisconsin diner she'd been in, the waitresses had worn pink-polyester ugly suits, but the phone rang before she could utter a syllable.

'Yes?' Grace snatched her receiver, listened, said, 'Got it,' and hung up. She looked over at Annie. 'Magozzi has a possible location. Interstate 94 and Wisconsin Highway 10, a diner called the Little Steer.'

'Shit!' Harley bellowed. 'What county is that? Who's the sheriff?'

'I'm on it!' Roadrunner shouted back.

Agent John Smith put his elbows on the table and his head in his hands. They were going to lose another one.

Lisa Timmersman didn't believe there was a hope on God's green earth of growing up thin on a Wisconsin farm. She had been a ten-pound baby born with her hand out for a cookie, to hear her father tell it, and for a while, looking at the rest of her hefty family, she actually believed she had just been a genetic fat bomb waiting to blow up.

It never occurred to her that growing up eating pure lard on homemade bread, and gravy on everything else, had anything to do with it. It was all she knew, and barely worth thinking about, since all the farm kids in her little country school looked pretty much the way she did.

And then skinny little Cassandra Michels transferred into her second-grade class from Milwaukee, told Lisa she was the fattest girl she ever saw in her life and that what she needed was an eating disorder. At that age, Lisa didn't have the slightest idea what an eating disorder was, or where she could get one. But that single remark from that single person taught her a very important lesson: that the people outside the small circle of her childhood weren't going to like her, not one little bit, all because she'd been born fat into a fat family and didn't have a prayer of changing that.

So, you carry a little extra baggage. Honey, that ain't such a bad thing. Makes for a softer place for a man to fall, and some day that's going to be a good thing.

Lisa had been eight at the time and didn't understand much of what her daddy was telling her, but for years she had nightmares about some gray area in her future where really fat hairy men would fall on her and squash her flat.

It wasn't her daddy's fault, who raised the food she ate, or her mother's, who put it on the table. All they'd ever done was let her know how much they loved her, and that she was pretty and smart and could be just about anything she wanted to be. They meant well, but they didn't have Cassandra Michels' perspective, and that was what she listened to.

When she was thirteen, her daddy put up a satellite dish and Lisa found the Food Network, where the people who cooked wore snappy white coats and clogs to work, which was totally cool. A lot of them were pretty fat, too, and no one made fun of them, which sealed the deal for her. Lisa was going to be a famous chef. She'd go to the culinary school in Chicago, or maybe Minneapolis, and then she'd buy a new front door for the house that fit so tight her mother wouldn't have to tuck blankets into the crack at the bottom to block the winter winds. And maybe one of those new shiny steel steam cleaners so her dad didn't have to kill himself scrubbing the milkhouse with a hose and a brush twice a day.

She got an after-school job at the Little Steer Diner out near the freeway, started out bussing and waiting tables and saving every dime she made. The soybean prices had hit rock bottom, and if she wanted to end up anywhere more glamorous than the high school cafeteria where they still wore those hairnets that fit halfway down your forehead, she was going to have to earn her own tuition. By the time she'd graduated from high school she owned half the menu and managed the place, and was precisely two months from the amount she needed to pay her tuition at the Minneapolis School of Culinary Arts. Her parents were so proud they kept saying how they were near busting, and that made Lisa shine.

She felt sorry for the other women three times her age who wore support stockings and shuffled from table to table taking orders, whose only dream was to make the monthly mortgage payment. Alma Heberson was having a particularly bad time this year. She'd lost her eldest son to a corn picker last year, and her husband had been knee-deep in the bottle and mean as a copperhead ever since. She'd been dead on her feet tonight and fighting a nasty cold, and Lisa offered to finish up her tables so she could go home early and get some rest. It wasn't a small thing, since Lisa had to be back at the diner before dawn to bake the pastry and make the soup of the day, recipe courtesy of one of the Food Network's newcomers, who Lisa thought would go far.

It was twenty minutes to closing when the last customer paid his bill and headed out. Maybe she could lock up a little early and get home in time to get a full five hours of sleep.

She hadn't finished closing the register drawer when the last straggling customer pushed open the door and let in the steamy night heat from the parking lot. Too early to turn him away, especially if the order was easy. It had been a pretty slow day, and the till was hurting. Besides, the customer was attractive and young with one of those pleasant, hopeful faces that made you think a little homemade meatloaf might just change his life.

'Can I help you?' Lisa smiled and ran her bleach cloth over a section of the Formica counter.

Deputy Frank Goebel was cruising north on one of those tar two-lanes that doubled as a section line between farm fields, which meant there were no lights other than his own, and the asphalt brandished the ever-present mud trails of whatever tractors had taken the same route during the day. Damn things were invisible at night, impossible to avoid, and the ride home was one long series of bumps. His tires danced and jittered over a thick tread line of mud that the day's heat had hardened into cement and the patrol skidded onto the right shoulder. He eased it back onto the road and sighed, bringing his speed down to thirty.

Not that he was all that anxious to get home anyway. He'd

lived solo in the little boxy rambler since his wife had left last Christmas, and small as it was, the house echoed every move he made, reminding him he was alone.

Couldn't save his kid, couldn't save his marriage, and lately he'd been wondering if he could save himself, or if it would even be worth the effort.

He winced at the buzz and click from the radio that announced a call from dispatch, and waited without emotion for Mary to go through the by-the-book introductory identifiers. He'd watched an old movie once where a cop on patrol got a call on the radio, and the dispatcher said, 'Hey, Bill, this is Dispatch and we've got a break-in at the bank.' Now how hard was that? What brainiac decided that Dispatch should have a number, every car should have a number, and every crime should have a number? So damn many numbers to remember that these days talking on the radio was like taking a math test. Hell, he could hardly remember his own car's call numbers at the end of a long shift, and he sure as hell wouldn't be able to guess the kind of call she was going to send him on because she'd never say it flat-out in English. Whatever it was, it wouldn't be good; not this late. Car accident, drunk driver, teenagers having a noisy kegger somewhere, driving the early-to-bed farmers nuts.

'Frank, are you there?'

That got his attention. No rigamarole, and a little panic in her voice.

'Jeez, Mary, you broke protocol. Was there a terrorist attack on the Tom Thumb, or what? Spew out some numbers for me or I'll think you're an imposter.'

'Shut up, Frank, and listen.'

Wow. Her voice was actually shaking.

'I've got a crowd of people from Minneapolis yammering at me over the speakerphone, including an FBI agent, and there's no number in the book for what they say is happening.'

Frank flipped on the roof lights and pulled over onto the shoulder. 'Okay, calm down, Mary, I'm listening.' He heard her take a deep breath.

'They said someone's going to kill one of the girls at the Little Steer tonight unless we can stop it.'

'*What?* How the hell do they—?'

'Don't ask questions, Frank, just take it as gospel and get the hell over there. We don't have much time.'

He turned on the siren, cranked the wheel and stood on the accelerator. Shoulder gravel rooster-tailed into the ditch and then the front tires caught tar and the back tires laid twin lines of rubber. 'Jesus, Mary, I'm twenty miles away!' he yelled into the radio. 'Isn't there someone closer?'

'No! There isn't! So just step on it! And leave your radio open.'

'You got it.'

Frank didn't do much talking after that, because he was doing sixty now on the road, trying to dodge the worst of the mud ridges the tractor tires had left, getting thrown from side to side, jerking the wheel, trying to keep the car upright. His palms were sweating, greasy on the wheel, and his heart was hammering.

Nothing you can do, Frank, nothing you can do, just get there in one piece, and who the hell would want to kill one of the girls at the Little Steer, and why, for Chrissakes? Who's on tonight? Alma for

*sure, she worked every night shift; and Lisa, natch, because she damn
near lived at the place, and oh God, no, not Lisa.*

She was a great cook, a great person, his daughter's best
friend, a frequent visitor to the house when there had been
a family living there, and two plump arms at the funeral
wrapping around his waist, squeezing the breath out of him
while she tried to hold his heart together, her tears soaking
the one and only tie he'd ever owned.

*Look at you, Frank, you can handle sixty on these goddamned
mud ridges, and that means maybe you can handle seventy, just ease
it up slow, pay attention, breathe, goddamnit, breathe . . .*

A green mile marker flashed by the right side of the car.
Fifteen miles to the freeway.

There were times Grace could remember her heart
actually hurting, as if some giant fist had it in its hand,
squeezing down harder and harder until she thought it
would surely be crushed. Those times all had names —
people horribly murdered because of her — kept sacred
in her memory like jewels in some Pandora's box that
only opened when another name was about to slip inside.
Kathy and Daniella, her roommates in college; Marian
Amburson and Johnny Bricker, foolish enough to want
to be close to her; Libbie Herold, sent to save her, her
lifeblood flowing on the other side of a closet door,
where Grace cowered, helpless.

Helpless then, helpless now, huddled with the rest of
them around the speakerphone at the big table, listening to
what was going on in Wisconsin as if it were a horrible
radio play.

Frank, where are you?

Coming up on the ten-mile marker. You got backup coming?

The call's out to everyone. Tommy's up at the northern end of the county, but I got Brad out of bed, he was the closest. Should make it to the diner in about forty. Three counties and WHP are sending cars, but they're all farther away.

Shit, Mary.

No answer at the diner. Maybe they all went home early.

Pray to God.

Agent John Smith leaned over the speakerphone. 'Agent Smith here, Mary. Give us the owner's name. We'll call from here and get mobile and home numbers for whoever was working tonight.'

They could hear Mary breathing hard, clicking on a keyboard. Then: 'Ted Kaufman in Woodville. And thanks. I've got my hands full here . . .' the shrill ring of another call coming through on her end interrupted her.

Roadrunner was covering ground to his computer station, long fingers moving even before he hit the chair. Precious seconds seemed to fly by. 'I have Kaufman on line two, John, pick up and do your thing.'

John took the call on Annie's desk because it was closest, and so he wouldn't interrupt the transmissions they were still getting over the speakerphone on line one. It was turning into a nightmare of noise now; the siren in Frank's squad wailing whenever he keyed in, Mary on Dispatch talking nonstop to the highway patrol and other deputies who were calling in.

John talked fast, too fast, and probably sounded crazed. 'Mr. Kaufman, this is Special Agent John Smith of the

FBI and I need the home and mobile numbers of anyone working at the Little Steer tonight.'

'Who did you say this was? Goddamnit, George, is that you? If I've told you once I've told you a thousand times . . .'

John dragged his fingers down his face so hard they left angry red rake marks on his cheek. 'Please shut up, Mr. Kaufman. I'm an FBI agent and we have a killer either in your diner now, or on his way to kill one of your employees. Now give me their phone numbers right now.'

Silence for a moment, then John heard, 'I gotta get my book. Hang on a second.'

John rolled his eyes upward to see Annie standing next to him. 'Jesus Christ,' he muttered. 'This is a fucking nightmare.'

Annie covered his hand with hers, and then he had to snatch it away because Ted Kaufman was spitting out phone numbers like a slot machine hitting the jackpot. He wrote them all down, then ripped off the tablet sheet and handed it to Annie. 'Split 'em up, call them all.'

'Except Lisa,' Ted Kaufman said through the receiver. 'It's just ten o'clock. That's closing, and she's there cleaning up for an hour after, regular as clockwork, every night.'

'We've been calling the restaurant, the phone rolls over to voice mail.'

'Huh,' Kaufman said. 'That's weird. Lisa always answers. Her mom's been sick.'

Smith closed his eyes.

*

Lisa had her arms braced on the Formica counter while she watched the young man eat her meatloaf sandwich. He was almost dainty, using a fork, chewing each bite for a long time, eyes closed and lips curled in the slightest smile.

'Unbelievable,' he said between bites, careful to make sure his mouth was empty. 'Sage, for sure, and what is that? A little thyme?'

Lisa beamed. 'That's right.'

'And shallots, not onions. You caramelized them first, didn't you?'

'I did.'

He took a last bite, and pushed the plate away with one finger. 'You ever watch the Food Network?'

Lisa slapped an open hand to her ample bosom. 'Omigod. Are you kidding? I never miss any of the shows.'

'That guy who does the show on great food at diners, what is it called?'

'Omigod again. That's Guy What's-his-name. *Diners, Drive-Ins and Dives*. He's so amazingly totally super.'

'You belong on that show.'

He had really blue eyes, or maybe they were green, but oh, Lisa felt them look into her and see what was really there. 'How do you feel about going on camera?' he asked.

Lisa felt her heart flutter. 'Excuse me?'

There was absolutely nothing Grace could do. Listen to Mary fielding calls to Dispatch in Wisconsin; listen to John shouting into the phone at Annie's desk, and then to Annie and Harley and Roadrunner frantically calling people who were on shift at the Little Steer, and now home, safe. All except Lisa, whoever she was.

She heard Charlie whine and looked to her right. He was on the chair next to her, eyes worried while her right hand twisted the hair on the top of his head. 'Oh, Charlie,' she murmured into his forehead, 'I'm sorry.' His tongue accepted her apology just as Mary asked Deputy Frank Goebel where he was and how much longer.

Five miles, Mary. Three minutes if I don't crash first. This road is shit.

It's Lisa, Frank. She's there alone. The Minneapolis people called the rest of them, and they're all home. I've got no help for you for at least another fifteen minutes. You're the man.

Frank saw the lights a full mile away. The clouds were low tonight, and the sodium vapors bounced from cloud back to earth, marking the place the Little Steer claimed for its own near the freeway.

He tasted the braised steak and garlic potatoes Lisa Timmersman had made for his lunch just today; he felt her arms around his waist at his daughter's funeral over a year ago; and in a very strange way, he saw things coming together to make a destiny he never would have imagined.

Everyone was back around the table in the Monkeewrench office, all of them leaning toward the speaker phone, listening hard, faces brittle and swept back like astronauts in a centrifuge.

Turn off the siren, Frank. He'll know you're coming and he'll bolt.

I love you, Mary, but fuck you. I want him to hear the siren. I want him to bolt. I want Lisa to live.

Sometimes there was no explanation for the way God worked in this world. Lisa Timmersman didn't understand why a nice young man with a really nice face who liked her meatloaf would suddenly grab her by the neck and slap a piece of gray sticky tape over her mouth; or why he'd tie her hands and ankles with those plastic things that Best Buy used to hold their bags together; and she didn't understand why anyone would carry around a knife that big.

'I'm afraid this might be very painful,' the young man said with a small smile, and that's when Lisa began to buck her way across the linoleum floor like an inchworm trying to outrun a snake. He laughed at that, and for the first time, tears squirted out of her eyes.

They were all back around the big table again, leaning toward the speakerphone, staring at it as if their eyes would help them hear something other than the deputy's siren. That's all there had been for the past several minutes; the constant wailing of that siren and occasionally in the background, a steady, whispered mumbling, probably coming from Mary.

'What's she saying?' Annie asked.

John Smith, who had known his way around a church a million years ago, folded his hands together as if he were in one now. 'She's praying.'

Mary, I'm there!

They all jumped at Deputy Frank's sudden shout.

I see Lisa's car and a red Ford F-150 parked around the side, can't read the plate – Jesus God there he goes!

In Minneapolis, they heard the siren, still wailing, the release of a seat belt, a car door flung open, and then there was Frank's voice, screaming.

Stop! Stop or I'll shoot!

The roar of an engine, the sound of tires screeching on asphalt, and then the gunfire. There were nine shots, and then Mary yelling into the radio.

Frank? FRANK!

There wasn't a fraction of a second small enough to measure the time it took for Deputy Frank Goebel to make his choice. Chase the bad guy as he sped out of the parking lot and onto the back roads, or go inside and see to Lisa. No choice at all really. No options.

He found her tied to one of the stools at the counter, clothesline around her neck, pulling her head back, blood seeping from the duct tape across her mouth. One of her eyelids was swollen shut, but the other eye opened when he bent over her and said her name. 'Hey, Lisa.' He tried not to hurt her when he pulled the duct tape from her lips, apologized because he knew it was painful, and then he took his knife to the plastic and rope that bound her, screw whatever evidence he was destroying, and called into his shoulder unit for an ambulance.

'Hi, Mr. Goebel.'

'Hi, Lisa.'

'He didn't cut me. He had a big knife and he said it

was going to hurt and then he heard the siren and ran away.' Blood was coming out of her mouth, garbling her voice.

Frank scowled hard and kept working at the ropes around her, trying not to look at her ruined face, trying not to remember that he'd been a second too late – just a second – to save his daughter from bleeding out when a drunk driver had crossed the freeway median and sent a sliver of windshield through her jugular. 'I'm glad, Lisa. Be still now.'

Chapter Twenty

Magozzi still hadn't gotten used to walking into his own house through the front door. Nothing looked right, and he doubted very much that it ever would again. He'd learned that there were a couple of life-changing mistakes it was almost impossible to undo: one was marrying the wrong person; another was – and God help any man who tried it – hiring a decorator.

He stood at the archway to his living room, knowing absolutely that he was not supposed to set foot on that stupid Oriental rug without taking his shoes off. Why the hell would anyone slap down an area rug on top of wall-to-wall carpet? There was no sense to that at all, and some very real dangers. His socks always tangled in the silly fringe around the edges, and you could see every misstep he'd made in shoes on the cream border.

Shoes, or not shoes. Funny how he could make rational snap judgments at a river crime scene, looking at a bloated body, yet found himself paralyzed at the entrance of his own living room.

His old battered recliner was gone; the big-screen TV was hidden behind the massive doors of a piece of furniture he still couldn't pronounce, and funny-colored pillows in weird shapes were scattered all over the place.

When the decorator had finished two months ago, there

had been a very specific place for each pillow; something to do with contrasting colors and textures, the cohesiveness of the room design – some bullshit like that. The pillows still pissed him off. It took several to cushion his head when he crashed on the sofa that was a foot too short for his six-plus feet, and they kept sliding off the new leather massage recliner he'd insisted on buying, even when the decorator made a prune face. Someday, when he was retired from the force, he was going to hunt down that woman and slap her silly with those pillows.

The phone rang while his second frozen dinner was still in the microwave. He never looked at the picture on the box when he bought them, never looked before he nuked them, but this one smelled really weird. 'Magozzi here . . .'

Grace never bothered with hellos before starting a phone conversation, especially if she was tired or stressed, and tonight she sounded both. 'Wisconsin saved the girl, the perp got away. I don't know where you got your information about the location of that diner, but make sure you tell the source they saved a life. Apparently the guy heard the siren coming and bolted before he could do some real damage. He pulled out of the parking lot just as the deputy was pulling in.'

'How is the girl?'

'Pretty banged up, pretty terrified, but she's talking. He tied her up and came at her with a knife, Magozzi, just like the one in Medford last night.'

Magozzi thought about that for a minute. 'Oregon's a long way from Wisconsin.'

'If he flew, it's possible, and, God love airports, they have cameras all over the place. The girl gave a pretty good description; they've got a sketch artist with her now, hoping for some distinguishing characteristics they can start comparing to security footage.'

'Witness sketches suck, Grace, you know that. They all look like celebrities. Did the deputy get a tag on whatever the perp was driving?'

'Better than that. He put nine bullets into it. They found it at a freeway wayside four miles away. Stolen, of course. They're guessing he had his own vehicle parked there and switched them out. He could be anywhere by now.'

'Cameras at the wayside? And how about at the diner?'

'Nothing at the wayside, and get this: he backed into the door at the diner so the camera couldn't pick up his face.'

'Smart. Any more news out of Medford?'

'No. The woman's still unconscious, and the cops and Feds are still processing. Prelim reports by tomorrow morning, they think, but still no leads.'

The microwave pinged and Magozzi popped open the door, releasing an unidentifiable miasma that smelled lethal. He peeled back the film to reveal an unappetizing brown mash.

'Listen, Magozzi, I'm dead on my feet. Anything else you need before I collapse?'

'Yeah. Do you know what Indian food smells like?'

'Doesn't matter what it smells like. It's good for you. Eat it.'

After he hung up, he examined the cardboard box that had contained his latest gift to the microwave, then poked a fork into the mushy brown stuff. It wouldn't win any beauty contests, but surprisingly, it was pretty damn good. Anant would be pleased.

Between mouthfuls, he picked up the phone and dialed Gino.

'This better be good, Leo, because you just woke me out of a sound sleep,' he grumbled.

'How are you already asleep? You just got home.'

'I was already asleep before I walked in the door. What's up?'

Magozzi relayed his conversation with Grace, which seemed to perk up his partner considerably.

'Hell, that's terrific news. Way to go, Judge. Send him a fruit basket.'

'I'll do one better than that – I'm going to call him right now.'

'Whoa. You found religion in the last half hour? Since when are you into validating drunken sots?'

'Since never. But he saved a life, unwittingly or not.'

'I think the unwittingly part means something, Leo.'

'Whatever.'

'Don't trip over your skirt on the way to bed, buddy.'

'Screw you, Gino. Go to sleep.'

'I hear, and I obey.' Gino hung up instantly, which meant Angela had put her hand on him, and maybe exhaled against his skin, and in that moment, Magozzi hated him.

Judge Jim was sitting in his office, reflecting on the history of technology. Invariably, all the powerful technological tools that were invented for the good of mankind ultimately fell into hands that turned them toward evil. Dr. Richard

Gatling invented his rapid-fire weapon because he thought it would end war. The A-bomb was invented for the same reason, and now every crazy fucker had one. The people behind weapons of destruction should have spent less time in their labs and more time on the streets, observing humanity. And now, the Web . . .

He jumped when his phone rang and he snatched the receiver when he saw Magozzi's name on the caller ID. 'Tell me you're calling with good news, Detective.'

'I am, Judge. Law enforcement on the scene at the Wisconsin diner wanted me to let you know you saved a life.' He heard the judge take a breath, then blow it out. 'You were dead-on with the location. Thanks to your info, the cops got there before the perp could do serious damage.'

Magozzi rubbed at his tired eyes while he waited for the expected thank-you-for-the-call, but all he got was silence. After five seconds of that, he started to get pissed. Just picking up the phone had been a courtesy; one the judge obviously didn't deserve.

Finally, 'And was the victim a woman, Detective Magozzi?'

'Of course it was a woman. Pink polyester, remember? What did you think? That it was a gay golfer?' Bizarrely, he heard the definitive sound of liquid being poured into a glass, and then the unmistakable noise of gulping. Jeez. What an asshole. Did the old bastard actually think Magozzi was going to stand here and listen to him drink himself to death? 'Listen, Judge . . .'

'Thank you for calling, Detective.' And then an abrupt disconnect.

Chapter Twenty-one

Tommy Espinoza connected with the world on the Internet. He did his shopping, he watched television programs, he got his news, and occasionally found a date. Nothing he did in his life originated anywhere else. He didn't really understand people who lived any other way, and when Magozzi and Gino stopped in his office, he assumed that they, like he, knew everything that had appeared online.

'You guys are famous,' he said when they crowded into his space.

'Oh yeah?' Gino was rummaging through the offerings on the snack table, all ordered online, delivered right to his door.

'Totally. You saw the morning shows, right?'

'Nah,' Gino said around a rippled potato chip. 'Angela won't let me watch the morning news since my last physical. Anything pops, I gotta go back on the blood-pressure meds, and let me tell you how those things suck.'

'Jeez, Gino, go to the gym, eat lettuce.'

'I'd rather die. So why are we famous?'

'Well, not exactly you guys, but MPD and Monkeewrench. The Wisconsin thing last night. The waitress is doing interviews all over the place from her hospital bed. It's been streaming all morning. Pull up a couple chairs and I'll show you some footage.'

A young field reporter stood next to a satellite van from a Milwaukee TV station, talking earnestly into a microphone while the sun rose over the alfalfa field behind him and a cow lowed in the background. 'This is rural Wisconsin. Farm country.'

Gino rolled his eyes. 'Jeez, buddy, what was your first clue? The cow? The hayfield?'

Tommy stabbed pause and glared at Gino. 'You want to hear this or not?'

'Probably not. It's just another asshole cub reporter trying to hit the anchor desk on the back of somebody else's misfortune. Fifty bucks the kid asks her how she felt when the guy tied her up and came at her with a knife. Duh.'

Magozzi sighed and circled his forefinger at Tommy.

'Forty miles from the closest town of any size,' the newscaster continued, 'over a hundred miles from any of the larger cities that foster crime. According to the locals, nothing bad ever happens here, but all that changed last night.' As he spoke, the camera panned left to show a long shot of the Little Steer Diner. 'Twenty-year-old Lisa Timmersman was alone in this diner last night, just about to close up when a last customer came in and viciously attacked her. She was beaten, duct tape was placed over her mouth, hands and legs tied to one of the counter stools. "I'm afraid this is going to be very painful," her attacker said as he approached her with a large knife.'

The film cut to Lisa in a hospital bed. One side of her face was black and blue, the eye swollen shut, black stitches cutting from her cheek to her lips. Tears welled as she recalled her ordeal.

'He wanted to kill me. I don't know why. I didn't even know him. And then he heard Mr. Goebel's siren. Deputy Goebel, you know? And he ran away. Mr. Goebel saved my life. He's a hero. A real hero.'

Cut to film that was presumably Deputy Goebel, walking away from the camera, holding up a hand to fend them off, saying, 'No comment.'

'Good cop,' Gino muttered.

'But Deputy Goebel wasn't the only hero in this near-tragedy,' the newscaster went on. 'A confidential source has told WKAL Milwaukee News that Monkeewrench, a computer company operating out of Minneapolis, was instrumental in saving Lisa Timmersman's life. They were the ones, along with an agent of the FBI, that notified the local sheriff that there would be a murder attempt at the Little Steer last night. How did they know this was going to happen? How did they know someone was planning to kill Lisa Timmersman? What is the FBI's involvement? These are questions that have yet to be answered, but WKAL is investigating. In the meantime, the police are asking for your help identifying Lisa's attacker, who is still at large. If you recognize the man in this sketch, please call the tipline number at the bottom of the screen.'

Tommy navigated away from the news report. 'There's a lot more in this report – interviews with Lisa's family and friends, small-town stuff like that – but it gets worse. By the time the *Today* show hit the air they had Monkeewrench's history and, amazingly, the whole story about the Internet murders, the FBI connection, and Monkeewrench finding the code that gave them advance warning of murders to come.'

'That sucks,' Gino was shaking his head. 'If we don't already have copycats, we'll probably get some now.'

'Trust me, we already have copycats by the truckload . . . oh, come on, Gino, shove your eyes back in their sockets. I didn't mean copycat *killers* – so far we haven't hit on any of those. But thanks to the media, the format of the code is all over the friggin' TV, in every newspaper, and the goddamned Web is on fire. So now we've got a bumper crop of assholes who know to capitalize letters one, three, six, and nine to get a little attention. I just screened over two hundred new pre-posts in the last hour, and that's just Minneapolis. Look at this one. "CiTy oF laKes, Bob banged Betty in the Boy's Bathroom." Jesus. It's a nightmare. We didn't know what was real and what was just a prank before, when this story was under wraps, but now we're getting buried. And to give you an indication of how bad it really is, Federal Cyber Crimes already has a new task force set up, just to deal with this, and since when did the government have a twenty-four-hour turn-around time on getting anything done?'

'What *are* they doing about it?' Magozzi asked. 'What can they do?'

Tommy shrugged. 'Most of them are stupid, like "Bob banged Betty," but the locals have busted a few cyber-bully kids who think it's funny to put up pre-posts about murdering whoever stole their milk money in the lunch line. But what are you going to do? Throw a thirteen-year-old kid in the pen for making terroristic threats?'

'Hell, yes!' Gino snapped. 'Christ, are there any parents out there anymore, or is it the hot new trend to let wolves and the Web raise your kids? If one of my spawn did something like that, I'd hog-tie 'em, smear 'em with honey, and throw 'em on a fire ant hill.'

'You would not,' Magozzi said.

'Well, maybe not my kids, but one of my neighbors' kids did that . . .'

'It's not just kids,' Tommy said. 'A few other nutters have been busted. Point is, the copycats aren't in the same league technology-wise as our murderer . . . or murderers. They're not using anonymity software, and they're not running through foreign servers, so it's a no-brainer to trace them. But the really bad guys are seriously dialed-in.'

'What I'd like to know is how the media got all this information,' Magozzi said.

Tommy shrugged. 'Who were the insiders on all of this shit, besides Monkeewrench, the Feds, and us? I'm thinking it's gotta be one of the hackers the FBI brought in, long on info and short on cash. I mean, the Feds have been using hackers forever, and most of them are straight-up dope when they get the call, either because there's money involved, or a commuted sentence. But it's always dicey when you get criminals to help you catch other criminals. So, you guys want to see more coverage, or do you want to see what I dug up on that list of vics you gave me yesterday?'

Gino asked, 'Anything in there we're going to like?'

'Well, it's not exactly an earthquake, but there are a couple of things that are kind of interesting.'

Magozzi looked at Tommy. 'Shoot.'

'I'll give you guys all the paper on this so you can take a closer look for yourself, but here's the short version –

Minnesota is the common denominator for six of the victims. And five of those six have criminal records right here in the Land of Lakes. What's that do for you?'

Gino made a sock face. 'Makes me want to move to Iowa.'

'Which vics have the sheets?' Magozzi wanted to know.

Tommy consulted a handwritten piece of scrap paper that looked like it was written in Aramaic. 'Elmore Sweet in Cleveland – and by the way, you guys were right about him being the same weasel from Ely. Justice is finally served.'

'Awesome,' Gino said, pumping his fist.

Tommy continued deciphering his notes. 'Then your North Shore guy, Austin, Chicago, and L.A. Your river bride is the sixth Minnesota link, but he-she-whatever didn't have a record, just a lifetime resident of our fair state.'

'All men.'

'Yep. The two women have no records and no Minnesota connection.'

'So what kind of crimes are we looking at?' Gino asked.

'Well, basically, you've got a Greatest Hits list of dirty deeds: the two pedophiles – Elmore Sweet and your North Shore hole in one; vehicular manslaughter, a nasty domestic, and a drive-by that popped a five-year-old girl asleep in her bed.'

Gino had that gleam in his eye that always terrified Magozzi, because it was usually the precursor to some spectacularly whacked theory. 'Bad men,' he pointed out. 'Bad, *dead* men, specifically targeted, who all had their own victims at one point. I know what this is. Couldn't be more clear.'

Magozzi and Tommy didn't even bother to ask, because they knew Gino would march out his latest and greatest without encouragement.

'We're looking at a bunch of vigilante killings, guys. It's the only thing that makes sense. And let's face it. We've been getting more and more of those lately.'

Tommy thought about that, tipping his head back and forth to shake the memories out of his brain. 'All those old people killing each other.'

'Exactly. And let's not forget our little snowman fiasco just last winter . . .'

'All right, all right,' Magozzi said irritably. 'So we've had some vigilante killings. They've always been around, just like any other motive for murder. But that's not what's happening here.'

Gino folded his arms over his chest. 'I got two words for you. Charles Bronson.'

'Who's Charles Bronson?' Tommy asked.

'Are you kidding me? Mr. Vigilante is who he is, or was. He might be dead, I'm not sure. Anyway, it's an old movie. Thugs kill his family, he loads up and off he goes, popping people right and left. That was a seriously popular movie, and you know why? Because sometimes the justice system lets people down, and until we stop letting pedophiles and murderers walk, we're going to have Charles Bronsons out there.'

Magozzi rolled his eyes. 'Damnit, Gino, I don't care how many vigilantes are out there, these are not revenge killings.'

'Why not?'

'First off, it's too risky, because there's a past personal connection. Second, revenge killers are focused on eliminating whoever they're pissed at, not in showing off trophies.'

'Maybe they all found each other on the Web and egged each other on, like Chelsea said.'

Magozzi shook his head. 'If you're out to avenge the death of a loved one, you're not going to pre-advertise on the Web. You want the guy dead. Why take the chance that someone can find out ahead of time and stop you? Vigilantes are on a holy mission; what's happening here is some kind of sick game-playing.'

Gino thought about that for a minute, then stuck his lips out as far as they would go. 'Well, gee, Leo, thanks a whole hell of a lot. There you go, popping a real pretty fantasy bubble once again, trashing one of my more brilliant theories. So if it's not pissed-off survivors, and it's not a single killer, then the victims aren't going to have anything in common. So what the hell are we looking for?'

'Damned if I know. But we're going to keep looking until we find it.'

Gino turned his attention back to Tommy. 'Did you print out complete files on all the victims?'

'Hey, I'm your man, of course I did. Everything's in there.' He pointed to an enormous box sitting by his door.

Gino's jaw went slack. 'You've gotta be kidding me. That box is bigger than my first house.'

Chapter Twenty-two

Chief Elias Frost had been sitting in the corner of the tiny ICU cubicle since Marian had gotten out of surgery. The nurses had tried to kick him out; even a couple of well-intentioned doctors; but he was having none of that.

'She won't be able to talk,' the doctors told him.

'You said she moved her hands.'

'That's correct. There's no paralysis.'

'Then maybe she can write.'

'Chief Frost, if she wakes up at all within the next forty-eight hours, it's going to be a miracle.'

'Then I'll wait for a miracle.'

He'd seen a few of those in ICU rooms just like this one over his twenty-odd years on the force. No reason he couldn't see another one. Especially this one.

Her last name was Brandemeyer, on loan from the useless piece of crap she'd married when marijuana and motorcycles were more of a magnet than a skinny kid who wanted to be a cop. She'd dumped the garbage when he started hitting her, but kept the name because there was a daughter. But he never did think of her with a last name. Just Marian. A single-name person, like Elvis or Cher.

No way in the world he could have recognized her face. It was all swollen and mottled from the surgery. But they had her hands outside the sheet, and he would have known them anywhere. Lord knows he should have; he'd held them often enough when they were an item in high school. Going steady is what they called it then, back when Medford only had one high school and everybody knew everybody else.

He looked at his watch and marked the thirteenth hour of his vigil. When he looked up again he had one of those horror-movie moments when the eyes of the dead person in the coffin suddenly open, and you think you'll have a heart attack right there in your seat with popcorn all over your lap.

Get a grip, Frost. You're so tired you can hardly see straight, and you've been looking at her too long, that's all. Willing her to live and waiting for her to die, and now your eyes are playing tricks. Look away, slow down the heart, take some deep breaths.

He did all that, but when he looked at her again, Marian's eyes were still open and staring.

Oh, Jesus, please, no . . .

He tiptoed over to her bedside, which was really stupid, after all the loud talking he'd done in the past hours, trying to wake her up. Why do you try to wake up people who are unconscious and try not to wake up people who were dead?

And then she blinked.

The doctor and nurses shooed him out while they did whatever it was you did when someone who was supposed to die decides to give it another shot. 'Two minutes for you, two minutes for the daughter,' the doctor told him when they were finished.

Frost went back to her bedside and touched her hand for

the first time in over twenty years. 'You're in the hospital and you're going to be okay' – he told her the things he knew she would want to know immediately. 'Alissa is doing all right, but she was exhausted. I made her stretch out on a sofa in the waiting room for a while. I'll go get her.'

Marian winced when she tried to move her head, then raised her right forefinger.

It broke his heart watching her struggle to lift that single finger as if it weighed a million pounds. 'You don't want me to get her?'

Frost's heart skipped a beat when she moved the finger a little more. He pulled out his notebook, laid it at her side, and put a pen in her hand.

In any hospital he'd ever been in, the Intensive Care Unit waiting room made the rest of the place look like a sci-fi bus stop, and this one was no different. No dinky cubicles with plastic chairs here. Soft furniture in gentle colors, carpet underfoot, lamps on real wood tables instead of that crappy fluorescent lighting that made everyone look half-dead. They had food and drinks on a long table with a cloth, televisions and computers, books and magazines, and a lot of plants. The plants always made him feel good, until he started thinking that they might live a lot longer than anybody in ICU. Families in crisis mode had long, agonizing waits in places like this, and someone had put a lot of thought into making it easier.

Alissa was curled on her side on a green sofa with little white dots. She was pretty like her mother, fresh-faced like her mother used to be before life wore her down. Frost laid a gentle hand on her shoulder and whispered her name. 'Your mother's awake.'

She was awake instantly, on her feet, hugging him hard, and he reminded himself not to make too much of that. People were always hugging people in places like this.

He waited until the glass door had closed behind her before he went to a phone, pulled his notebook out of his pocket, and flipped it open. Marian had managed only three letters in faint, wavering print: 'ENG.'

'Ginny, it's Ethan.'

Dead silence on the line, and Ethan knew what that was about. Nobody thought Marian would get through the first night, let alone the second, and everyone at the office had been dreading this call.

'It's okay, Ginny, she's still with us. And she woke up, which is a good sign, but it's still touch and go.'

'Oh thank God. I was afraid you were going to say—'

'I know. Listen, who's on the desk today?'

'Theo.'

Chief Frost rubbed at his face. Theo was two weeks on the job and had about three whiskers on his whole face. 'Anybody else?'

'Just me, and I've got every light on the board blinking. The press is driving me nuts. So you want to talk to him or not?'

'Yeah, I guess.'

Theo had a spindly little frame and the face of a twelve-year-old boy, but a voice that boomed like he had an amp plugged into his chest. He could probably scare a criminal to death as long as they never saw him. 'What do you need, Chief?'

'Marian woke up . . .'

'GREAT!'

Frost winced and held the phone a little further from his ear. 'Anyway, she managed to write down three letters. E, N, G. Could be the beginning of a last name, a first name, maybe initials, I don't have a clue. Check with the people she works with at the bar and the diner, see if it means anything to them. If you don't get anywhere on that track, hit the phone books, the computer, whatever you can think of.'

'Will do. Did you ask the daughter?'

'I will. She's in with her mother now. I'll call you back if she has anything for us. If not, keep working it.'

'No problem. Uh, have you been watching the tube this morning . . . ?'

The question was so out of left field Frost almost hung up on him.

'. . . because, the thing is, there was this attack on another waitress in Wisconsin last night. Tied her up, knocked her around, then came at her with a knife, kind of like what happened to Marian. I thought maybe it might be worth a call to that FBI agent who put us on to the scene in the first place to see if there's any connection.'

Frost took a breath. 'Son of a bitch, Theo, you may have some cop in you.'

'Yes sir. You want his number?'

'Oh. Yeah. Thanks.'

Alissa came out before he could place the call, and he spent some time talking to her before he showed her what Marian had written. She stared sad little holes through those shaky, barely formed letters, and nearly wept when she finally shook her head. 'I'm sorry. I'm sorry. I don't know anybody with a first or last name that begins with ENG. I know all her friends and the people she works with. But you know what the traffic is like at the diner and the bar. It could have been a customer she never mentioned.'

'Maybe. We're checking on that right now.'

Like any human being on the planet, Alissa's eyes were drawn to the television in the waiting room. Didn't matter if you were in a sports bar, an airport, or even a hospital, Svengali lived in pixels these days, and if there was a screen around, it didn't take long before everybody's attention was drawn to it. Personally, Frost hated that you couldn't get away from the damn things. He'd gone to Europe once, gotten out of a taxi at an airport where about a thousand people were standing with bags in hand before they went into the terminal, all staring up at a screen the size of an old drive-in movie. There was nothing really interesting about it – just a bunch of rockers in a music video that sounded like cars crashing – but everyone seemed hypnotized by the image. They just stood motionless in front of the thing, no one talking, no one interacting, all looking up, oblivious to anything around them. That had creeped him out big time. Reminded him of *Soylent Green* or one of those other futuristic movies where everyone lived in some kind of a weird zombie state, as if the brains had been sucked right out of their heads.

But maybe it wasn't such a bad thing to be mindless in an ICU waiting room; to get a brief respite from the bad thoughts and fears that kept you just on this side of screaming. Alissa looked almost vapid, which was about as close to serenity as she was going to get for a while.

She made a soft noise in her throat, and Frost looked at the TV. They were showing a full screen of one of those nonspecific police sketches that always end up looking like somebody you know.

'What is it?'

'Nothing. That man looks a little like one of my teachers, is all.'

'How much like him?'

She gave him a sheepish smile. 'Not much. The mouth, a little.'

Frost tipped his head and looked at the guy. 'Looks like Owen Wilson to me.'

'I'm going to go back in and sit with Mom now, okay?'

Frost didn't answer. He was just another automaton in front of a television, mouth-breathing like an idiot while he read the crawl line under the sketch that identified it as the attacker of the Wisconsin waitress Theo had told him about. 'Alissa?'

'Yes?'

'What's your teacher's name?'

'Mr. Huttinger.'

'First name?'

Alissa pursed her lips as she tried to remember. 'Cliff, I think . . . no, Clinton. That was it. Clinton Huttinger.'

Frost kept his disappointment to himself. Why couldn't it have been Engleburton Huttinger, or something like that? 'Okay.'

'He was the best English teacher I ever had, actually. A really super guy.'

After she went back to her mother's room, Chief Frost tried to talk himself out of jumping to conclusions because he wanted an answer so damn bad, but all he kept seeing was his own high school report cards with all the classes abbreviated to three letters because the space was too small.

He had Theo back on the phone within minutes. 'Go, Chief.'

'ENG might be an abbreviation for English.'

'You think the guy's a Brit?'

'Just listen, Theo. Don't repeat anything I say out loud. I don't want anyone in the office or out of the office getting wind of this, because I'm going on my gut here and nothing else, and I don't feel like trashing the life of someone who might be a decent guy.'

'Got it, Chief. Go ahead.'

'There's an English teacher at the high school . . .'

'Ah. English. ENG.'

'Right. Name of Clinton Huttinger. I need his photo and five other similars for a spread. Don't let anybody see what you're doing, just put the package together and get over to the hospital as soon as you can.'

Frost waited in the downstairs lobby, facing the big glass doors, but he heard Theo coming long before he saw him. Didn't matter how well you packed and settled your belt if you were as rail-thin as Theo. Damn thing banged on his bony hips, and handcuffs and light and everything else clattered with every step. He sat down next to his Chief and pulled the photo spread out of a large envelope.

'Fast work, Theo, and it looks good. Which one is he?'

Theo pointed.

'Jesus. He looks like an altar boy.'

'Actually, he was. Also Teacher of the Year and voted students' favorite past three years in a row.'

'Is there a sheet on him?'

Theo snorted. 'Sort of. He ran into his elderly neighbor's burning house to save her cat. The officer on site wrote him a warning on interfering with fire fighters.'

'Terrific. I picked a hero.'

'Hey. A lot of people thought Ted Bundy was Mr. Wonderful.'

'Yeah, I guess. I've got a nurse, a doctor, Alissa, and you for witnesses when we show the spread to Marian. It's going to be tight in there, but I want this covered seven ways from Sunday in case we get anything. By the book, every second. Let's go.'

It was worse than tight when they all crowded into Marian's tiny room, because everyone had to stand at the head of the bed, where they could see the silent identification if it happened.

Marian looked at Frost, then at the photo spread, then back at Frost. He felt his heart fall to his stomach when he saw a tear fall from the corner of her eye. He'd been way out in left field with this leap, and way off base. He'd let her down, and he wondered if he'd ever get over that.

Then he watched her finger, stronger now than when she fumbled with the pen and paper earlier, but still wavering as it moved slowly, but certainly, to the photo of Clinton Huttinger.

Chapter Twenty-three

The problem was that Grace's brain had fallen off the genetic assembly line before they'd installed an off switch. Annie, Roadrunner, and Harley all had some sort of mindless activity where their brains literally seemed to shut down in a kind of weird living death, which gave them respite from the frenetic mental gymnastics required in programming. Grace's brain just kept working like the Energizer Bunny, and the only way she could blank out the endlessly repeating lines of programming language was to focus that laser attention on something else she was passionate about.

Now, this was simple. Basic. Look at the artichokes. Assess the green, the darker tinge at the edge of the leaves that screamed no, not perfect, move on. And then you find the mother lode, fresh off the truck, firm leaves lightened at the tip by the good California sun, drops of liquid crystal when you pushed your thumbnail into the flesh. Perfection.

Grace was a million miles away from her computer, totally focused on smelling Italian parsley, elephant garlic, waving her arms over vine-ripened tomatoes like a Jewish mother at Shabbat, pulling the aroma to her nose.

She'd walked into Whole Foods pissed, because she'd had to drive the few blocks to the store instead of walking. It was a little cooler than yesterday, perfect weather for a sidewalk stroll, but there were other considerations that

184

made that impractical. Walking to the store on a lovely summer day was a pleasant notion, but if you had to carry more than one bag, you wouldn't be able to pull your gun fast enough if the need arose. And today there would be three bags, maybe four, because she was making lunch for all of them.

Lately she'd been thinking about her passions, about how the only two she had – work and cooking – had nothing whatever to do with people. Magozzi had made a ripple in her smooth pool of solitude. The man simply would not give up. He continually banged on the door of her life, foolishly ignoring all the signals that would discourage a lesser man, as if persistence could break through the barriers she had carefully put in place. She was a pragmatic woman, cognizant of her simple biological needs as a human being, accepting that weakness that occasionally succumbed to the mandate of human physical contact. She knew Magozzi wanted much more, and deserved it, but there were sad limits on what Grace was capable of giving. Fear had always defined her life, and she was beginning to think it always would. It was like trying to live underwater after you had exhaled all the air in your lungs, desperate to take a breath, terrified of the consequences.

She thought of the concern of Annie, Harley, and Roadrunner, who kept telling her she was isolating herself from the only thing that mattered – a lasting relationship. It seemed they didn't ever look inward to see the obvious: they were all isolated. Annie's flirtations and Roadrunner's obsessive exercise and Harley's ever-changing and short-lived liaisons kept them as separated from lasting human connection as she was. Perhaps there was no hope for any of them, except for the connection they had to each other, the one constant in all of their lives.

John Smith was sitting upstairs alone in the Monkeewrench office, staring out the window and wondering what the hell to do with himself. The past forty-eight hours had been a workaholic, adrenaline junkie's fantasy; but the problem with being both of those things was that time was always your enemy – either there was never enough of it, or too much of it, like now.

Most agents at his stage in life had plenty of places to redirect their focus and energy when the action died down. They had kids, grandkids, a wife, and a social life. He had none of those things, which simplified the job. The problem was, he wouldn't even have the job in a few months, and the thought of only himself for distraction was truly depressing.

The Monkeewrench crew, on the other hand, didn't share his lack of imagination – they all seemed to have their own places of retreat where they recharged their batteries and shut off their minds. And with the exception of Grace MacBride, they'd all offered to include him. But he hated exercise, which precluded Roadrunner's offer of a bike ride; and he hated opera even more, so he'd politely declined Harley's offer of sitting with him in a room and listening to people screech out some hackneyed story line. He had no idea what Grace's sanctuary was – he only knew she'd taken off in her Range Rover early this morning. The only remotely intriguing offer had been Annie's, but he really had no idea what one did in a spa, and he was pretty certain there wasn't much they could do for him, anyhow.

Jesus, what was happening to him? He'd even tried to play fetch with the weird dog as a last resort, but the mongrel completely ignored him and just sat by the door after his mistress had left, staring up at the knob. Dissed by a dog – the story of his life.

When he saw Grace MacBride's Rover pull into the driveway, and heard the door open and close downstairs, he felt an odd sense of relief and moved toward the elevator.

He found her at the massive kitchen island, unpacking grocery bags that were yielding a farmer's market worth of fresh produce, meat, and shellfish. She acknowledged him with a brief glance and nod of her head. 'There's coffee and fresh pastry in the breakfast room.'

'Thank you. You're cooking?'

'I will be.'

'Can I help?'

'No. Thank you,' she tacked on at the last minute as a civilized formality, but there was no question in his mind that he had just been dismissed. 'This is how I unplug,' she added.

Smith nodded. 'I understand. Good-looking artichokes.'

He left the room; he left her alone, and this was unexpected. Also unexpected that he would notice the extraordinary perfection of a vegetable as underappreciated as the artichoke.

She laid out the ingredients she would need to prep first;

honed the knives she would use and laid them in perfect order on the cutting board, and heard the clink of John Smith's coffee cup on a saucer in the adjacent breakfast room.

God, she hated people. They cluttered up the planet and kept bumping into you; diverting your attention and distracting you from productive work. She softly put down the last honed knife, took an exasperated breath, and walked to the breakfast room. 'Can you handle a knife without cutting your hand off?'

John Smith looked at her. 'Yes. Unless you want me to prepare the artichokes. I'd rather use scissors.'

Grace's eyebrow went up before she could stop it. 'You're a cook.'

'Recreational.'

'I'm going to braise them, then stuff them.'

'Okay.'

They worked together in the kitchen for maybe half an hour without saying more than twenty words. When Grace heard the eight-inch chef's knife clatter against the board, she risked a sideways glance at John Smith mincing garlic, then quickly looked away. He'd prepped the artichokes perfectly; he'd made a pretty terrific vinaigrette for the arugula that she tasted and couldn't criticize, and the only thing he'd ever asked was where to find the lemon, and did she want Meyer or regular. It was like watching herself disconnect from everything by connecting to food. In one way it was upsetting. Was she really so like FBI Special Agent John Smith? A man with no life except his work and the Zen escape into food that demanded nothing and yielded all you thought you could ever expect? Dear God. He was two decades older than she was, and empty.

'You feel like you're looking at your future?' He asked that after an hour, when they were nearly ready to plate, and Grace almost doubled over, as if he'd hit her in the stomach. There weren't many choices when someone was so on point, so she spoke the truth.

'Maybe a little.'

Smith smiled as he wiped away a stray drop of olive oil from where it didn't belong on the edge of a plate. 'You're very young. Lots of time left.'

Grace stabbed a perfectly grilled shrimp from the platter and offered it to him. Only Magozzi had ever received food from her fork before. A strawberry, she remembered, dipped in dark chocolate. 'You were just as young once, with just as much time.'

'But I was stupid. You aren't. I think I overdressed the arugula. And the shrimp breaks my heart.'

Grace shook her head and turned to the sink to wash her hands before she did something stupid, like smile at an FBI agent.

As she was retrieving the last of the serving dishes she'd need from Harley's kitchen cabinets, Smith's phone rang. 'Smith here,' he answered, tucking the phone between his shoulder and ear while he washed the garlic off his hands.

'FBI Agent John Smith?'

'Speaking.'

'Agent Smith, this is Chief Frost, Medford, Oregon, PD.'

'Good to hear from you, Chief Frost. How is your victim?'

'Better. She came out of the coma and did a positive ID of her attacker on a photo spread. An English teacher here by the name of Clinton Huttinger.'

'That's excellent news. Do you have him in custody yet?'

'He's hiding under a rock somewhere. Not at home and he called in sick to work, so we've got both places under surveillance. The thing is, while we were checking out his background for places he might go to hide, we found out he's got a sick mother who lives in Wisconsin.'

Smith's brows lifted. 'Really.'

'Yeah. And so we're looking at the Wisconsin attack that was on the news today, and it looks like ours and theirs have a lot in common.'

'Yes, we've been thinking the same thing. Both waitresses, both tied up and attacked with a knife. And now we know he's got a Midwest connection.'

'Exactly. I know it's thin and kind of a stretch since they happened so far apart on subsequent nights, but I thought it might be worth sending our photo their way. You've got a contact over there, right?'

'I do indeed.'

Frost was silent for a few moments. 'Uh . . . those computer wizards you're working with – how good are they?'

'You wouldn't believe it if I told you. What do you need?'

Frost sighed. 'Well, we've got enough with the positive ID to get a warrant for airline records to see if our boy may have traveled on the night in question, but it's going to take some time. The airlines all get a grace time to have their legal beagles check our warrant to cover their butts before they let us look at manifests, and we've got a hell of a lot of airlines to go through.'

Frost cleared his throat and looked up at Grace. 'Hmm. Let me see what I can do to speed up the process.'

'That would be appreciated. I'm not suggesting anything under the table, of course.'

'No, of course not.' *That's why you asked how good our computer wizards were.*

'I just figured the FBI might have some special kind of clearance. You have a fax number for me? I don't want this photo anywhere near the Web after what you told me about how these guys are operating. We don't want to spook him.'

'What do you need?' Grace asked once he'd hung up.

'The victim came out of the coma and gave Medford a positive ID from a photo spread, but they can't find him. They noted the similarities between the Wisconsin attack and theirs, and think he may have flown out there, but the airlines are dragging their feet releasing manifests.'

Grace sighed, popped a single shrimp into her mouth. 'What's his name?'

He hesitated only a moment. 'Clinton Huttinger.'

'Give me five minutes.'

Smith stared after her as she left for the upstairs office, feeling like he'd just taken the first step onto a slippery slope he'd been avoiding for his entire life.

Chapter Twenty-four

Chief Frost hadn't been in an airport in years. After a lifetime of watching white tinsel contrails decorate the blue sky over his head, he still couldn't convince himself that any plane he boarded wouldn't plummet back to earth. Worse yet, it wouldn't plummet fast; it would take a long, long time so he could be good and scared before he got good and dead.

The fear mystified him. He wasn't afraid of high-speed car chases, confronting armed robbers or even walking into a domestic, but just sitting there listening to the roar and thrust of those fragile metal tubes shooting up into the air over the terminal made him sweat.

Last time he'd been on a plane he was a teenager, looking around at all the other passengers reading magazines, chatting and laughing, comfortable as could be to be mounted on a rocket filled with thousands of gallons of explosive fuel. If they thought it was okay, it had to be, right? A fatherly type sitting next to him saw through his thin ho-hum veneer and patted his hand. 'Flying scares me shitless, too, son,' he said, and that's when he realized everyone else was faking, pretending they actually thought airplanes were airworthy when they knew damn well they were going to crash. He never trusted people or planes again.

'You look a little pale, Chief.' Theo took the seat next to him, bracing knife-sharp elbows on nowhere thighs. It was a wonder they didn't slice right through what little flesh he had.

'I don't like airports.'

'Me neither. I hate flying. Everybody thinks skydiving is such a big macho thrill game. I always thought jumping out of a plane made a hell of a lot more sense than staying in one.'

'Yeah?'

'Yeah. Huttinger's flight is still on time. Should be touching down in the next fifteen minutes. And we're cleared through security if you want to go to the gate.'

'Not yet.'

Theo pulled out his notebook. 'I checked in with Ginny. They're still tossing the house with the on-site Feds. They pulled his PC first and sent it off to Cyber Crimes, but so far they haven't found the laptop.'

'He's got it with him.'

Theo smiled. 'And we've got a warrant. Judge said we had the go-ahead to search his nostrils with a power drill if we wanted.'

Frost looked at him. 'Judge Krinnen said that?'

'Actually, I left out a couple of really colorful words. I'm telling you, the man surprised me. He's like a million years old and as soft-spoken as a little girl and he scared me to death. You ever see his gun collection?'

'Didn't know he had one.'

'Hemingway would eat his heart out, and the judge was real set on showing me every one and describing what kind of damage it would do to Clinton Huttinger if he ever got a bead on the guy.'

Chief Frost sighed, pushed himself up out of the hard plastic chair and adjusted his belt. 'Can't say I blame him. I want to kill this guy myself.'

Goddamnit, he shouldn't have said that out loud. You didn't have that kind of luxury when you were a cop about to arrest a suspect who nearly killed a woman you'd loved twenty years ago. Police brutality wasn't a charge your career recovered from. It was always there on your record in black and white, and sometimes, God forbid, it gave the suspect a cause of action and let him walk. Now he'd really have to suck it up and treat Huttinger with an overdose of care and respect, and the prospect made him sick.

He'd spent the two-hour drive down here looking at the scenery, sucking in the intense greens of an Oregon early summer, smelling the pine coming in through the open window; but all he really saw was Marian's tortured eyes, and all he'd smelled was disinfectant and old blood and adhesive.

It was the same when he walked through security and showed the pass that let him carry fifteen pounds of metal on his belt down to the gate. The sensors beeped when he passed through the archway, and they sounded like the monitors measuring Marian's life back in the ICU.

It wasn't really a long walk to the gate. It just seemed that way. Halfway there Theo stopped for a cell call, then hurried to catch up. 'Crime Scene might have found the knife in Huttinger's dishwasher.'

'There goes that evidence.'

'Maybe not. It's serrated. They can pull a positive blade match from where he cut her.'

Frost stopped in his tracks, thinking autopsy. You didn't excise flesh and bone for a weapon match from a live person, which meant Marian was dead. He didn't have to say anything. All Theo had to do was look at his Chief to know what he was thinking.

'Oh, damn, Chief, I'm sorry. I didn't mean that. Marian's doing fine. Getting better.'

Frost closed his eyes and exhaled.

'But the thing is, well, the throat wound was pretty ragged, you know? So the surgeon had to do some trimming before he could close it. He'd done a turn as county coroner a few years back, so he knows evidence. He took care trimming and saved the flesh for a possible match someday.'

Frost was looking out the window at the 737 pulling up to the gate. His smile was slow in coming, and just a little scary.

Clinton Huttinger was one of the first off the plane, and never in a million years would Frost have passed him on the street and thought that this was an evil man. He looked just like the pictures Theo had pulled off the Web. Clean-cut, well-dressed but not pretentious, a little half-smile permanently placed on lips that told everyone who saw him what a fine, gentle fellow he was.

'Mr. Huttinger?'

'Yes.' The smile broadened. 'Can I help you?'

He didn't even go pale when Frost started the very careful process of placing him under arrest. He just stood there with a baffled little-boy smile, cooperating in every way possible, looking to all the curious passers-by more like a Boy Scout than a crazed killer. Frost played to the gathering crowd, apologizing to Huttinger for the necessity of hand-cuffs, inquiring as to their comfort.

'They're fine, Officer.'

'Chief.'

'Excuse me?'

'It's Chief Frost, Medford Police Department.'

'Oh. Pardon me. It's just that I won't be able to carry my bags with my hands behind my back.'

Frost smiled benevolently. 'Of course not. We'll be happy to carry them for you. Just the single case and the laptop?'

'That's right.'

Theo moved to pick up the luggage but the Chief inter-cepted him, bending to pick up the hard-bodied Samsonite case with the metal reinforcements at the corners, then standing quickly, suitcase swinging as he turned back to face Huttinger. Centrifugal force was an amazing thing, he thought, as the case swung wide and fast with the turn, headed directly for the gentle English teacher's crotch. Huttinger took a quick, panicked step backward, and Frost managed to stop the case's momentum with an inch to spare. He looked head-on at Huttinger and smiled.

'Whew. That was a close one.'

Huttinger didn't say a thing, but he wasn't smiling any-more.

Chapter Twenty-five

Gino was leaning back in his office chair, head thrown back, digging the heels of his palms into his eyes. 'Are my eyes bleeding? Because they feel like they are.'

Magozzi peered around the towers of paper that dominated the space between their desks to assess his partner's current ocular condition. 'I can't tell because you have your fists punched into your eye sockets. But if they weren't bleeding before, they probably are now.'

Gino sat up, flipped over another sheet of paper from his stack, and stared at it like a mortal enemy. 'Is there an ink shortage, or what? I swear to God, anything in print is getting smaller day by day. I always used to wonder what kind of people bought those cheap magnifier reading glasses they always have in baskets at drugstore check-out counters. Now I know.'

'Old guys like us.'

'Yeah. Exactly. So what are you squinting at?'

'North Shore and Chicago cases.'

'Find any connections?'

Magozzi leaned back in his chair and rubbed at the knots in his neck, which made really creepy, crunchy noises when he pushed on them. 'Nothing ties these two together, for sure. None of the same players as far as law enforcement goes, and two totally different crimes – one pedophile and one gang banger. How about you?'

'I was looking at the Elmore Sweet transcripts, but I started to get nauseated, then I started to get pissed, so I thought I'd read something lighter for a break.'

'*War and Peace*?'

'L.A. He was the guy who was driving after his fifth DUI revocation and killed that family on 35W a few years back. Guess he decided to relocate.'

'Maybe he was getting threats from the vics' family.'

Gino shrugged. 'I'll look into it.'

'Any overlaps with Sweet and L.A.?'

'Not that I can see. At least not yet. I still have some more dead trees to get through before I can tell you for sure.'

Magozzi sighed and returned his attention to the file he was reading. 'I guess all we can do is make a list of our major players, and we'll compare notes once we get through all this paper.'

'Which is going to take forever. You know how many names I have swimming in my head right now? Perps, vics, next of kin, witnesses, family members, lawyers, cops . . . This is a nightmare.'

'Maybe we should get Smith on board. He's sharing with us; only seems polite to share with him. After all, these are his cases, too.'

Gino's mouth curled into a smile. 'I like your train of thought, Leo. Very devious, like something I'd think of. Give him a call.'

While Magozzi was trying to reach Smith, Detective Johnny McLaren ambled in and set a big box of donuts on Gino's desk. 'Here's your cliché of the day.'

Gino could literally feel his pupils dilate. 'Are you kidding me, Johnny? Are you angling for beatification, or what?'

'I won the donut raffle this week. Thought I'd share the wealth.'

'What donut raffle, and why the hell don't I know about it?'

'Because you never come to my poker games. The biggest loser of the week has to buy for the biggest winner.'

Gino reverently lifted the lid of the box and selected a glazed disk of heaven. 'You are my hero.'

McLaren eyed the stacks of paper on Gino's and Magozzi's desks. 'Jesus. That's a Muir's Forest worth of pulp – were there just fifty new homicides that I didn't hear about?'

'Just our one river bride, but it might be connected to a bunch of other ones all across the country.'

'No way.'

'Yes, way. It could be huge. We're even working with the Feds and Monkeewrench on this.'

Johnny's red brows peaked into twin Vs. 'Sounds interesting. A hell of a lot more interesting than the Little Mogadishu drive-by Tinker and I pulled yesterday. We solved that homicide in about one second.'

'Oh yeah?'

'Yeah. The perp was a shit driver – couldn't shoot and steer at the same time, so he wrapped his car around a telephone pole. When the first responders yanked him out through the window, he was still holding the gun.'

'That's priceless.'

Magozzi finally hung up the phone, greeted Johnny, then

turned to Gino. 'Smith's tied up and can't help us right now. They've got a hot lead on the Wisconsin guy.'

'Excellent.'

'Who's Smith? Who's the Wisconsin guy?' McLaren asked.

Gino gestured to the files on their desks. 'All part of this mess. You want in on it? We could use an extra pair of eyes big time.'

McLaren shrugged. 'Sure, why not? Our docket's clear right now. I'm officially on vacation anyhow, so maybe the Chief will throw me some overtime.'

Gino pulled a chair for McLaren, and he and Magozzi gave him a quick overview and two of the murder files.

Magozzi said, 'Right now we're just looking for a link between the victims.'

'Cool. Cop work. I can do that.'

'Write down every name you see, and anything else you think might be interesting.'

An hour later Johnny finished with the first file and spent five minutes leaning back in his chair with his mouth open, trying to hit his eyes with eye drops.

Gino snatched one of his pages out of the saline shower. 'Jeez, McLaren, take the rainstorm to the can, will you?'

Johnny wiped at the water on his cheeks. 'I hate these damn things. Could somebody tell me why you can never get this crap in your eyes unless you're standing in front of a mirror? I know where my eyes are, and even if I didn't, I'm looking straight up at Mr. Nozzle and still can't hit the target.'

Magozzi reached for his phone when it rang. 'Your eyes were closed, McLaren.'

'No.'

'I was watching. It's a reflex. You see the drop coming down, you blink at the last second. Gino, take him to the can and staple his lids open.'

'No problem.'

'I heard that, Magozzi.' Grace's voice came over the phone, making him smile. 'And I like the new greeting. A lot more creative than saying "Homicide, Detective Magozzi." Whose lids are you stapling open?'

'McLaren's.'

'What if I'd been a customer?'

'I would have said you'd misdialed and gotten the mayor's office.' He heard a soft chuckle, which was really weird. 'Stop laughing, Grace. You're scaring me.'

'I'm happy. We got him, Magozzi. Clinton Huttinger, aka Teacher of the Year, aka attacker in both Medford, Oregon, *and* Wisconsin. Medford PD just arrested him at the airport.'

'That's great news, Grace. Really great. Any chance he's connected to any of the other murders?'

'None. The Medford cops checked on that, and he's got solid alibis in public places for every one of the others, including your bride. Sorry, Magozzi. But he knew the pre-post code, so his computer may tell us something. We'll let you know.'

'I need a date, Grace.'

Silence for a few seconds. 'Leave your cell on, Magozzi. It might be late, it might not be at all.'

Chapter Twenty-six

John Smith was at the window table in the Monkeewrench office, looking out through the leaves of a tall tree with a trunk as big around as his Great Aunt Harriet five years after she discovered fast food and Twinkies. He wondered how old the tree was. Decades, certainly; maybe centuries, or however long trees lived. Maybe this one had witnessed the migrations of the Ojibwa and the Sioux, the growing pains of a city that kept changing its identity, depending on which industry or immigrant population was dominant, or maybe Harley had planted it last year. John didn't know, and would never have wondered about such a thing three days ago. It disturbed him enormously that such questions were starting to occur to him, and he blamed Monkeewrench for putting him at a table where a tree constantly distracted him.

Why did he care how old it was? Such musings were the provenance of people who wore funny wide shoes and hung wooden beads around their necks. If you couldn't kill it or pick it and throw it in a stewpot for supper, nature's bounty had never held any interest for him. For the most part, it was messy, sometimes dangerous, and always annoying. Especially insects. They'd been bad in the often humid climate of Washington, D.C., but in Minnesota they were enough to drive a man insane. The one and only time in his career he'd been tempted to draw his weapon was when a swarm of gnats had descended on him in the motel parking lot.

And what was so wrong about killing all the insects? Who cared if the frogs died with them? The only thing frogs were good for was keeping the insect population down, and clearly they were lousy at that. So if the insects were gone, the frogs could either find another job or go extinct. That was the way of the world . . . and, come to think of it, a pretty good description of the Bureau's mandatory retirement policy.

His cell phone lay forgotten on the table next to him, still warm from almost an hour of calls informing those who needed to know that Clinton Huttinger had been arrested in Oregon and was now under lock and key. A surprisingly big part of John understood that he had been a very small part of capturing this particular psycho (*making the world safe for waitresses everywhere!*), and every time he passed the news along in that dignified, self-effacing manner that the classes in Quantico had drilled into him, he felt a little flutter in his stomach, a sense of that satisfaction his father had talked about when he locked a bad guy into the back cage of his squad, and the feeling was like a narcotic. Too bad it had happened for the first time so near the end of his law enforcement career.

'Penny for your thoughts, man.' Harley's big mitt came down on his shoulder, making him jump. Funny how such a big man could move so quietly.

John looked up at him. 'Murder, mayhem, chaos – the usual.'

'Holy crap, John, I think you may have come close to a rib-tickler there. Are you okay?'

'Actually, I am very well, thank you. Passing on the news that Clinton Huttinger is off the streets was very . . . satisfying.'

Harley set his bulk down in a chair and stretched out his legs. 'We all kicked some bad ass there, didn't we? So that's who you've been talking to all this time? The big guns in D.C.?'

'Yes.'

'That's good to hear. At first I figured you were having phone sex, you were on that cell so long; then I was afraid you were having some kind of special freaky moment with that tree, the way you were looking at it all serene. For a second there you looked almost happy. Very un-Fed.'

John rolled his chair to face him. 'I was actually thinking about killing all the frogs, if that makes you feel any better.'

Harley raised a brow. 'Frogs, huh? That's a pretty weird target for a crime fighter.'

'It was a very convoluted train of thought.'

'That's never bad. Someday we'll get snockered together and you can tell me how you got there. Not that I care. Personally, I hate frogs. Always did, ever since I ran over one with the lawnmower at foster home number seven. Freaked me out big time. And speaking of that, we just put the dead-people software to bed.'

John took a breath as he tried to fumble his way through Harley's maze of thought. Foster home number seven? How many had there been? 'The dead-people software?'

'Yeah. Remember? The thing you brought us on board to do? Roadrunner's spinning the thing through the beta version now, and when that's tight, we'll have a product that can tell you in two seconds if you've got film of a real dead body or a setup. So the whole damn day is just plain good. Huttinger's in jail, and you've got the software you wanted.'

'Oh.'

'"Oh"? That's all you've got to say? Get your dancing shoes on, Mr. John, because the champagne flutes are polished and I'm ready to dust off the big boys.'

John almost smiled, and it looked a little silly, as if smiles rarely found a comfortable spot on his face. 'You know, half the time I have no idea what you're saying, but I do enjoy the way you say it.'

Harley guffawed and clapped him on the back just as John's cell phone started skittering across the desk. 'Tell whoever's on the other end of that thing to lose your number. We've got some celebrating to do.'

Harley walked away, giving him some privacy, which John thought said a lot about the man. He snapped open the cell and listened carefully for a time, and felt that elusive and rare moment of semicontentment he'd been enjoying seep away. 'I'll pass it on and get back to you,' were the only words he uttered during the entire conversation. When he snapped the phone closed he looked down at his watch, wondering where the afternoon had gone, where the years had gone, and how the world had changed so starkly while he was right there in it, a blind witness.

Everything seemed to be swirling out of control, falling

apart – his watch included. There were little things on the face he'd never noticed before. A fleck of dirt under the glass between the two and the three; a dull spot where the metal had worn off on the minute hand. Cheap junk, deteriorating less than a year after he'd bought it. He thought of his uncle, in the ground for over a decade now, wearing the Swiss watch his own father had given him the day he put on the blues. *I should have snatched it off his wrist while the coffin was still open,* he thought, and then closed his eyes, startled that such a thing had occurred to him. When he opened them again, Harley was back in the chair opposite, fingers laced over his barrel chest.

'Bad news, Smith?'

'We have a new problem.'

'Huh. Interesting. So far we've got actual murders broadcast over the Web and schoolteachers gone mad. The way I see it, the only things left are ICBMs on their way from China or a comet on a collision course with Earth. Which is it? And, Christ, I hope it's the comet, because that would take longer than ICBMs from China, which gives us time to get ripped.'

The smile was totally inappropriate, and John had to fight the impulse to cover it with his hand. 'That was Chelsea Thomas on the phone.'

'The hottie profiler you sent Magozzi to see?'

John frowned. 'Who told you she was a . . . hottie?'

Harley grinned, thinking that Special Agent John Smith had probably never ever uttered that word before in his entire politically correct life. He shrugged and his leather jacket exuded a saddle smell. 'Rolseth called with a howdy-do the day she brought the murder films to City Hall. He doesn't mince words when it comes to describing women, if you know what I mean. Unless his wife is around. Then he's Prince Charming on a horse.'

Nonplussed at all the unsolicited information, John caught himself wondering if Detective Rolseth was a philanderer. 'Oh. Well, yes. Agent Thomas is the profiler I sent Magozzi to meet, and she's been involved in the murder cases from the beginning. Her specialty is actually the increase of youth crime fostered by Internet communities. She assiduously monitors the youth social sites – YouTube, Facebook, and the like, and stumbled across a few of the murder films in the course of her work that hadn't been caught by the servers.'

'Wow. Great titties and a monster brain. Can't get much better than that.'

John scowled and puffed up a little. 'She's a brilliant agent with a stunning intellect and has an unquestionable loyalty to law and justice that has absolutely nothing to do with her physical appearance.'

Harley blinked at him. 'John. Get over it. Great titties are a good thing. Not an insult. So what did this female goddess tell you on the phone that sent your feel-good swirling down the toilet?'

'Firstly . . .'

'Is that an actual word?'

'Yes, it is. Firstly, that everyone in the Bureau is celebrating the capture of Huttinger, as if he were the end of this. They've all forgotten the other murders.'

Harley rolled his upper lip and moved his black beard.

'Nobody's forgetting. You just have to celebrate the little victories, otherwise you reach for the razor.'

Smith rubbed at his eyes. 'We didn't have a victory. We caught a fluke. A loser who stumbled into the place where the real monsters play. Those are the ones we have to stop, or we haven't accomplished anything.'

'Jesus, Smith. What do you mean, we haven't accomplished anything? So what if Huttinger was just a copycat. We nailed his ass, and who knows how many he would have hurt with a little more practice. The white hats won one today.'

Smith sighed. 'I guess.'

Grace, Annie, and Roadrunner slipped into the other chairs at the table and just looked at him. It was kind of creepy.

'Sugar, you look plumb worn out,' Annie said. 'Gracie must have busted your balls in the kitchen this morning.'

'Not at all.'

'"So why the long face?" said the bartender to the horse. We stopped a bad guy, we had a good day.'

'He just had a downer call from Chelsea Thomas,' Harley explained. 'The firstly part was all wrong, but I straightened him out on that. So – what's the secondly part, John?'

Smith shrugged. 'This thing keeps expanding in directions nobody expected, getting bigger and bigger all the time. Ever since the media publicized the code the murderers used, there have been thousands copying the "CiTy oF" format to post nonsense, and no way to separate the chaff from the real thing without tracing each one individually. The people in Cyber Crimes are afraid we're going to miss a pre-post of a real murder while they're chasing down false leads.'

Roadrunner smiled. 'No sweat. I'll just modify the program we're already using to set up an automatic trace on every post that uses the code. If they're traceable, the program puts them in the slush file. But if they use the same type of routing the real murderers used or some kind of anonymity software, we'll get an alarm. That should help.'

Harley patted him on the head. 'Cool, little buddy. I wasn't going to think of that for another three seconds.'

'How long will it take to put something like that together?' Smith asked.

'Give me half an hour. And call Cyber Crimes and tell them it's coming. Last time I tried to send them something they fried me as spam.'

Smith grabbed a pad of Post-it notes and scribbled an e-mail address. 'Can you send that off to Chelsea Thomas to load on her computer, too?'

'You got it. And if that's all you need, call the restaurant, Harley. I'm starving.'

Roadrunner headed for his station while Harley stood up and stretched his tattooed arms wide. 'Glory hallelujah. I've got pasta on my mind. You like pasta, John?'

'I really should get back to the motel.'

Annie flapped a hand. 'Oh, screw that, darlin'. We're going out, and you're comin' along.'

'So what's the deal with Huttinger?' Harley asked as he lumbered over to the mini-fridge. 'Is he talking?'

'Not yet, but he's processed, and the locals are about to commence the first round of questioning.'

'Well, I hope they put the son of a bitch in a rack and yank the truth out of him joint by joint. He slimed into this twisted network of maniacs somehow, so there's gotta be something he knows that we can use. Here you go.' He set a tiny bottle of beer in front of Smith.

'What's this?'

Harley rolled his eyes. 'Man, do you need work. That's a shortie. A mini-beer, right out of the mini-fridge. We've got thirty minutes to kill, and happy hour is now enforced by law.'

'I really shouldn't.'

'Don't give me that no-drinking-on-the-job crap. I didn't buy that for a minute. Job like yours, you can't tell me there aren't really pissy days when you come home and take a sip or two to destress, and you've had a few pissy days in a row. Besides, livers are evil and must be punished.'

John blinked at the bottle. 'You have an opener?'

Grace sighed, then reached over and unscrewed the cap. 'They invented twist-off caps a while back, John.'

'Oh.'

'So who has Huttinger's computers?'

'His laptop and the CPU from his home office are with our Computer Analysis and Response Team in Portland. They'll work on forensic recovery around the clock.'

'How good is Portland's CART?'

'Excellent. Our field office there also houses the Northwest Regional Computer Forensics Laboratory, so the Bureau has a very solid local team on this. They'll also be sending copies of the hard drives to D.C.'

Grace sighed. 'We might be able to help if you got us copies of those drives, John.'

'I've made the request on your behalf already, and paperwork for that clearance is in the pipeline.'

'Paperwork?' Harley growled. 'Man, that's scary, because paperwork usually means nothing gets done. Jesus. We offer up our services on a silver platter, and you've got to jump through hoops to get it?'

And that, in a nutshell, was what was wrong with the Bureau, and centralized bureaucracies in general, Smith thought; if you wanted to accomplish anything, you had to check with somebody who had to check with somebody else, who had to check with somebody else, ad infinitum. In the meanwhile, time got wasted, opportunities got lost. Would it really be so bad if the powers that be put a little more faith in the people on the ground they'd hired to get the job done in the first place?

Dangerous territory, he chided himself. *This morning you turned your back when MacBride hacked into airline computers; now you're sitting in front of an open beer you absolutely are going to drink; and in a few minutes, you're going to get hard drives without authorization for people with no clearance. What are you going to do next, John?* Grace watched John Smith's face reflect the battle his conscience was having with his good sense. 'John. Huttinger didn't just know the code, he knew the routing all the murderers used. He made contact with these people at some point, and it's probably on his computer. I know your people are good— '

'No, we're better,' Harley interrupted.

Smith took a breath and another sip of beer, then pulled

out his cell and punched in a series of numbers. 'Mark, this is John in Minneapolis. Expedite copies of Huttinger's hard drives to me here, will you? No, no clearance numbers yet. My authority.'

Grace was smiling at him when he hung up.

Chapter Twenty-seven

It was eleven o'clock by the time they returned to Harley's from the restaurant. John had had two glasses of wine on top of the shortie, and there wasn't enough pasta in the world to counter that much alcohol for a non-drinker. He remembered now why he never drank – it made his mind fuzzy and his eyelids droop. 'I'm afraid I have to get to bed. Thank you all so much for the excellent evening.'

'John's right,' Grace said. 'We should all get some rest, and I, for one, plan on doing just that in my own bed tonight.'

'That's not a bad idea, sugar,' Annie said. 'First of all, I don't have a thing left to wear in my closet here, and I miss my bunny slippers.' She looked up at Smith, and he could have sworn she batted her eyelashes at him, although that could have been the kind of wishful thinking that happened when you had an elevated blood alcohol. 'You shouldn't be driving, John Smith.'

Harley nodded. 'Yeah. Stick around, Smith. The motel you're at sucks and if I've got anything here, it's space.'

Harley put John Smith in what he called the Big Boy's Room – a mahogany-paneled suite next to the Monkeewrench office that boasted a four-poster bed big enough for Henry VIII, a steam shower, a sauna, a wet bar with single-malt scotch and Waterford lowball glasses and a cigar humidor that John thought was a table safe.

He barely noticed most of the accoutrements, although he was quick to see the black cashmere pajamas laid out on the bed. The rest of the Monkeewrench crew had already gone home, with the exception of Roadrunner, who had been checking the alarm settings on his computer when I bid him and Harley good night.

Bicycling home after midnight was a concept John simply couldn't get his head around. Such a thing in D.C. would be suicide, but apparently Minneapolis was a whole different story. People jogged and biked and walked under the moonlight in this Midwest Mecca, blissfully unaware that in other metropolises such a venture would be lethal.

'Roadrunner does it all the time,' Harley reassured him as he showed him his quarters for the night. 'Towels in the bathroom, extra blankets in the cupboard, anything else you need?'

'Nothing I can think of. Thank you for putting me up for the night.'

Harley snorted. 'No prob. Trust me – you won't be sorry. The bed is sweeter and softer than chocolate mousse, the sheets are Italian, and I make a killer frittata. Besides, everybody else is gone for the night, and this place echoes when I'm the only one in it. It'll be a good thing to have a breakfast partner.'

John was slipping his suit jacket onto the silent valet next to the bed. 'Yes. For me, too.'

Harley folded his beefy arms across his chest and regarded the man curiously for a moment. 'No family, huh?'

Smith shook his head. 'Married to the job.'

'I hear you. So what's going to happen when your job divorces you?'

'I'll know the answer to that in six months.'

Harley frowned. 'Mandatory retirement?'

Smith nodded. 'This is my last case.'

'That's too bad, because you're damn good at your job.'

'Thank you. Likewise.'

'What are you planning to do with all your spare time?'

'I suppose I'll pick up some useless hobby. Maybe do some consulting on the side.'

'I've got a lot of useless hobbies. They all get old after a while.'

'You don't need hobbies, Mr. Davidson – you've got a family.'

Harley rocked back on his heels, then smiled. 'It's never too late to make one, John Smith,' he said as he closed the double oak doors behind him.

The steam shower was amazing. John sat on the marble bench and watched clouds curl around his legs for a long time before he remembered to leave the volcanic steam and find his way to a bed that had micro weight settings to accommodate his frame. Cashmere was an amazing material, he thought, slipping into the pajamas and crawling under a comforter that made him remember his mother, tucking him in, kissing his nose, of all things, telling him that morning was bright, and it was coming.

Hours later, just as the light of a coming morning began to change the colors in his room, he heard a slight pinging in his dream; the sound of his microwave in his D.C. condo telling him his frozen turkey dinner was ready, ready, ready.

A part of his brain knew this was an erroneous message; that he wasn't in his D.C. condo, and that the pinging meant something else, but eventually the pinging faded and he heard nothing but the soft susurration of his breath, moving in and out.

In the Monkeewrench office, next to John Smith's Big Boy bedroom, Roadrunner's computer was flashing blue on a black screen.

'City of Lakes, Many, Everywhere,' it read, pinging every time the letters reappeared.

Chelsea Thomas balanced a bag of take-out Vietnamese on her knee while she struggled with the ancient, temperamental lock on the front door of her uptown duplex. The place had been described as 'historic' and 'charming' by the real estate agent who'd leased it to her, but she failed to see the allure – cosmetically appealing adjectives were just verbal plastic surgery as far as she was concerned, and no compensation for the fact that the place was over a hundred years old and had more leaks, creaks, and groans than a nursing home. Not to mention the fact that there were no closets – apparently, people in the old days, at least in the Midwest, didn't have any clothes or shoes.

Just two more months and the posh river condo she'd purchased would be ready for occupancy. She still had four months on the duplex lease, but didn't mind one bit making double payments for a while. Money was no problem, and never had been.

In her old world, this lot would have long since been razed and redeveloped to accommodate a ten-thousand-square-foot replica of a Tuscan villa, like the one she'd grown up in. And was conspicuous consumption such a bad thing if it meant functioning door locks and plumbing and, gee whiz, maybe a closet? Well, apparently it was in this zip code, which was inhabited by people who made an art form of dressing down and worshiped historical detail like a religion. She'd tried to replace the rusty old broken lock with a brand-new deadbolt during her first week in the duplex, and the owner had nearly swallowed her tongue at the request. *Omigod. Surely you must be joking. That lock is original to the house. Original. You California people have no respect for history. None at all.*

Chelsea got the 'California' slam a lot here, even before people knew that was where she'd grown up, and she hated that. Bad enough that she was born blond, grew up looking like a cheerleader, and had a diploma from Beverly Hills High; worse yet that she sailed through post-grad degrees while everyone was thinking she must have slept her way to Ph.D.s in an academic version of the casting couch.

She might as well have been a Hollywood celeb, like her uncle and her grandfather, or one of those bling-obsessed Housewives of Orange County, or Atlanta, or wherever, with their heavy loads of silicone and light loads of brain cells.

Oh, yes, she understood the allure of glamour and fame more than most, growing up in the rarified environment she had, which was why she was so well qualified for the job she was doing now. Any culture that prized notoriety and image above all drove people, especially young people, to all sorts of extremes to achieve that single goal. In the insular world of her past, it was SOP for a lot of her contemporaries to do as many drugs as possible as early as possible, get boob jobs and nose jobs and lipo at sixteen, make sex tapes as soon as the bandages came off, and engage in any other shenanigans that would set you apart in a place that wasn't easily impressed by bad behavior, but rewarded it with celebrity if you could deliver.

But if you were an angry, disenfranchised, parentally neglected kid in Iowa, with no Hollywood pedigree and no paparazzi following your Porsche from club to club, you didn't get attention. Which is where the Web came in, where the Web was changing everything. And as far as she was concerned, it was just a matter of time before that kid in Iowa decided to blow the Paris Hiltons and Britney Spears and Lindsay Lohans out of the water with something truly spectacular.

Nobody at the Bureau understood that in quite the way she did, and nobody had been particularly fearful of such a scenario, until she'd told them they should be. They hadn't exactly laughed at her, but they'd made it perfectly clear that eavesdropping on teenagers was a waste of the Bureau's time and resources. Six months ago she'd been wasting her own personal time eavesdropping on YouTube when she discovered a plot by two high school seniors to blow up their Texas school. Like all bureaucracies, and most shortsighted businesses, if something worked before, it was taken for granted that it would work again. So when new threats emerged on the Internet, they just assumed their tech whizzes could find the source and catch the bad guys. The problem was, criminals adapted much faster than law-abiding citizens, and with the sophisticated anonymity software available, the bad guys were golden, at least in this brief point in time, before law enforcement could catch up. It took vision and a general lack of faith in humanity to anticipate hideous crimes that hadn't even been invented yet, which is essentially how she'd created a new position for herself above and beyond her work as a profiler.

She ate in front of her computer, watching it download the software program Roadrunner had sent her. Why was it computer geeks always used cutesy little handles instead of something more dignified, more befitting their intelligence? And he was brilliant, this Roadrunner character, at least according to John. His modification of a program to clean up all the nuisance 'City of' posts was pure genius. She prayed the alarm wouldn't buzz tonight as she crawled into bed, exhausted.

As it turned out, her prayers were answered. The alarm didn't sound until sunrise.

Chapter Twenty-eight

Magozzi woke up before sunrise to a hot, swampy summer morning that promised misery to all and certain death to his decrepit, wheezing window air conditioner. The next home improvement project was going to be a practical one – central air.

Gino had begged to keep the Cadillac for a couple days, so this morning he was chauffeuring Magozzi to work for a change, even though it meant backtracking an extra ten miles. When Magozzi stepped out of his house he was already at the curb, lounging in the driver's seat with his eyes closed, AC cranked to arctic blast, the stereo wailing vintage Springsteen.

Magozzi hopped in on the passenger's side, and Gino bolted up in his seat. 'Christ, Leo! I didn't even hear you,' he shouted over the noise.

Magozzi punched the stereo off. 'I can't imagine why. Are you trying to get popped for a noise violation, or what?'

Gino smiled a little sheepishly. 'Glory days, buddy. Glory days.'

'Why are you in such a good mood? You hate mornings.'

'Are you kidding? We helped save a life and bust a complete psychopath yesterday, and we don't even have any paperwork to do on it. That's just about as perfect as this job ever gets.'

'Yeah, I guess.'

'Did you hear if they pulled anything off Huttinger's computer yet?'

'Everything's still in lockdown with the Feds in Oregon. Monkeewrench is waiting on copies of the drives.'

Gino shook his head. 'Man, I can't believe that freak was actually Teacher of the Year.'

'Scary.'

'No shit, it's scary. Parent-teacher conferences are never going to be the same.' Gino put the car in gear, then reached over and cranked the stereo again.

When they got to City Hall, two squads were coming up out of the underground garage, lightbars flashing. Even over Gino's music, Magozzi could hear the sirens spit out a wail a few seconds later for the intersection, and tried to remember what this week's policy was. The battle was ongoing: half the denizens of City Hall wanted a quiet zone around the building to keep from going deaf every time a squad pulled out on a call; the other half wanted sirens on the second the cars hit daylight as a warning to sidewalk pedestrians. The one and only hard-and-fast rule was that sirens were not turned on inside the garage, which was one of the dumbest three-page memos he'd ever read on the job, detailing the decibel level of a siren inside a closed concrete structure and the potential of hearing loss. Duh.

'Ten bucks says those guys are going on a donut run,' Gino said as he reluctantly departed the posh cocoon of their loaner.

'In your dreams.'

'Yeah, in my dreams. You know, I haven't had a good

donut since they closed the Melo-Glaze. You know what they're making there now? Dog biscuits. Frigging boutique dog biscuits. If that's not a waste of good, industrial kitchen equipment, I don't know what is. I mean, we've all had dogs before, we know what they eat. And I can tell you one thing, it's not pistachio-encrusted, truffle-infused, carob-coated petit fours. Which actually aren't that bad.'

'You *ate* dog food?'

Gino shrugged and hitched his pants up. 'I didn't realize it was a goddamned dog bakery last time I went.'

In the office, they found Johnny McLaren and his partner, Tinker Lewis, standing around the filing cabinet, looking at the little television on top.

'What's with the TV?'

McLaren snorted. 'It's stupid day at the airport again. Some jerk forgot a package next to a chair in baggage claim and they had to evacuate the terminal.'

Magozzi glanced at the screen, saw a shaky long-lens shot of hundreds of passengers hightailing it away from the terminal while the Bloomington PD Bomb Squad moved in. He shook his head, thinking of the thousands of dollars that would be spent having somebody's lunch box hauled away in a total containment vessel and moved to a detonation site.

McLaren said, 'I don't get it. There's great security at the airport. You can hardly get in the damn place.'

Gino snorted. 'Are you kidding me? Every time Angela's parents fly in she's crossing her legs half the way there and by the time I pull up to the curb she's out of the car like a rocket, tearing inside to use the can. And let me tell you, that's woman's purse is huge. She could carry a tactical nuke in that thing, and nobody stops her. There is no security at passenger pickup.'

McLaren was troubled. 'That can't be right.'

'You ever been to the airport, McLaren?'

McLaren flipped him the bird and continued staring at the television.

'Well, when you're finished wasting taxpayer dollars watching the idiot box, get your ass over to our cube so we can talk about all that help you're supposedly giving us.'

'Yeah, yeah, yeah, just a couple more minutes.'

They drifted to their desks, and Gino sat down and swiped a pile of crumbs from his blotter. 'This whole plan to try and connect the victims drove me to drink more Chianti last night.'

'Worked for you last time.'

'Not this time. I'm thinking I should switch over to Pinot Grigio, just for the summer. Might be a little more inspirational.'

Magozzi tipped his head at the sound of feet hitting the hall floor hard. Someone was running somewhere; maybe to the same place the squads had been heading when he'd come in. Officers running in City Hall was like kids running in grade school; it wasn't unheard of, but it prickled the hairs on the back of your neck, just because you didn't hear it that often.

'Aw, shit,' McLaren called from across the room. 'They've got another one.'

'Another what?'

McLaren blew a raspberry at the TV. 'Another call on a

suspicious package . . . oh, terrific, this one's ours, boys, smack-dab in the middle of the Convention Center. Can anybody tell me how the media gets this stuff before we hear about it?'

Running footsteps in the hall, Magozzi thought, and stepped out of Homicide in time to see Joe Gebeke heading out, once again decked out in his gear. Déjà vu. 'You going to the Convention Center, Joe?'

'Oh yeah, and guess who's there today. The National Library Association and about ten million boxes of books we're going to have to check one by one. Two more days and I could have gotten a free pass into the boat show, but no, it had to be today.'

Magozzi took a step or two down the hall with him, which wasn't easy. The man had a stride like a race horse. 'Say, have we ever had two of these suspicious package calls in one day before?'

Joe stopped and looked at him for a long second before answering. 'Sure we have, Leo. No sweat.'

'Okay.'

But after Joe hit the front doors and the hall was empty, Magozzi could hear phones ringing all over the building.

Chapter Twenty-nine

Barney Wollmeyer didn't feel that twist in his gut anymore when his squad was called to the airport. It had happened too many times, and it was starting to get boring. That was a bad sign. For this kind of duty you had to be calm, thorough, and methodical, but it didn't hurt to be a little scared shitless, either, and he was losing that. Time to turn over the lead to someone younger, someone less jaded, who still thought maybe there was a bomb in the Neiman Marcus bag, and not a birthday present for someone's grandkid.

Bloomington PD's bomb squad had covered the airport from the beginning, and were arguably the best in the state. Best equipment, the best men – and absolutely the most experienced, since airports were primary targets, at least in the minds of those who ran Homeland Security. Barney never got that. Why was a bomb at the airport any more frightening than a bomb in the middle of a shopping center? Funny how people assigned different levels of fear to something as silly as location. Dead is dead, after all; didn't matter much where it happened, but get a suspicious package anywhere near an airplane and everybody's heart rate doubled.

Everybody else on the squad hated the suit – the way you could hear your breath inside the hood, and the steady beat of your pulse in your ears. Barney loved it. At home he had six kids and a wife with a high-pitched voice that hit your ears like Chinese music. He loved them all more than life, but oh, God, the sound of his own breathing was soft and restful, and he only heard it in the suit.

He looked over at his partner, toddling spread-legged across the last road between the parking lot and the doors to baggage claim. The kid wasn't used to walking distances in the heavy suit yet, in spite of all the practice. It was different when you were breathing hard because the adrenaline was pumping and it was about a hundred degrees outside on top of it.

Aubrey would be one of the candidates Barney would tag to take his place as lead on the squad. He was old enough to have experience under his belt, young enough to have the strength and guts, and new enough to the duty to still be scared. Perfect. And Lord knew he needed it. What kind of sadistic parents named a kid 'Aubrey,' for crying out loud? You almost had to volunteer for bomb squad duty to live down a name like that.

They'd shut off the power grid to baggage claim, and the lower level of the terminal was dim and gloomy with only the faint light creeping through the front windows. The carousels were still and quiet, luggage jammed onto the metal fins, going nowhere. He saw backpacks and garment bags, Louis Vuitton cases butted up against cheap black nylon marked with pink duct tape, and there he saw the commingling of a diverse society that flew together, shoulder to shoulder, went to the same places, and maybe came home to a safe place in the Midwest.

Barney didn't like this part. Airports weren't supposed to be empty and quiet. He was used to seeing passengers crowded around the spinning circles, hearing the annoying announcements spit out almost nonstop over the public address system, dodging running kids and rolling suitcases that all seemed a lot more dangerous than some innocuous box sitting unattended. The best part of his job was making sure that all came back.

The box was against an interior wall behind carousel number three. Heavy cardboard sealed with standard strapping tape, the same size as the boxes his wife used to store old tax files. Utterly unremarkable except for one thing: in a place where every single item had ID tags and addresses and routing labels slapped all over them, this box didn't have a mark on it.

Barney took a little deeper breath than he had so far and set up the portable X-ray. It was real-time, but the viewer was small, and a little fuzzier than the big monsters upstairs at security check-in. He took a knee and leaned forward to bring his face closer to the screen.

Aubrey stood patiently a few steps away, sweating in the suit, waiting for his look at the screen. He'd been on enough of these runs to know that this was where the scenario ended. Barney would step aside and give him a look at the X-ray of clothes or stuffed animals or whatever was inside, and then it was just a matter of procedure and time before he could strip off the hood and get a breath of good air, or at least as good as the air at the airport ever gets.

Finally Barney pushed to his feet and stepped aside and

Aubrey moved in and hunkered down in front of the machine. He looked for a few seconds, then remembered to breathe. 'Sweet Baby Jesus,' he murmured, and Barney nodded.

'We're going to need the Hazmat suits.'

Chapter Thirty

Magozzi was staring at the television screen, noticing only peripherally that the phones in Homicide weren't ringing. Apparently people postponed killing each other when there might be a larger, more all-encompassing threat. There was a Ph.D. thesis in here somewhere.

'Okay, I got the list right here,' McLaren said, rattling a sheet of paper. 'Five bucks to pay, or you don't play. What's in the boxes, boys, what's in the boxes?'

Gino raised a hand with a fiver. 'Nothing. They're empty.'

'You sure you want to go that way, Rolseth? Four guys in Vice already bet that way, so if you're right, you have to split the pot. Try to be more creative.'

'Okay. Porn.'

'Nice one. And it's all yours. Leo? You in?'

'Yeah. I'm doubling down on a note.'

'What kind of note?'

'You know, some "Ha-ha made you look" kind of thing.'

'Whoa. Another nice one. Tinker?'

Tinker was still staring at the television. 'No thanks. Take a look. They've got the first one from the airport at the detonation site in Rosemount, and there goes the robot.'

Magozzi closed his eyes. He'd been out to detonation sites with the squad – everybody in the department had after bomb threats had become all too common. He'd watched from behind the steel barrier while the remote-control robot whined up to the dummy bomb, its metallic arms busy, and every face behind the barrier, his own included, was gleaming with sweat. It wasn't a real threat. Everyone there knew there was no bomb inside that container; but the procedure itself was filled with tension, and every man and woman felt it as if it were the real thing.

'There's nothing in the damn boxes,' he grumbled. 'Probably just another stupid kid's prank, like at the mall the other day. The media just gets a hard-on from titillating the public. Makes for good ratings. Problem is, if they keep giving it airtime, it'll keep happening. They're creating a little culture of celebrity-starved psychopaths, just like Chelsea said.'

Gino turned his head slowly to look at Magozzi. '*Titillating* and *hard-on* in the same sentence, Leo? You're running off the rails.'

Tinker Lewis had been a Homicide Detective for longer than he cared to remember; a cop for twice as long, and he'd seen this before. Every now and then there was a weird year – who knew why – too many mosquitoes, too few jobs, too many really hot and humid days, or maybe even something odd, like the alignment of the planets or some such crap. He never bothered to wonder why; he only knew that in those years strange things happened. A lot of vandalism, like two weeks ago when twenty cars on a side street in a pleasant neighborhood had all their windows broken out by something like a baseball bat wielded by someone who was really pissed. Kids, probably, raging for reasons you could never understand, using senseless violence as the pointer toward a society they thought had failed them.

Then there had been the murders. Not a lot of them, over the past few weeks, but they hadn't been pretty. The domestics were more gruesome than usual; the robberies more vicious. And then there was this home-invasion thing. That phrase hadn't even been in his vocabulary a decade ago. What madness prompts your average burglar to intentionally break into a house where people are asleep in their beds? What sadism feeds the need to terrify people you never met while violating their property? What's the problem with doing it like it's always been done? Certainly there was far less risk in breaking into houses when people aren't home, taking what you want and walking away free? Something was changing. Something was different, and it pulled his sad eyes even further down on his face, because it spoke more of evil than simple criminality.

Take your pension. Get out now, Tinker.

His wife had been telling him that for some time.

God knew, the pension was good after all these years, and it didn't hurt to be married to one of the country's top heart specialists, who made more money on surgery Monday than he did in a whole year.

He was thinking of all these things as he watched the television; watched the number of boxes adding up. *It's just kids,* he thought. *Getting their rocks off terrorizing the whole damn city, just because they could; just because they raged and raged. These days they smashed the windows in twenty cars, broke into houses to scare sleeping families, or maybe, just maybe, they stashed a few suspicious boxes in places that would send a whole city into panic mode. That's what it was. That's what it had to be, because the alternative was unthinkable.*

Chapter Thirty-one

Joe Gebeke was at one of the bathroom sinks splashing water on his face when Magozzi walked in.

'That was fast. False alarm at the Convention Center?' Magozzi asked, then did a double take when Joe glanced up at him in the mirror. He didn't look so good.

'We're not finished yet. Not by a long shot.'

'And they let you come back?'

Joe braced his arms on the sink and looked at the drain. Water dripped from his chin and made tiny sounds on the porcelain. Finally he straightened, looked around the room, then stepped closer and almost whispered, 'They sent me back because I haven't finished my recertification for Hazmat yet.'

Magozzi felt like he was missing something. Between meth labs and chemical spills, Hazmat had gotten a lot of press time, and almost everyone had seen the rigs on the road at one time or another. Leave behind a can of hairspray or a case of wine at the airport, Hazmat was likely to show up, just like it had this morning. Even the media didn't try to hype it up anymore, because eventually the thing that looked like a can of hairspray tested out to be a can of hairspray, leaving a lot of reporters looking like the boy who cried wolf, and a lot of other people pissed because so-called 'breaking news' made them miss their favorite show.

'Okay . . . ,' he said to Joe. 'You've got something questionable in the Convention Center box, just like they did at the airport, and Hazmat comes in. Happens all the time. Better safe than sorry, right? So why are you whispering?'

Joe got red in the face. 'It isn't two boxes, Leo. It's five. At least, it was five the last time I heard. There's a new one at the Mall of America; two more at the Metrodome. Every single box is absolutely identical, and every one of them has a Mason jar in it, you know those things your mom used for pickles and shit?'

Magozzi nodded.

'Well, they're all filled with some kind of liquid. Could be water – some sicko's idea of a joke – or it could be nitro, or something a hell of a lot worse. It's going to take a while to find out, because there's something under each jar. Something they took the trouble to wrap in lead sheeting so the X-ray can't penetrate. It's creeping a lot of us out.'

Magozzi felt his fingers go numb, and wondered where his blood was headed.

Down the hall in Homicide, Gino switched channels when the one they were watching broke away to a commercial. This one had amped up the coverage, with a split screen of live feeds from the package sites, and a female anchor who looked suitably concerned as she interviewed a terrorism expert.

'How the hell do you get to be a terrorism expert?' McLaren asked.

Gino shrugged. 'They're probably all retired spooks.'

'Oh yeah? Seems like it'd be a good gig. Play James Bond for a while, then get a nice, fat contract to show up on TV whenever the shit hits the fan.'

'Sign up now, McLaren. I heard they're looking for orange-haired agents with borderline albinism to plant in the Middle East.'

'Do the words "Miss Clairol" and "spray-on tan" mean anything to you, Rolseth?' Johnny returned his attention to the terrorism expert, who was clearly his new idol.

Gino was shaking his head in disgust. 'They just always have to jump right to the doomsday scenario every frigging time, don't they? I mean, this is probably just a sick, twisted prank, but oh no, it's Muhammed Muhammed Whoever, blowing up the Heartland. I'm telling you, it's just like the weather warnings. Remember last Sunday, when they were crowing about how this summer was going to be the worst drought in recorded history, how the crops were going to die on the vine, food prices were going to skyrocket, and by August, we'd all be rioting over the last can of corn on earth? And what happens the next day? We get five inches of rain in two hours, and suddenly the rivers are going to crest and the entire Midwest is going to get wiped off the face of the map in biblical floods. Jesus. If there are any terrorists, it's those gel-haired assholes on TV who tell you every raindrop's a tornado and every mugging is the end of Western civilization.' He stopped for a breath and looked at Tinker, who was gaping at him, absolutely speechless.

McLaren, on the other hand, who always appreciated a good rant, was beaming at him. 'Man, two snaps up . . .

Hey, Magozzi, long time in the can. We thought you fell in.'

Gino looked up at his partner's rigid face and felt his insides go cold.

Chapter Thirty-two

Red hair or not, Johnny McLaren had one of those pale faces you never associated with the Irish. Neither round and rosy nor dark and haunted, his was one hundred percent affable, and, as the ladies were fond of noticing and slow to respond to, boyish. It hadn't looked boyish since Magozzi told them what he'd learned in the bathroom.

It took the media about five minutes longer to learn about the Mason jars, and now the coverage was nonstop, and about as close to grim as Minneapolis television ever got, which meant the anchors weren't smiling. Magozzi and Gino had gone back to their desks, but McLaren and Tinker were hooked to the TV like dogs on a leash.

'Jesus, Mary, and Joseph,' McLaren murmured, and for the first time Magozzi heard Ireland in the lilt. 'They found another one. How many is that?'

'Seven,' Tinker said.

'And how many bomb squads have we got?'

'Last time I checked, we had four. In the whole state.'

Magozzi looked across the desk at Gino, whose eyes were fixed on the TV. The sound was muted, but the picture was bad enough. They had a graphic of the city up, with seven blinking red dots, marking the location of each suspect box. While they watched, three more lights popped up in the center of the city.

'Shit.' Gino pushed speed dial on his cell. 'Angela. Where are you? What library? Okay, that's okay. Where are the kids?'

Angela's irritated voice came through loud and clear when Gino held the phone away from his ear. 'Oh, gee, Gino, I don't know. Was I supposed to be watching them?'

Gino winced. 'All right, all right, I'm sorry, okay?' And then he told her what was going on, listened for a long time before turning toward the wall and murmuring some things Magozzi couldn't hear before hanging up.

'Everything okay?' Magozzi asked his partner.

Gino looked miserable. 'I told her to pick up the kids and take them on a little field trip.'

'Where to?'

Gino took a breath. 'Out of the city. Wisconsin, maybe.'

'Christ, Gino . . .'

But Gino didn't hear him. He'd raised his eyes to the television, where at least half a dozen new red lights were blinking.

Things were getting out of hand. Most Minnesotans watched the news coverage, decided for themselves whether the threat was real or exaggerated, and the only measure of the majority decision was the number of cars on the freeway heading for Wisconsin, because nobody wanted to attack Wisconsin. Ever.

'Lot of cars on the bridge to Hudson,' Gino commented, his eyes on the television.

Magozzi nodded. 'Where're Angela and the kids?'

'Somerset. She got the last room at a great bed-and-breakfast near the Apple River.'

'Feel better now?'

Gino nodded. 'Big time.'

Magozzi glanced at the caller ID when his cell rang, then picked up. 'You're watching this, right?'

Grace never worried about anything, except the bag boy at Whole Foods pulling out an AK-47 and shooting her dead. 'Of course we're watching it, Magozzi. We have been, since seven a.m., when we got a pre-post. You need to check the messages on your cell more often, especially when your switchboard is jammed.'

Magozzi thought about that for a minute. He always checked for messages, hoping one of them would be from Grace. But not this morning. This morning things had started to happen really fast, and his heart did a little flip-flop at the thought that he'd lost precious time on a potential murder. 'You're calling me, so I assume it's local. Did the post give you any ideas on the potential victim or location?'

'It's not another murder, Magozzi. We think the pre-post was about the boxes.'

'What?'

'All it said was "City of Lakes, Many, Everywhere." Half an hour later the TV was nonstop boxes. The post was untraceable, like the murder posts, but it didn't follow the same routing as the others. Your profiler friend, Chelsea, is in the know, according to John, and she says it's something else entirely.'

'She is not a friend. We had a beer and a burger and a

gallon of milk while we talked shop about serial killers and Internet stuff. Did she bother to mention what "something else entirely" means?'

'She's even got a name for it. Chaotic terrorism. You know how little boys get a kick out of popping out of closets and scaring the crap out of you?'

'That was really sexist, Grace.'

'How many little girls pop out of closets to scare people?'

'Not enough, but I get your point.'

'So Chelsea thinks this is the post-puberty version. Disenfranchised dweebs hiding in their basements, power-tripping on scaring a whole city to death. The coverage of the murder posts probably gave them the idea.'

Magozzi pushed wrinkles into his forehead. 'So she doesn't think it's real.'

'Obviously it doesn't have to be real to stop a city. The threat is enough, but it's still terrorism, plain and simple.'

Magozzi started rummaging in his desk drawer, looking for aspirin. 'So our choices are a terrorist attack or a teenager attack?'

'And if it's the latter, you better get those monsters in cuffs by the morning news or every media-addicted creep in the country is going to try to outdo what happens here. Go to work, Magozzi. We can't find them, so it's all on you.'

When Magozzi hung up, Gino was peering over his computer screen at him, powdered sugar parentheses enclosing his mouth. 'I choose teenager attack.'

'Huh?'

'You said "terrorist attack or teenager attack." I pick B. What else did she say?'

After Magozzi gave him a rundown, Gino folded his hands over his paunch and leaned back in his chair. 'If it's a terrorist attack, we're all screwed. If it's a teenager attack we can waterboard a couple thirteen-year-olds and no one will ever try it again.' His eyes drifted over to the television and his mouth turned down. 'I don't know, Leo. Mason jars with liquid, lead sheeting to beat the X-ray . . . ? Seems like pretty sophisticated shit for a screw-up kid.'

Magozzi nodded. 'That's what I was thinking.'

One of the newer hires out of Vice – a tall, loose-limbed guy who looked like he just got out from behind a plow – walked into Homicide and found McLaren. 'Hey, Johnny. I'm guessing nobody bet on Mason jars.'

'Nope.'

'So give me my fiver back.'

'Sure thing, Scarecrow. But I'm afraid there's going to be a processing fee.'

'I don't think so, you red weasel. Processing fee means I book you on gambling charges.' His eyes drifted up to the TV. 'This is some scary shit.'

McLaren squinted at him. 'You see, that's the part I don't get. You get a bomb scare at a school, you automatically think it's a kid making trouble. I don't get the panic button on this one.'

'Are you kidding? All that crap at the schools and the mall in the past few months? Amateur hour. This one was really put together.'

'So out of the thousands of dopes in this city, we finally hit one with an IQ in triple digits. Had to happen.'

'You whistling in the dark, McLaren?'

'You bet your ass I am.'

'Well, keep your head out of the sand, because even if this scare is a bust, it doesn't mean the next one will be. Al-Jazeera already picked this up. They're streaming news from Minneapolis, if you can believe that. It's like a play-book on how to terrorize people.'

'Jeez, Scarecrow, get a grip. And don't trip over your petticoats on the way out.'

'Fuck you, McLaren. You Homicide sissies make damn sure you hit the scene after the perp is long gone. Call me when you get a sack, and I'll take you on a meth bust.'

'So did you walk all the way over here to bust my balls or what?'

'Nah. I'm the town crier. You got anything to eat over here?'

'Last donut just hit Rolseth's gullet. You might be able to get him to cough it up if you use some of those cool macho meth-bust moves.'

'Man, you're testy today. Listen. They're pulling together surveillance footage from all the box sites that had security cameras, which means all of them, which means about four million hours of tape, and the brass is begging for help from anybody with a uniform and one good eye.'

'You actually saw the Chief?'

'Oh, hell, no. He's been locked up with the mayor and the governor since this thing started. They only let him out long enough to parse out the hourly updates on TV.'

'Yeah, I caught a couple of those. Poor guy is starting to look a little undone. I think I actually saw a hair out of place during the last one.'

'You ask me, he's allowed. The man's got a lot on his plate today. Anyway, we're going to set up in one of the old conference rooms on three, so anybody without an active case, come on up and watch some movies with us.'

'Tinker and I can help you out.'

'Good deal. Bring popcorn.'

Chapter Thirty-three

The task force room in City Hall had been transformed into a makeshift media center full of laptops, TVs, and volunteers from every department and every precinct, squinting at screens and taking notes.

The confusing olfactory potpourri that had always been a trademark of the space still lingered, even though it had been officially retired for years. As Magozzi stepped into the room, his nose picked up the familiar old scents of sweat, bad cologne, cleaning chemicals, and cigarette smoke, along with the newer contributions of the current occupants. He caught a whiff of breath mints, a fleeting hint of patchouli, and the cloying, pervasive stench of microwave popcorn that had been steamed to death in fake butter.

And then there was Grace MacBride, whose sensory ghost trumped all in this place, at least for Magozzi. He'd met her here for the second time in his life, almost two years ago, after he'd basically accused her of murder and a laundry list of other horrible misdeeds. Probably not the kind of courtship ritual little girls dreamed of.

'Leo?' Gino gave him a nudge.

'What?'

'I've been regaling you with brilliant insights for the past thirty seconds at least, and you're acting like you just popped a handful of Oxys.'

'Sorry. What were your brilliant insights?'

Gino snuffled, and rearranged some southern part of his wardrobe. 'For one, where the hell is our chalkboard? You and I solved many a murder brainstorming on that thing, and I loved it like a child.'

'Probably got stashed in storage someplace.'

'They can't just take an important piece of our life and mothball it without checking with us first.'

'Sure they can. Some killjoy with asthma complained about the chalk dust, so they replaced all the blackboards with whiteboards.'

'Whiteboards *suck*.'

They wended their way through the tables and desks and found McLaren and Tinker in the far corner of the beehive, both hunched over a laptop, noses practically pressed to the screen. 'How's it going?'

McLaren shook his head without looking away from the black-and-white security footage. 'This is damn near impossible. Everybody at the mall is carrying a shopping bag, damn near everybody at the library convention is wheeling around a suitcase full of books . . . and none of us have seen any boxes get dropped yet. The locations must have been scouted, because they're all out of camera range.'

Gino grunted, still pouting over the chalkboard. 'That's a little spooky.'

'Yeah, no kidding . . . Tinker, wait. Back up a few frames and play it in slo-mo for me.'

Tinker clicked the mouse a few times and McLaren jabbed a finger at two kids who were milling around at the Mall of America. 'Check out those guys. Look familiar?'

Tinker stared for a moment, then shook his head. 'Just a couple of skate punks. The mall is full of them.'

'Yeah, but I think I've seen these dudes before, in some of the footage we checked out earlier. Maybe from the Metrodome. Go back.' He pushed away from the desk while Tinker worked the mouse some more. 'So, you solve your case already, or what?'

Magozzi shook his head. 'We're stuck in neutral, getting nowhere fast.'

'I know what you mean – I went through those two files you gave me and came up with nada. I have a list of names for you, but I gotta tell you up front that nothing clicked. The most interesting thing I pulled was the blood alcohol on your river bride – that guy should have been wearing a biohazard warning label. I'm surprised he had a liver left, especially with all the meds he was on.'

'Meds?' Gino asked.

'Yeah. He had AIDS.'

'He did?'

'Yeah. Don't you guys read autopsy reports?'

'Not recreationally, like you, McLaren,' Gino grumbled. 'Besides, we already knew how he died.'

Tinker tapped the screen. 'Rolling tape, Johnny.'

The four of them turned their attention to the computer screen and watched a motley assemblage of humanity unwittingly pass beneath the all-seeing eyes of the Metrodome security cameras. Ten minutes later, Gino slid his eyes to look over at Magozzi. 'The Tiara Club film was way more entertaining.'

Magozzi nodded.

Gino started fidgeting. 'Man, this is more boring than what we were doing back in the office. What do you say we break for lunch, then . . .'

'Stop!' McLaren said, then pointed to the screen. 'See? Same two kids. Exact same skater punk clothes, same faces.'

Magozzi and Gino were now breathing down McLaren's neck. 'I think Johnny's right,' Magozzi said. 'What kind of time frame are we looking at?'

Tinker scrawled down the time stamp, then went back to the mall footage and compared them. 'About two hours apart. You might have something, Johnny.'

Gino shrugged and pushed up the sleeves of his wrinkled white button-down. 'Or not. Could just be bored kids making the rounds. And I gotta tell you, these two don't look bright enough to tie their own shoes, let alone pull something like this off.'

'Yeah, but the same two guys at two different sites? I don't know, that's kind of a coincidence.'

Gino blew out a breath. 'If they show up at another site, then I'll jump on board.'

'Pull up some chairs and we'll check out some more tape.'

Gino rolled his eyes. 'Great.'

It took another half hour before McLaren found what he was looking for – the same two kids, loitering around the Crystal Court in the IDS building, about half an hour after they'd been filmed at the Metrodome. 'Goddamn. These could be our perps. Two kids.'

Just like Chelsea suspected, Magozzi thought.

Gino leaned back and rubbed his eyes. 'We've still got a

problem. We didn't see them drop any boxes. So this doesn't prove anything.'

'Yeah, but it might be enough to bring them in for questioning. If we can figure out who the hell they are.'

'Good luck with that. How are you going to match identities with a couple faces in a city with a few hundred thousand people? We can't question them if we don't know who they are or where they live.'

'I have an idea,' Magozzi said quietly.

The other three detectives looked at him hopefully.

'Do you remember that facial-recognition software Monkeewrench developed?'

McLaren scrunched his face up for a moment, then his eyes widened. 'Yeah. That was the program that basically tied up the old Nazi case, right?'

'Exactly. You input the photo of the person you want to identify and the program cross-references with images on the Web and looks for a match.'

Gino smiled. 'And there's one thing you can count on – kids have their pictures plastered all over the Web.'

Chapter Thirty-four

Gino spent most of the ride to Harley's on the phone with Angela. He hung up just as Magozzi turned onto Summit Avenue.

'Everything okay at the B and B?'

'Better than okay. There's a pool and a restaurant that has cheese curds on the menu. And here I am, fighting crime with an empty stomach and a bad donut hangover.'

'What's the mood on the street?'

'She said people are pretty spooked. Nobody's actually letting themselves believe the threat is credible, but so what? They're still white-knuckling it in Somerset, Wisconsin, just in case. One hell of a big power trip for our doer, or doers.'

'Reminds you how vulnerable we all are. The price of a free society.'

Gino nodded emphatically. 'Exactly. What a big problem *that* is. But, fortunately, I have a great solution – martial law for a few months with you and me in charge. Shut down the Web, beer and fresh donuts for the troops. And all our generals will drive confiscated Caddies just like this one.' He let out a miserable sigh. 'This is depressing. Do you really think kids are behind this?'

'I don't know. What's scarier? Criminally warped kids on the rampage or real terrorists?'

'I don't think you can split hairs when it comes to terrorism, which is what this is, plain and simple, no matter who's behind it. But at least if it's kids, there's probably nothing in any of the jars except water or something else lame, right? I mean, I'm no Chelsea Thomas, profiling goddess of the modern world, but I know how those little antisocial bastards' minds work. They go for the big bang, but they usually don't have mass slaughter on their minds.'

'The Columbine kids had bombs, and they obviously had mass slaughter on their minds. Hell, they probably used blueprints from some terrorist website.'

Gino scowled. 'Thanks for that. And by the way, the Web is really starting to piss me off. It's like a meet-and-greet for sociopaths all of a sudden.'

'Access and anonymity. If you're a scumbag, it's the perfect storm. But in the end, it's the same old criminals, just a different venue.'

'Yeah, I suppose. Too bad we're always playing catch-up and doing damage control.'

'That's what this job is about. It's what this job has always been about. You win some, you lose some, and you do as much good as you can along the way.'

Gino grunted. 'Christ, Leo. You're sounding like one of those scary, late-night TV inspirational speakers. And here I am, wondering what our new shrink friend would say about the kind of personality that picks a career where your chance of failure is about as good as your chance of success.'

'She would say we're noble, gallant, right-fighters. Maybe

even modern-day superheroes. She has to think that way, because she picked the same field we did.'

'Masochism?'

'Yep.' He pulled into Harley's driveway and parked behind the airport-rental Fed-mobile that obviously belonged to John Smith, then smiled a little when he saw Roadrunner, waiting anxiously on the front steps for them.

'Damnit,' Gino said under his breath. 'I can't get used to seeing the skinny guy in jeans. It's just wrong.'

Roadrunner waved as they approached, then held out his hand. 'Hey, guys. You have a disk for me?'

Magozzi handed him a CD in a plastic sleeve and gave him an affectionate pat on the shoulder. 'Three clips of the same two kids at three of the box sites. How long do you think it's going to take?'

Roadrunner's brow wrinkled. 'I don't know . . . the program is pretty bloated, out of sheer necessity. We've tweaked it a little since the last time we used it, but it could still take a while. Come on in, make yourselves at home, I want to get started on this right away.'

Roadrunner ignored the elevator and took the stairs three at a time up to the office, while Gino headed straight for the kitchen, Magozzi on his heels. They startled John Smith, who was standing by the refrigerator, drinking a glass of orange juice. The poor man looked almost embarrassed for having been caught in the midst of a perfectly normal, human act. 'Good afternoon, Detectives.'

Gino's eyes scanned the empty countertops in disappointment. 'Afternoon, Agent Smith.'

'Good work with the surveillance footage. Let's hope it

will help bring this situation to a quick resolution. I was informed that five of the boxes have been cleared.'

Magozzi nodded. 'That's right. No explosives, plain glycerin in the jars.'

'So eight more to go.'

Gino snorted. 'Eight more that we know about. There could be another hundred out there that we just haven't found yet. Or maybe the frigging bastards are still out there planting the things, we don't know. Nobody's taking a powder on this thing. Not your guys, not ours.'

'How is your murder investigation progressing?'

'It's not,' Magozzi said.

Smith looked troubled. 'Last we spoke, you mentioned a Minnesota connection with the seven male murder victims, which seemed like a promising detail.'

'We're still working that angle,' Gino said. 'Nothing so far.'

'But it's quite a coincidence, you must admit.'

'You're telling me. Minnesota is suddenly up to its eyeballs in Web-related homicide, and now this crap with the boxes.' He shoved his hands in his pockets and regarded his shoes for a moment – an innocent pair of physical ticks that meant nothing to anybody except Magozzi, who knew his partner's pre-attack body language better than his own.

'And as long as we're on the topic of coincidences,' Gino continued, as Magozzi knew he would; 'here's another one. A week ago, you rode into town for a cyber-crime sting before you even knew about the Minnesota connection. Or *did* you know?'

John blinked a few times, genuinely blindsided, in Magozzi's opinion. 'We absolutely did not know. We never even considered the fact that the Web murders could be related until Monkeewrench found the pre-posts. And, frankly, just because they were all pre-posted doesn't mean they're related. As I'm sure Dr. Thomas mentioned to you, there is a great potential for deviant communities to form and escalate on the Web. The fact that seven of the victims have ties to this state is really the most compelling evidence for a connection we have so far.'

Gino frowned. 'So maybe we've got a deviant community escalating right here.'

'It's a possibility.'

'So why *did* you pick Minneapolis for a base of operations if you didn't know anything before you got here?' Magozzi picked up Gino's pass.

Smith almost smiled. 'You two are an impressive interrogation team.'

Gino puffed out his chest a little. 'Thank you.'

Smith nodded graciously. 'We're here because Monkeewrench is here. Regardless of the competency of our Cyber Crimes Division, we felt it critical to utilize all resources available for this investigation. And I think we can all agree that there is nobody better at what they do than Monkeewrench. We did offer to set them up with an office in D.C. for this assignment, but they preferred to work from their home office. We agreed to accommodate them.'

'So this really is just a coincidence?' Gino asked.

Smith frowned. Apparently he was as uncomfortable with

the word *coincidence* as everybody else in law enforcement. 'It appears that way.'

Grace, Annie, and Harley all pulled up chairs next to Roadrunner and watched as he loaded the clips from the surveillance footage onto a dedicated computer that ran the facial-recognition software.

'Are you going to limit Web-search parameters, buddy?' Harley asked.

'No.' He turned around in his chair. 'Should I?'

'It's gonna take forever if you don't. Start out small and match against a few social networking sites first.'

'Okay. I'll start the search with MySpace, YouTube, and Facebook. They're the biggies.'

Annie, who was looking particularly fetching in a floral-printed silk caftan today, gave Harley a rare compliment. 'That's the most sensible thing that's come out of your mouth in days.'

Harley waggled his eyebrows at her. 'Everything out of my mouth is sensible. You're just finally getting it, doll face.'

'Keep the dream alive, Harley,' she snipped back. 'Sophistry becomes you. And don't ever call me doll face again, or else I'll . . .'

Grace tuned out the ongoing tête-à-tête between Harley and Annie and let her eyes drift up to the wall-mounted television they rarely watched but had kept on since the box fiasco had started. Every channel, on network and cable, was still running nonstop coverage of Minneapolis in chaos. How long would it take before this scenario replayed itself in other cities across the country, and across the planet? Probably not long. Global interconnectedness had seemed like such a great idea at its inception, but like all powerful things, it had its dark side – a seriously big dark side – and they were on the frontlines.

Annie had apparently burned out her war of words with Harley, because she was watching the television now, too, her lips pursed in a glittery pink pout that matched the shimmering silk poppies on her dress. 'This is just plain craziness. Look at those freeways – plumb full of nice people who are scared to death to stay in their own city. That's not right, and we need to do something about it.'

Grace sighed. 'The only real solution is to change human nature, and that we can't do. The Web might be inciting bad behavior and providing a global audience, but in the end, we're still talking about bad people, not bad technology.'

'The thing that drives me crazy is there are too goddamned many places on the Web where the bad guys can hide,' Harley grumbled. 'If we took away their hiding places, maybe they'd think twice.'

Roadrunner spun his chair around. 'I just launched the facial-recognition software. Now it's a waiting game.' He looked at Harley. 'And there's nothing we can do about their hiding places, Harley.'

'Oh yeah?' Harley grumbled. 'There's lots we can do, if we have the cojones to do it.'

Roadrunner rolled his eyes. 'Oh yeah? Like what? We've been tap-dancing in and out of these hostile servers and sites for the past week. The people we're looking for know how to stay stealth, and every single post that predicted crimes has been bounced around the globe through anonymity software, botnets, networks of firewalls, you name it. There is such a thing as untraceable.'

'I know that, dipshit, I worked with you on all the traces we tried. My point is, we need to cut off the head of the hydra. There are foreign servers we know about that are protecting bad guys seven ways to Sunday and won't grant access to law enforcement. So what are we supposed to do, play nice? Follow international laws that promote cyber crime? Hell no. We shut 'em down. Every time we find a foreign server tag associated with a crime? Bang! Denial-of-service attack. Viruses. Whatever. And we'll just keep shutting them down the minute they go back on-line.'

Annie gaped at him. 'Sweet Jesus, Harley, you've lost your mind. We can't do that.'

'Why not?'

'First of all, it would probably incite an international incident. Second of all, we would surely end up in those orange jumpsuits.'

Roadrunner was smirking at Harley. 'Besides, *dipshit*, do you know how many servers there are in this country alone, let alone the world? You might as well try to empty the Pacific Ocean with a teaspoon.'

Harley scowled back. 'Okay, so maybe shutting down servers isn't the answer. My point is, our lawbreaking has always been in proportion with whatever crime we're trying to solve. But the crime is escalating, and so we have to, too. Laws don't keep up with technology, and those laws deserve to be broken.'

'I agree with you, Harley,' Grace said quietly. 'The problem is, there will always be criminals out there, whether or not we shut down servers or compromise the anonymity networks that protect them. All we can do is try to keep up, and help the cops make an example of the criminals we do catch.'

'Pretty ironic that four people who repeatedly break the law spend so much time fighting crime,' Annie said, scrutinizing a chip in her new manicure.

'Did I hear something about breaking laws?' Gino's voice preceded him into the room, along with Magozzi and Smith.

Harley chuckled. 'Just international law. Nothing you need to worry about, buddy.'

'How's it going with the surveillance footage?' Magozzi addressed the room, but his eyes were fixed on Grace.

'Hi, Magozzi. The program is running now.'

'Pull up some chairs, darlings,' Annie drawled. 'We've got some time to kill.'

Ten minutes later, Roadrunner let out a whoop and Harley started laughing so hard, he doubled over, and everybody in the room descended on Roadrunner's computer.

'What is it?'

Harley took a few seconds to catch his breath. 'We got a match,' he pointed to the enhanced picture of one of the kids from the surveillance tape. The program had pulled up a second picture from MySpace. 'Can you believe it? This kid was smart enough to use anonymity software that's so complicated, you practically need two brains just to install and config it, but there he is, right on MySpace, full name, city, and state. What a dumbass.' He looked at Magozzi. 'How many Kyle Zellicksons do you think live in Minneapolis?'

Magozzi smiled. 'Pull up the white pages and we'll find out.'

Chapter Thirty-five

'Oh my goodness.' John Smith slid into the middle of the Caddie's backseat and started playing with all the electronic controls at his disposal. The back windows went up and down; the rear AC fan went on and off; and some really annoying rap blared out of the back speakers before he figured out how to shut it off. 'I don't know what this orange button does.'

'Lumbar support,' Gino said, snapping his shoulder harness with a proprietary click, as if he thought absolutely nothing of this kind of ride. 'But you won't get it in the middle. Right side, right seat, left side, left seat. The middle passenger suffers. It's kind of a junker.'

Magozzi closed his lips on a smile and backed out of Harley's driveway.

'Is this standard for MPD, or just Homicide?'

'Confiscated from a drug dealer,' Magozzi said, toughing down on the accelerator because Gino was a corrupting influence and made him want to show off. 'Gino bribed one of the garage evidence guys so we had sweet wheels while ours were being fixed.'

'What do you usually drive?'

'A tacky brown sedan with no heat and no AC and enough get-up-and-go to get up and fall down.'

'I see. So what's the bribe for this kind of transportation?'

'Gino's wife's lasagna. She'd cook your heart out.'

'Hmm.' John stretched his arms out over the backseat. 'What are the chances of a retired Federal agent tucking into your department?'

Magozzi shrugged. 'We've always had a little problem with the Feds. The SAC here is pretty much of an asshole.'

'And it's a tough gig,' Gino added. 'No picnic. They put me on the dunk tank at the MPD festival last year.'

'What's a dunk tank?'

'That would be man's ultimate humiliation. You sit on this little seat over a tank of water, and the public throws balls at a target that tips the seat so you fall in. If the seat's high enough above the water, the impact flattens your balls.'

John thought about that for a minute. 'Are you serious?'
'I am.'

Magozzi squealed the Caddie's rubber at the turn off Snelling onto Lexington. 'You want the lead on questioning these kids?'

Smith shrugged. 'Your city, your precinct.'

'I think the Feds trump the cops on terrorism.'

'That is where the working-together part comes in. Besides, when it comes to terrorism, I'd let a Brownie troop take down a possible witness if they wanted.'

Gino turned to look at John in the backseat. 'You're starting to talk like a cop.'

'I'm practicing so I can get lasagna and a Cadillac.'

'Good God, Leo, are you listening to this guy? A week in the Midwest and he's starting to get funny.'

John closed his eyes. Another item for the slippery-slope

list. Violating Bureau policy, violating Federal law, consuming alcohol on duty, and now stepping away from stern and proper agent demeanor. He was shedding pieces of who he was, who he had always been, like a dog with mange. He cleared his throat, straightened his tie, and put on his Bureau face. 'I am also certain that both of you have more experience interrogating juveniles. We don't get many offenders that young at the Federal level.'

'They're not juvies,' Magozzi reminded him. 'Eighteen, both of them.'

'Barely. I am also a little uncomfortable questioning these boys in particular. Technically, we don't have a great deal to support their involvement.'

'Bullshit,' Gino snorted. 'Little bastards are in this so deep we're going to have to rip their balls off and stuff them in their ears to get them to talk. And personally, I'm looking forward to that.'

Magozzi caught a glance of John's alarmed look in the rearview mirror. 'Gino hasn't done that in a really long time,' he said genially.

The house was a surprise – one of the largest in a new development of McMansions people bought on credit to impress their neighbors with how much money they supposedly had. Magozzi knew the inside by heart. Lots of electronics, lots of granite and upscale appliances in a kitchen they never used, lots of bills hidden away in a drawer somewhere. People with real money never bought places like this, because there was something tacky that shone through all the pretense of luxury like a Target T-shirt under a cashmere sweater.

The doorbell was a melody – didn't anybody have normal doorbells anymore? – and whoever was inside took a while answering. Magozzi took point, as always; Gino was off to the side, and John Smith hung back a little, ceding the lead to the cops, who did this kind of thing a lot more than he did.

The man who finally came to the door was dressed in what old movies had taught him wealthy men wore at home in the evening. In his peripheral vision Magozzi saw Gino cover his mouth quickly, and he didn't blame him. The idiot was wearing one of those silly shiny robes over his white shirt and suit pants. 'Good evening, sir,' he said respectfully, flipping open his badge case and holding it up. 'Are you Mr. Zellickson?'

'Yes, Officer. What can I do for you?'

'Detective Magozzi, MPD. This is my partner, Detective Rolseth, and this is Special Agent John Smith of the Federal Bureau of Investigation. Is your son Kyle at home?'

Mr. Zellickson looked genuinely confused. 'Yes, he is . . . did you say the FBI?'

'That's correct, sir.'

'What on earth would you want with my son?'

Magozzi smiled briefly. 'Just a few questions, sir. We think he and a friend of his may have inadvertently witnessed something pertinent to a crime we're investigating and hoped he'd be willing to help us out by answering a few questions.'

'Really. Well, of course he'd be happy to help if he could . . .' He pressed his lips together and frowned at John

Smith. 'I don't understand the FBI connection. Does this have anything to do with the boxes today?'

Goddamnit, Magozzi thought, he wasn't as dumb as his doorbell. 'Yes, it does.'

'Good heavens. I can't imagine Kyle seeing anything and not mentioning it . . . this whole thing is terrible, and to tell you the truth, I think it frightened him a little.'

Magozzi nodded. 'I'm sure it did. The point is, witnesses often see things without realizing what they saw, so they never think to mention it until someone asks them about it.'

'Oh.' He chewed on his lip a while and tugged at his pants, which Magozzi thought was always a bad sign. Bull readjusting the jewels before taking a stand. Worse yet, Mr. Silk Robe wasn't opening the door and inviting them in. 'I do want to be helpful, Officers. Please don't misunderstand. But Kyle is my son, and having the three of you show up at my door at this hour wanting to question him about what happened today makes me very uncomfortable. I think I'd like to call our lawyer.'

Magozzi nodded. 'Then that's exactly what you should do, sir. As a matter of fact, if you have any reason to believe that your son might have been involved in the placement of these boxes all over the city— '

'Good God, no! It's not that. I just meant . . . it's so ridiculous. Kyle was valedictorian of his graduating class. Four-point-oh since he was a freshman. Voted most popular, most likely to succeed . . .'

Gino made a face and rolled his head. 'Oh, man, you gotta be kidding me. You have a kid with a four-point-oh?

I got a sixteen-year-old who thinks four-point-oh is an IQ score. You're a lucky man, Mr. Zellickson.'

Kyle's dad blinked at Gino, and then smiled tentatively. 'Thank you. He's a great kid.'

Gino gave him a lopsided smile. 'Obviously. Let me know when he's between girlfriends. My daughter may not be the brightest bulb on the tree, but she's a sweetheart, and a looker to boot, and I'd sure like to see her hooked up with a young man who takes education seriously.' He shoved his hands in his pockets and shrugged at Magozzi. 'Come on, Leo. Let me tell him what's up. The guy's got the army at the door and has every right to be concerned.'

Magozzi looked down at his shoes and pretended to think for a moment.

John was watching the two cops without saying a word, thinking he'd learned more in the past three minutes than in all his years of law enforcement.

'I suppose,' Magozzi finally said.

'Great. Okay, Mr. Zellickson, this is the deal,' Gino said. 'We got some surveillance video from some of the sites where the boxes were planted, and we caught a pic of Kyle and his friend' – he pretended to consult his notes – 'Clark, something . . .'

'Clark Bradley?'

'Yeah, that's the one. They weren't carrying a box or anything, and we're not thinking for one minute they were involved, but they were pretty close to a spot where one of the boxes was found, so we figured maybe, if we were really lucky, they might have seen something . . . like somebody setting down a box, for instance. And what's so freaky about that? A guy setting down a box? You'd never think twice about it. But in this case, maybe it means something.'

Kyle's dad frowned. 'Where was this?'

'The Metrodome.'

The man got manicures, Magozzi realized, wondering why that still gave him the creeps. His hand was pressed against his chest as if to quiet a relieved heart, and his buffed nails glinted on the black silk of the silly robe.

'Oh, for crying out loud,' Mr. Zellickson said, smiling for the first time since he'd opened the door. 'They have open skating at the Dome on a couple of floors whenever nothing else is going on. Kyle and Clark go all the time. They love their Rollerblades.'

Gino opened his hands and grinned. 'And they were blading on the film.' His grin disappeared. 'However – and I'm telling you this as a father, because I'd want to know if it were my kid – neither one of them was wearing a helmet.'

Mr. Zellickson's eyes narrowed. 'I will definitely talk to him about that. Come in, gentlemen. Kyle's in the basement doing some homework. With Clark, as it happens. You can talk to them both at the same time.'

Gino beamed at him. 'How lucky can we get?'

Kyle's mother pretty much hated the basement, which suited Kyle just fine since it meant she didn't come down here very much. Once in a blue moon the tornado siren on the corner blew its brains out and busted everybody's eardrums, and that was the only time she came down to the space Kyle had made his own. He and Clark had tacked up band posters on the wall, and hidden under those were the really fab posters of girls with big hooters hanging down to their belly buttons that made you want to do things to yourself no matter who was looking.

Clark was kind of a superdweeb. He'd been wearing jackets with zippers instead of snaps, duh, when he and Kyle had first hooked up, but he was a pure CSI genius. He'd seen every show about a million times, and watched all the cop and autopsy shows on cable until he nearly fried his brains out with a TV Ph.D. in how to do crime and make assholes out of the cops. Better yet, he carried a bong in his backpack and scored a lot of green from somewhere, because he always had a Glad bag full in his jockey shorts.

They were slumped on the sprung-out couch in the basement room mainlining tortilla chips and chocolate, watching the big screen Kyle's dad had hung on the wall to keep his precious progeny occupied while he and the mother of the year did whatever the hell they did upstairs. Last time he'd checked they'd been watching some reality show about a bunch of weird people trying to beat each other at stupid games on a deserted island. Tonight they were glued to the coverage of all the boxes that were turning the city upside down.

Have you done your homework, Kyle?

We're doing it now, Dad. Clark and I are watching the PBS special on the Civil War for history class.

That's good, Son. I heard that was a good series. So you're not watching the network news?

Nah. It's all about the boxes, and that's a little scary, you know?

It is, a little. Your mom and I were thinking we might all head up to Duluth tomorrow to visit your grandparents.

'Well, that sucks,' Clark said quietly, just in case Kyle's dad was still at the top of the basement steps, trying to think of something else to say. Most of the time he worked about forty hours a day, which made him the ideal dad in Clark's opinion, if you had to have one at all. But occasionally, when he took a day off because the world was ending or he had a killer hangover, he took a shot at father-son bonding with Kyle, and those days were just plain creepy. He'd come down to the basement and ask them how they were doing, and they'd say they were doing fine, and he'd say, 'No shit,' as if that kind of talk would put him in the cool-dad category or something.

'You and Mom want to watch this with us, Dad?' Kyle called up the stairs. Kyle was kind of brilliant at parental management. He knew damn well if he invited his parents down, they'd assume they were actually watching that stupid Civil War thing and didn't need any supervision; plus, it allowed them to tell themselves they'd be good parents if they trusted the boys and just stayed upstairs, watching the Great Mystery Boxes show while they had a few cocktails.

As predicted, Kyle's dad said thanks very much but they'd stay upstairs so they didn't interrupt the boys while they were watching a homework assignment, which meant it was perfectly safe to light up some green.

Kyle turned on the HEPA air machine, opened the windows, and pointed at the big screen. 'Oh, that is so sweet. Look at the traffic cams.'

Clark focused on the screen for a while, grinning at the

endless lines of cars frozen on all the freeways out of town. It wasn't like earlier this afternoon, with all the cars dodging and speeding and one spectacular rollover on 94 into Wisconsin, but all the same, he felt his gut tighten and ripple like that super fool who hip-hopped to super-abs. 'It's kind of weird, watching this, isn't it?'

'Weird, how?'

'Well, they're idiots. Assholes. Freaked out over nothing. They've blown all the boxes, for Chrissake. They know they're empty, and look at those fools, still running.'

'They don't know if they found them all.'

'I want to tell somebody,' Clark said.

'Who?'

'Carrie Wynheimer, for one.'

'She's a loser. Wears a push-up bra.'

'So what? It's pushing up something.'

Kyle snatched the stick away and pulled a load into his lungs, thinking he might have made a big mistake hooking up with Clark.

They were both mellowed out by the time the sun started sinking and the basement started to get murky. Bad thing about basements and their little window slices at ground level, especially when your parents planted yew bushes to hide the top four courses of cement blocks, as if no one knew they were there.

They'd watched a lot of the news coverage of the panic in the city. At first it had been fun to see the traffic jams and wide-eyed residents packing up their minivans with kids and pets. After a while it got old. And then the doorbell rang.

The door to the basement opened onto the hall just beyond the foyer, so Magozzi was front row center to read the body language of the kids when they came upstairs.

Gino had wanted these kids to be the perps, partly so they could sew this thing up fast, and partly because he hated all teenage males. That kind of prejudice was the price of doing business when you were the father of a drop-dead sixteen-year-old daughter. Magozzi hadn't known what to wish for or what tack to take until he heard the footsteps plodding up from the basement. The way he figured it, you didn't stop running up any flight of stairs until you were at least twenty, unless you were nervous about what was at the top.

Kyle came first. His house, his lead on the stairs. He was a good-looking kid, blond and blue, with a pleasant, intelligent face.

'Hey, Dad. What's up?' his eyes immediately shifted to the three strangers standing in the foyer, and his brows tipped in polite curiosity. No tell there. Total innocence. Christ, the kid was good.

Clark came and stood a step behind his friend, un-intentionally showing Magozzi the pecking order. Funny how people positioned themselves in a physical display of hierarchy without ever being taught such a thing. Then again, wolves did it. Why not kids?

Mr. Zellickson, proud papa, put his arm around his son. 'This is my son, Kyle, and this is his friend, Clark. Boys, these two gentlemen are Minneapolis police officers, and this is Agent Smith of the FBI. They'd like to ask you some questions about anything you might have seen at the Metrodome today.'

'Sure thing,' Kyle said pleasantly. 'Although I can't think of anything unusual. Just the usual slew of 'bladers and skaters we see there most of the time.'

Magozzi smiled and nodded. 'How about at the Crystal Court?'

Clark's face went stiff, Kyle's smile faded, and Mr. Zellickson looked puzzled. 'Uh . . . I thought you said you saw them on surveillance film at the Dome.'

'That's right. And at Crystal Court, and the Mall of America, and I don't know how many other sites where we found boxes. We're still going over the film.'

'Oh, Jesus.' Clark was swallowing hard, over and over again, and beads of sweat popped on his forehead.

Magozzi and Gino both took a step backward as the boy suddenly folded in half and threw up on the Zellicksons' oriental foyer rug. 'It was just a joke,' he wailed, and then threw up again.

'Shut up, for Christ's sake,' Kyle screamed, but as it turned out, Gino barely had time to read them both their rights before Clark started talking.

Magozzi looked down at the mess on the rug and felt bad, then turned up the edge with his toe and immediately felt better. Damn thing was a fake, just like the house and the pretense of a perfect family and the golden boy who was starting to look really tarnished.

Then he saw Mr. Zellickson's world falling apart on his face, and felt really bad all over again.

Officer Haig answered the call for a squad with a cage,

which made Gino and Magozzi very happy. The man was in the last quiet year of twenty as a workhorse on the streets, and there was no retirement present that could hold a candle to bringing in some most-wanteds while a hundred cameras were rolling. Magozzi went out to talk to him before Gino and John brought out the little monsters.

'You hit the jackpot, Haig.'

'Yeah? What have you got?'

'Box boys.'

Haig's forehead wrinkled. 'You mean the kids who pack up your stuff at the supermarket?' He studied Magozzi's grin for a second, then his graying eyebrows went up to say hello to his hairline. 'No fooling?'

'No fooling. You saw the mess of cameras and reporters at the house, right?'

'You mean the ones who've been blocking the streets and sidewalks and the entrances all day? Nah. Didn't notice them.'

'It's worse now than when you went out. All the networks, a ton of cable stations, and a few foreigns have the place surrounded with satellite vans. Looks like the Martians have landed.'

'Don't worry about it. I'll just zip down into the garage like always . . .'

'No.'

'No?'

'I want you to off-load these boys at the front entrance. Maybe go around the block a couple times before pulling in so the media catches sight of you. We'll be right behind you to help walk them up the steps, but you take the lead with one of them and go slow, got it?'

'Wow. I'm going to be on TV.'

'Comb your hair, Haig. The whole world's going to get a look at it by tomorrow morning.'

'Cool.'

Chapter Thirty-six

The media ranks had swelled in the past few hours, vans filling the streets, photogs and reporters milling on the sidewalks and front steps of City Hall. They were all hooked into Dispatch, Magozzi knew, and all had heard that the possible perpetrators of the box fiasco were being brought in. That had been the plan.

Gino looked up at the windows and saw faces at almost every one, watching what was going down. 'This is about as big as it gets, Leo,' he said. We're going to be all over the news.'

'Let's hope it works.'

'It's not going to work. We'll haul these kids off to Federal prison in front of the cameras and a million idiots out there will still think they could do what they did and not get caught. We'll be chasing this tail for years to come. What a rush, closing down a city and getting the attention of the world. Look at this. In less than a week we've got murders on film and a fake terrorist attack, and maybe neither one of those things would have happened without the Internet. Goddamn Web is escalating everything, just like Chelsea said. Somebody's gotta get a handle on this, 'cause there's no going back.'

Officer Haig led Clark up the stairs to City Hall, pausing every few steps, supposedly to look for the men behind him, but actually giving prime shots to all the cameras flashing behind him.

Gino and Magozzi, flanking Kyle on their way up the steps, were forced to stop whenever Officer Haig stopped, and the media cashed in on film of the terrified boys that the satellites sent around the county and the world.

'Jeez, Leo,' Gino said when the hard lights hit his face, 'what happened to Haig's hair?'

Magozzi was trying to look professional and a little mean. A really good-looking woman with BBC all over her microphone was in his face, asking if these were the two perpetrators who had engineered and planted the boxes that had had the world holding its breath all day. 'No comment,' he said, pushing past her gently while dozens of other voices yelled out questions. He leaned toward Gino and whispered, 'I told him to comb his hair, and believe it or not, he pulled a comb out of his back pocket. Looked like Fonzie next to the jukebox, sweeping back the strands, getting ready for the girls.'

'He's pushing sixty, Leo. He's no Fonzie.'

John was trailing behind a few steps. Even in this media age, the Bureau still clutched at the threads of dignity from times past, avoiding the limelight. Hungry reporters and camera operators looked at him curiously, wondering if he was a person of importance, then turned away as if he were an unknown escort on the red carpet, not worth the film.

City Hall was blessedly quiet when they finally managed to get their prisoners inside, but behind closed doors, you could hear the muffled sounds of celebration. A lot of off-duty cops had stuck around after their shifts to revel in the happy ending to a nightmare day, clap each others' backs like the warriors they were, and get the latest gossip.

'We're going to have to give the Chief a couple minutes, John,' Magozzi said. 'Will you and Haig take the prisoners down to a holding cell?'

'My pleasure.'

McLaren ran into them in the hallway on the way to the Chief's office. 'Swe-eet,' he greeted them. 'Well done, guys.'

Gino always tried hard to play the curmudgeon, but nobody could ever accuse him of being unfair or ungracious. He reliably gave credit where credit was due, and today was no exception. 'Are you kidding me, McLaren? We were just your delivery boys. You had the sharp eye, Monkeewrench had the brains, and we had the courage to go bust a couple Clearasil geniuses who puked the minute they saw a cop. Kind of like *The Wizard of Oz*.'

'Man, I wish I'd been there. Did they really puke?'

Gino smiled. 'Yes, they did puke, and oh, it was pretty, my friend. A sight to behold. Normally, you don't want to see recycled candy bars and nachos, but this was very satisfying.'

McLaren gave them both high fives. 'Cool. Well, I'm outta here. Just wanted to stick around long enough to give you props.'

'Likewise,' Magozzi said. 'You want to catch a beer with us later?'

His pale face turned slightly pink, and then he grinned. 'Sorry, guys, but I've got a real cutie lined up for dinner.'

Gino nodded his approval. 'No shit? Way to go, dude.'

Johnny's grin got bigger. 'JDate rocks.'

'I hope like hell you told her you were a Belfast Catholic before you agreed to meet her.'

'I know her story, she knows mine. Everything's kosher.'

'Hey, at least you're working your way into the lingo. Best of luck, friend,' Gino said, meaning it.

'Thanks. And hey, speaking of cuties . . . there's a profiler from the FBI somewhere around here waiting for you. That's some hot property.'

'Chelsea Thomas,' Magozzi informed him.

McLaren's red brows lifted. 'Ah, so you know her. Lucky you. She's way outta my league.'

Gino shrugged. 'Oh, I don't know, McLaren. She might be the kind of woman who picks the ugliest Christmas tree on the lot or adopts the blind, one-legged puppy at the pound.'

'Rolseth, you are such an asshole. Anyhow, have a good night, guys, and wish me luck.'

Chelsea Thomas was waiting for them outside the Chief's office, and she did look hot . . . and different. She was dressed in a suit, but it wasn't a Fed suit. Magozzi was no fashionisto, but he knew really great, expensive clothes when he saw them – Annie Belinsky had schooled him in that.

'Detectives. Excellent work today.'

Her smile was infectious, and Magozzi and Gino both succumbed. 'Yep. Everybody did their part, and it turned out great.'

'Yes, it did. You can't imagine how important this is as a deterrent. What kind of impression did you get from talking to them?'

Magozzi thought about that for a minute. 'Actually, they weren't the monsters I was expecting.'

'New kind of monster,' Gino said. 'Stupid little bastards with too much alone time and no sense of consequence who think they can get away with anything.'

Chelsea nodded. 'Their brains aren't fully developed at that age. Actually, they're boys, so their brains never fully develop.' Her smile flashed again.

Magozzi's brows lifted. 'Wow. You're in a great mood.'

'Aren't you?'

'Absolutely. Want to grab a beer with us later?'

'I'd love to, but I have to get to the airport. The Director wants me on the morning talk-show circuit tomorrow to get as much publicity on this as possible. Save the interview tapes for me, will you? And congratulations again.'

Gino looked over at Magozzi. 'We're zero for two on the happy-hour buddies. I think we're stuck with each other.'

'I think we're going to be stuck here all night, anyway.'

Chapter Thirty-seven

Grace was standing at the marble counter in Harley's kitchen, picking her way through a chicken pot pie – she was eating purely for sustenance, not pleasure, so it seemed appropriate that she do it standing up. Huttinger's hard drives had arrived, and they were all staring down a long night's work.

She looked up when John Smith walked in a few minutes later. He was clearly exhausted, which was understandable, and yet there was something almost peaceful in his face, as if gravity had granted him a temporary kindness.

'You've had quite a night,' she said, laying down her fork. 'We caught the news. Congratulations.'

'None deserved. The credit belongs to all of you and your extraordinary software, and to Detectives Magozzi and Rolseth, of course. They're quite an impressive pair.'

'Yes, they are. But I'll bet they didn't feed you,' she raised her plate in an invitation. 'There's more in the oven if you're hungry.'

'What about the others?'

'They ate earlier.' She started to move toward the oven but he stopped her with a gentle hand on her shoulder. 'Don't interrupt your meal. I'll get it, and thank you very much. It smells delicious. When on earth did you find time to make this today?'

'I make them in advance, and keep them in Harley's freezer for nights like this.'

He asked for permission to sit after he'd filled his plate, and Grace pulled out stools for both of them. They sat side by side, looking straight ahead, eating in a silence that was oddly comfortable for two people who didn't really know each other at all.

'I have a boat,' John said abruptly, ruining everything.

Grace chased a piece of carrot around her plate, letting the statement hang there. Damnit. And it had all been going so well. She should have known he'd turn out to be just like everyone else. It was one of the reasons she avoided people. 'Hello' always turned into some inane conversation that would interest her not at all. What did she care if he had a boat? Now he'd tell her how long the boat was, what he'd named it, where he parked it, or docked it, or whatever it was you did with boats, as if all this information would be important for her to know.

'This is important,' he said, which was almost as weird as saying 'I have a boat.'

She looked up from her plate, annoyed with herself for being a little curious. 'I have no interest in boats,' she told him. Best to nip conversations like this in the bud.

'Neither do I. But I like where they take me.'

'Right. On the water.'

He almost smiled, but he didn't look at her. 'Not where they take me physically, where they take me in my head. I called my boss tonight and resigned. When I get back to D.C., I'm going to get on the boat and just sail away.'

Grace couldn't help herself. She actually turned her head and looked at him, because, damnit, that was interesting. And stupid. 'That wasn't very smart, John.

You're going to lose part of your pension. Why would you do that?'

'Because you looked at me the other day, saw your future, and didn't like it. I don't like it much, either. So I'm going to change it. You want to come along?'

She snatched up the plates and walked to the sink. 'Don't be ridiculous.'

'Okay. Do you want me to cover the leftovers with plastic or tinfoil?'

'Tinfoil.'

He went right to the correct drawer and pulled out the tinfoil. Grace watched from the corner of her eye. Harley had about fifty drawers in his kitchen. How the hell did he know where it was? Did he sneak down here when they were working and inventory everything? She spun away from the sink and folded her arms over her chest. 'Why did you ask me that?'

John shrugged. 'Because I didn't know how much butter you put in the crust. A lot, and plastic wrap would make it soggy—'

'Not that, the boat thing.'

'Oh. Because you're a great cook and you don't talk much.'

Upstairs in the office, Harley, Roadrunner, and Annie were deep into Huttinger's hard drives, and were about to break when Harley roared from his station, '*NO WAY!*'

'Christ, Harley, give us a warning when you're going to go ballistic in a quiet room,' Roadrunner complained. 'What's up?'

Harley spun his monitor around for his gathering audience. 'I just found a hit list.'

'What?'

He tapped his finger on the screen. 'Look. Every single name. All seven of the Web murder victims. This is completely off the chain.'

They all looked over Harley's shoulder and read:

```
Richard Groth, Duluth, Minnesota.
Elmore Sweet, Cleveland, Ohio.
Cy Robertson, Chicago, Illinois.
Evan Eichinger, Seattle, Washington.
Sean Pasternak, Los Angeles, California.
Gregory Quandt, Austin, Texas.
Alan Sommers, Minneapolis, Minnesota.
```

'Where on God's green *earth* did you find this, Harley?' Annie asked.

'Better you should ask how, because I was friggin' brilliant. Huttinger visited this creepy Ilovetokill.com website a lot, so I signed into the site – and this is the brilliant part – typed in a few of the vic names. This is the thread that popped up. AND . . . the date on the thread is December of last year, over a month and a half before the first murder.'

'Shift back in the thread, Harley,' Annie told him. 'What comes before the list?'

'Okay, I'm going to give you the CliffsNotes, because the thread's about twenty miles long. Basically it's a bunch of freaks bragging about how many people they've killed, how they killed them, what they did to them before and after they killed them . . . it just goes on and on. But then one of the posters who calls himself "Killer" – real creative, huh? – says, "I've killed twenty so far this year, and I'm shooting for twenty more. I'll kill anybody anywhere just for fun."'

Annie made a face. 'Sounds like some sick psycho blowing a lot of hot air.'

Harley shrugged. 'Maybe, but then a new guy popped up, and get this: his handle on the website is Hole In One.'

Roadrunner's mouth dropped open. 'Jesus. That was in the post of the first murder, the one up north.'

'Bingo. Now look at the single line he posted before typing in all the names and locations.' He scrolled up to the top of the hit list, one line below Killer's post about killing anybody anywhere.

```
Hole In One: Bullshit, Killer. Prove it.
Start at the top.
```

Roadrunner was shaking his head. 'I take it these guys are untraceable.'

'Good guess, little buddy. We are never, ever going to be able to find these people.'

'Not this way,' Roadrunner said.

Annie looked at him. 'You know another way?'

Roadrunner shrugged modestly. 'I had a thought.'

Chapter Thirty-eight

Magozzi, Gino, and McLaren were back in front of the Homicide TV the next morning, watching none other than their very own Dr. Chelsea Thomas chewing up the scenery on one of the big morning news shows. Aside from her impressive intellect, which came through clearly and unpretentiously over the airwaves as she elucidated the dangers of suggestible, unsupervised youth, the viral nature of the Web, and other stirring and salient topics, she definitely had the 'it' factor. And probably along with the rest of America, the hosts were eating her up like a bonbon. Magozzi figured she'd have her own talk show by noon.

McLaren was mesmerized, but Gino was fidgeting and fussing like he always did when ruminating over some dire injustice. Magozzi steeled himself for the rampage he knew was coming.

'Holy shit,' McLaren chuckled in amazement. 'Did you guys just hear that? She's, like, descended from Hollywood royalty. No wonder she's so good on camera.'

Gino narrowed his eyes. 'Yeah, I heard it. And what a crime that is. She's smarter than hell, she's making great points, and those hacks just have to march out the celebrity-frigging-angle. They're goddamned living examples of what she's warning them about. And, to her credit, she looks pissed off about it.'

She *did* look pissed off. 'That's actually a good point, Gino,' Magozzi complimented him.

'Thank you, Leo. And you know what else is really stupid about this? Everything we thought we were going to accomplish by sewing this thing up nice and fast and publicizing the hell out of it is circling the drain right now. Nobody's talking about anything else on the whole planet and those two little fuckers got the rock star moment they were looking for. They probably already have agents negotiating interview deals for them.'

'They're going to prison, Gino,' Magozzi reminded him. 'Twenty-four hours ago they were dreaming about freshman keg parties at the U of M this fall, and now they're staring down hard time at a Federal pen. I don't think that's the rock star moment they were looking for.'

'Oh yeah? Just you wait – they'll get all fluffed and buffed for the courtroom and their scumbag lawyers will throw down the bright-young-men, second-chance card, and some bleeding-heart jury's gonna go easy because it'll be stacked with parents who can envision their own feral offspring doing something just as stupid. It's a total washout as far as I'm concerned, it's gonna happen again somewhere else, and probably sometime soon, and meanwhile, nobody remembers that there are films of actual *murders* getting posted on the Web, and a few pesky maniacs out there playing games with human lives so they can brag to their little cyber-freak buddies about it online.' He took a deep breath. 'It's complete and utter bullshit, and I'm going back to my desk, because there are seven unsolveds that are riding shotgun right now, when they should be driving.'

McLaren stopped drooling over Chelsea Thomas for two seconds and regarded Gino with a candid eye. 'You're really negative this morning, Rolseth.'

'Yeah. I am.' The great thing about Gino was that once he got something off his chest, it was business as usual. 'By the way, how did your date go last night?'

McLaren gave them a vague shrug, but didn't offer any more information, which both Magozzi and Gino took as a good sign. With a guy like McLaren, who ran off at the mouth about how every woman he'd never met wanted to be his love slave, silence was telling. Maybe the little leprechaun might have something going after all.

John Smith was gazing out the Monkeewrench office window at the same tree that had recently inspired genocidal frog thoughts in him. As ambivalent as he'd always been towards any sort of flora, he realized he'd grown genuinely fond of this particular tree in the past few days, and he was going to be sorry to leave it.

'What the hell, Smith?' Harley bellowed from the other side of the room, where he and the rest of Monkeewrench were still working. 'You hung up with Washington five minutes ago and you're still staring out the window. Did your boss in D.C. put you in a fugue state of boredom, or is there a naked centerfold out there I should know about?'

Smith smiled a little, then put on his game face before he turned around. 'I've been called back to Washington. My flight is tomorrow afternoon.' Suddenly, he had four solemn pairs of eyes on him, and he had no idea how to respond to that.

'Seriously?' Roadrunner finally asked.

'Yes.'

The room stayed silent for a few moments, until Harley put his jackboots up on the ledge of his desk and pushed away with a big grin. 'Well, then, my friend, tonight is the night for those belly dancers and cigars I promised you. We're gonna send you out in style.'

Smith nodded graciously. 'I appreciate your generosity, but I do have things to attend to . . .'

'Yeah, yeah, yeah. You have to get back to your shit-bag motel and prepare for a debriefing, whatever. Do it hung-over on the plane tomorrow, dude. Tonight, you're ours.'

Smith's mind quickly flashed through his time spent here with these strange and brilliant people, and every slippery-slope step he'd taken along the way; then he thought again about the tree and the frogs and the bad people he was fighting, hand in hand with good people who seemed to have their own definition of justice, and their own way of administering it.

'I would be honored,' he finally said. 'And if you don't mind, I'd like to invite Detectives Rolseth and Magozzi as well.'

Grace smiled at him. 'I'll call them.'

When Magozzi saw Grace's name on his cell, he lunged for it and knocked it off the desk.

Gino glanced over at his partner scrambling after it on his hands and knees and nudged McLaren. 'Grace,' he said, and McLaren nodded.

'That's really sad.'

'Kind of.'

Magozzi finally caught his sliding cell and flipped them the bird as he answered. 'MPD Homicide, Magozzi.'

'Very dignified, Magozzi.'

'I am a very dignified man,' he said from the floor, and Gino burst out laughing.

'Two things, Magozzi. First, John's been called back to D.C. tomorrow so we're taking him out for a farewell dinner. He specifically asked for you and Gino to come along.'

God, he loved listening to her voice. He felt a slobbering moon face coming on and stiffened his jaw so he'd look macho. 'I guess we could do that. What restaurant?'

'That Greek place on Kellogg.'

'I don't think I like Greek food. That's the stuff with the funny olives that taste bad, right?'

'It's Greek/Mediterranean/American. They've got squab. You like squab.'

'I *love* squab. Remind me again, is that a fish or a mammal?'

Grace chuckled. 'It's a bird.'

'Oh, right. What was the second thing?'

'I'm faxing you a thread from a creepy website Huttinger visited all the time. We think it might be how this whole series of Web murders started. Somebody put up a virtual hit list – every victim's name and location, posted before any of the murders happened.'

'Holy cow. Can you trace whoever put it up?'

'No, not a prayer.' She was quiet for a moment. 'But . . . we're working on something. See you at nine.'

Chapter Thirty-nine

Judge Jim hadn't driven much since his last revocation due to an unfortunate alcohol-related traffic incident a few years back, but damn if his big SUV didn't fire right up – a testament to the importance of a superior battery. But now that he was back behind the wheel again, he remembered how much he loved cruising the freeway with all the windows wide open, the sublime, aftermarket sound system cranked up to ear-bleed level. It brought him right back to his high school days, when he'd worked summers as a bag boy at the SmartMart in Bemidji – the day he'd quit that job was the day he'd finally earned enough money to upgrade the stereo in his green, Bondo-bucket, AMC Rebel.

This morning, he was in a much pricier vehicle, with a much pricier stereo, but the feeling was the same as when was sixteen. He'd selected the overture to *Tannhäuser* as the theme music of the day – a piece he felt was the perfect accompaniment to his ultimate and impending victory over a grave injustice that desperately needed rectifying.

His former yard looked fairly well kept, which was a surprise; in fact, there were even some new plantings in the gardens. Perhaps Number Four had actually sacrificed a modest portion of her generous monthly subsidy to invest in a little home improvement. Why she would do such a sensible thing was beyond him, but he had a sneaking suspicion that it had something to do with the age and physique of the gardener who'd been responsible, because she would die before she lifted a shovel or touched dirt of any kind.

There was also a new sprinkler system – he'd learned that the hard way, tripping over one of the heads during his relocation project.

The chair was heavy, but in this glorious moment of final closure, he felt like he could lift the world. Once the Corbusier was in place, near the bay windows of the sitting room, he looked to the sky with a big smile, then looked to his fly with an even bigger smile, and proceeded to engage a sprinkler system of his own.

'Judge, you're killing us.'

'That wasn't my intention. Do I know you?'

The young officer sighed. 'Probably not, but I sure know you. You make way too much work for us.'

'I've heard something along those lines from a couple detectives with whom I'm rather well acquainted.'

'Right. Look, I can haul you in for indecent exposure, public urination, vandalism, trespassing, illegally disposing of property, driving after revocation . . .'

'And that's all?'

The officer was clearly frustrated, but he kept his wits, which Wild Jim appreciated.

'Listen, Officer. I understand your aggravation, and I want you and all of the MPD to know that this was my last act of childish rebellion. And that is a solemn promise. Justice has been served, finally, at least in my world. So, if you can find a way in your heart to grant me a reprieve, you won't be doing forty hours of paperwork.'

The cop shook his head. 'You just had to urinate on your ex's lawn?'

The judge smiled. 'Technically, I pissed on a piece of my property I was magnanimously gifting to her. And sometimes, spontaneous urination just can't be helped. You're too young to be suffering from prostate maladies, but I have occasional incontinence issues.'

The officer kept his face stony, but there was a twinkle in his eye. 'I have an ex-wife, too.'

'Ah. So perhaps you understand my bladder-control problems after all.'

After his near scrape with the law, and an hour or so spent navigating a significant amount of bureaucracy and the wrath of Number Four, Judge Jim retreated to his condo. He changed into his best black suit, which had been languishing in a plastic dry-cleaning bag in his closet for God knows how long, poured himself a brand-new bourbon he'd selected from the connoisseur's stock at Cherry Hill Fine Wine and Spirits, and, at last, began tidying things up once and for all.

He spent the remaining portion of the day organizing some very interesting documents he'd recently compiled, then carefully arranged them in an accordion file, which he stuffed into a duffel bag; he cleaned and oiled his Winchester rifle, which also fit nicely inside the duffel bag; and then he made dinner reservations at his favorite seafood restaurant. Last on his punch list were two phone calls, one of which would have to wait until the last possible moment.

There was nothing left to do before dinner, so he refilled

his glass, lit his best cigar, and wandered through his condo, thinking of the time he'd spent here. It hadn't been a bad place. In fact, it had been rather convenient, and the Mississippi River view was unparalleled. And without the ominous presence of the Corbusier continually monopolizing the space and his mind, the living room looked so much better; elegant, even. Maybe there was something to that whole feng shui nonsense. Damnit, he should have gotten rid of the thing a long time ago.

The final stop of his own home tour was at the photo shrine of his son – the only part of the condo he would truly miss. He reverently picked up his favorite picture, the one where he and Jessie were mugging for the camera on the eighteenth green of Woodland Hills Country Club. The little shit had actually whacked a hole in one that day. It was like all the luck he'd ever have was funneled into that very last game of golf, into that very last, eighteenth, cup. God, life was strange.

He ran his fingers over the glass, then at the last minute, decided to put the photograph in the duffel bag along with the gun and the files.

Chapter Forty

It wasn't an Irish pub, but Magozzi was happy enough to be within spitting distance of Grace McBride for a change, although she seemed a little distracted. Magozzi took it personally, of course, but there was the promise of great food, the certainty of great wine, since Harley had brought a few bottles from his famous cellar, and scantily clad women already on the stage and weaving through the tables of the restaurant and bar, so the brush-off was mitigated. Slightly.

They were all jammed together in an entry with four thousand of their closest friends, most of whom would certainly get a table before they did, since they had arrived first. Magozzi cozied up to Roadrunner, who was painfully shy at confronting strangers one-on-one, and yet totally comfortable in crowds where he wasn't likely to be singled out. 'I don't get it, Roadrunner. Mr. Foodie at a restaurant that doesn't take reservations? What happened to the chef's-table treatment? Where are the minions kneeling at our feet with caviar and foie gras?'

Roadrunner was resplendent and clearly tickled to be out of jeans and back to normal in navy-blue Lycra. 'Actually, we've never been here before. The food could suck, but Harley promised John belly dancers.'

Magozzi looked at him. 'John? Would that be Special Agent John Smith of the FBI? Mr. Straight and Narrow?'

Roadrunner chuckled. 'He's not so bad. And he's probably never seen a belly dancer up close and personal. It was more of a threat than a promise.'

'Terrific. Happy to hear you're all bonding with your old enemies. But the thing is, there isn't a woman in the world, I don't care what she can do with her belly, that's going to risk coming close to Smith with Grace hanging on to his arm like that.'

Roadrunner glanced over at the twosome, heads tipped together as they tried to talk over the din. 'They cooked together and have been pretty chummy ever since. I think Grace likes him, and you know her, she doesn't like anybody. Kind of a happy moment to see her moving beyond the tight circle, isn't it? Like she's letting go of something.'

Magozzi glowered. 'It's just so goddamn precious it makes me want to puke. I mean, he's good at his job, and he kind of grows on you, but the guy's a million years old.'

Roadrunner gave him an alarmed look. 'Jeez, Magozzi, I didn't mean she liked him like *that*. More of a father–daughter kind of thing.'

'Uh-huh. Whatever. All I care about is when we're going to get to eat. I'm starving.'

'The hostess said half an hour after Harley tucked a wad of bills in her halter top. We're supposed to wait in the bar.'

'So where the hell is the bar? Maybe they've got pretzels.'

Roadrunner pointed the way, but stayed in the entry, watching the dancers.

They didn't have pretzels in the little room with its worm-wood bar and blue mystery bottles reflecting in a mirror, but they were developing a very healthy respect for Gino, who had no compunction whatsoever about flashing his badge and demanding any kind of food that wouldn't eat him first. Magozzi came up next to his partner and clapped his hand on his shoulder.

'Thank God. Reinforcements,' Gino said. 'What kind of place is this, Leo? They got dancers with little jiggly bellies they sure as hell didn't get here, 'cause there's no food and I'm about to eat my hand. Now, I don't mind showing my face at a farewell dinner for Smith, but for Chrissake I'm not sleeping with the guy, so there'd better be something to eat.'

'Tell me about it. Six o'clock, latest Mom ever had dinner on the table, and Pop nearly had apoplexy. I'm telling you, the world is going to hell when dinnertime jumps past when the kids go to bed.'

Gino nodded a chin starting to bristle this many hours past the last shave. 'Let us become inebriated as quickly as possible, and toast the days when you ate supper and still had time for baseball in the corner lot before dark. Do you realize it's past nine?'

'I do.'

The bartender brought out a plate of tiny little meatballs on a stick propped on a bowl of white stuff with green flecks and set it in front of Gino with an arrogant flourish. 'Sir,' he said snippily.

Gino scowled down at the meager offering and opened his sportcoat to show his gun. 'Listen, you little puke. I am

MPD Homicide and today I have saved the world. These are not meatballs. They're dots on a toothpick. Now get your ass back to the kitchen and try harder.'

The barkeep had a lot of white around his dark eyes when he opened them that wide and backed away.

Surprisingly, it was relatively quiet in the little room off the entry. Most of the patrons collected their drinks and carried them out to the main room so they could watch the belly dancers.

'Detectives.'

Magozzi jumped at the voice behind him and the hand on his shoulder, and spun to see Special Agent John Smith, who had been standing too goddamn close to Grace.

'I want you to know it has been a privilege and an honor to watch real law enforcement at work, and I thank you both for the opportunity to witness it. And Detective Magozzi, you are the most fortunate of men. You have the affection of a most extraordinary woman, which is in itself the accomplishment of a lifetime.'

Magozzi felt like a cartoon character with his mouth hanging open like that, and all he could do was nod like one of those stupid plastic birds on the glassy edge of a killer tropical drink. Happily, the bartender returned at that moment with a meat platter of giant meatballs and a gravy boat of the white stuff with green flecks. Gino dug in without breathing.

'Okay, guys, I don't know what the hell this is, but it ain't bad. Barkeep, you're the man. Give us three big ones of whatever alcohol goes with this stuff.'

The bartender, probably remembering his glimpse of Gino's weapon, almost bowed. 'It's lamb kabobs, sir, with cucumber sauce, most frequently accompanied with ouzo.'

'Well, it's friggin' excellent, is what it is. Bring us some of that oo-stuff to go with it.'

Magozzi had his hand around a narrow glass of the oo-stuff when his cell vibrated against his hip. He flipped it open, frowned at the readout, and waited for the caller to identify himself.

When you were a cop and got a call from an unfamiliar number on your personal cell, you didn't say anything until you knew who was on the other end. A county deputy in Alexandria had made that mistake five years ago while he was running regular rounds of the local bars, checking for underage drinkers. He answered his cell with his name, and a drunken ex-con with a grudge, a snoutful, and a long memory for the name of the cop who had put him in Stillwater promptly shot him in the back. The drunken shooter got twenty years and the deputy got a bagpipe funeral.

'Good evening, Detective Magozzi. This is Judge James Bukowski.'

That made Magozzi unhappy. The man was getting intrusive, taking advantage. 'How'd you get this number, Judge?'

He heard the judge sigh just before a belly dancer literally bellied up to the bar next to John and jingled her bells and clicked her little metal clackers at him. Magozzi backed away a few paces.

'How I got your private number is irrelevant, Detective.

Please pretend for a moment that I might be a man with something important to say, and listen very carefully. We don't have much time.'

'I'm listening.'

'Would you mind giving me your approximate location?'

'St. Paul. Downtown.'

'Thank you. Unhappily, it is a bit farther away than I'd anticipated, so I will have to be brief.'

'Music to my ears, Judge.'

'I am quite certain it is. Are you familiar with the Woodland Hills Country Club Golf Course?'

'Just off Minnehaha, right?'

'That is correct. The man who killed Alan Sommers – the River Bride, as the media refers to him – will be meeting me on the eighteenth green in a very short time.'

Magozzi rolled his eyes and put his forefinger on the cell cover to flip it closed. 'Excellent. Have him give me a call in the morning, will you?'

'Alan Sommers died at 11:17 according to the knock-off Rolex he was wearing. The watch face was broken in the struggle.'

Magozzi's hand tightened on the phone and he felt the slip of sweat under his fingers. No one knew that. Just him, Gino, and Anant. They'd bagged the watch and held it back. 'Jesus,' he murmured.

'Splendid. I have your attention. Now, as I was saying, the killer is meeting me very soon on the eighteenth green. His intent, I am sure, is to kill me, since I threatened to reveal his identity. My intention is that you and Detective Rolseth intercept and arrest him. A little present for both of you, for being the good cops you are, and also for being respectful to a drunken old man. You will find a key to my condo in my pants pocket. Give my computer to your friends at Monkeewrench. It will tell you everything you need to know. Is that clear?'

Magozzi was already heading for Gino and Smith, jerking his thumb toward the exit while he kept talking. Whatever was in his face made both men follow him instantly without question. 'What you've *said* is clear, Judge. What you *mean* is a little murky.'

'That will change, Detective Magozzi.'

'You sound almost sober.' He heard a dark chuckle at the other end of the line.

'I always sound sober, and never am. I don't know the identities of all the killers, Detective Magozzi, but I suspect this man's computer will give you an excellent start in solving all the Web murders you've been working on. That Huttinger . . . *person* . . .' his voice was rich with contempt; 'was not part of this . . .'

'Whoa, whoa, wait a minute. Part of *what*? What the hell are you talking about?'

'Patience, Detective. We're running out of time, but it is important to me that you know those waitresses should never have been attacked. I hope you can believe that. Now. Look at your watch. You have exactly twenty-eight minutes to make it to Woodland Hills. Twenty-nine, and I'll be dead. Thirty, and your killer will be gone. Please leave now.'

When the line went dead, they were already halfway to the front door, badges held high to carve a path through the jam of people. 'Gino, mark the time. We've got twenty-seven and a half minutes!'

Wild Jim flipped his cell closed and laid it on the passenger seat next to him before he got out of the car. He breathed in pond smell from the eighteenth-hole water hazard, and saw moonlight reflecting on the flag stuck in the cup.

He started walking from the parking lot next to the club-house, out to the green, and felt the hairs on the back of his neck stand up. Hole in one, he thought, remembering Jessie's last shot from the tee, miraculously skittering into that cup and breaking all the club records, because no one had ever done that before. It was a par-three hole, singled in the father–son tournament for the very first time when Wild Jim and his amazing son, Jessie, had taken home the silver trophy. Had they been talking then? He couldn't remember. What he did remember was Jessie's face when the crowd at the green let out a roar, telling the twenty-five-year-old kid he was something special.

He'd never thought of the course being frightening; then again, he'd never been here since that last grand and glorious day of sunlight and applause.

At night, everything changed. Trees laid down shadows on the grass in front of the moon, and men who killed for fun hid behind their trunks, waiting.

John sat in the back of the Cadillac, listening to Magozzi's and Gino's scattered descriptions of who Wild Jim was while he stared fearfully out the side window, watching the freeway mile markers flash by at speeds that were really quite frightening. High-speed chases were normally the purview of local cops, rarely Federal agents, and it took a full ten minutes before John stopped being terrified and started getting one of those adrenaline highs he'd heard about.

'So this man is a drunken judge kicked off the bench who happened to be near the river the night your bride was drowned, and probably saw the body.'

'That's about it,' Gino said pleasantly. He liked high-speed chases, even when they weren't chasing anybody, and especially in the Caddie.

'And you believe he saw the killer, why?'

Magozzi looked manic at the wheel with the dash lights hollowing out his face and showing the tension there. 'Don't know. It's kind of hard to explain.'

'Do we have any kind of a plan?'

Gino turned around to look at him. 'Hell, no. Usually we make up our plans after everything's gone down, just to fill in the lines on the report, you know?'

Magozzi swerved around a cone with a blinking light on top and nearly put them in the median. 'Goddamn road construction,' he muttered, utterly unfazed.

John tightened his seat belt and cleared his throat. 'So basically we're going to some golf course in the middle of the night to intercept some crazed killer who's going to kill your alcoholic ex-judge.'

Gino punched the recline button and smiled. 'Well, what do you know. We have a plan after all. Check your load, Smith. You're going to have to hide behind a tree and maybe shoot somebody.'

'I've never actually shot at a real person.'

'Yeah, well, there's a first time for everything.'

Wild Jim Bukowski, fierce believer in law and justice, padded across the short-clipped green in the pair of maroon Uggs he'd taken to wearing when he'd exited the world. He flinched at the sound of a cricket in the grass, and nearly collapsed at the mating call of a male frog in the water hazard. He shouldn't have been afraid. This was what he had wanted, what he had planned, and now at the end of his journey he felt the rapid heartbeat of fear and wondered if he could find the courage to sustain him.

There was a flutter of leaves in the carefully tended woodland surrounding the green. Wind, or man? He froze close to the flag and heard the pounding of his own heart. There was a breeze, and it whispered terror in the leaves, making his eyes sharpen against the moonlight. It was too soon.

Gino wasn't reclining in his seat anymore, but sitting bolt upright, frantically trying to program the Caddie's GPS to find an alternate route that wasn't closed for construction. Despite the air conditioning, sweat was beading on his forehead. The ninety-mile-an-hour whiz on the freeway had ended abruptly when they'd taken the Hiawatha exit. The highway was down to one lane, jammed with the vomit of cars from the Twins game and the detritus of construction that was so constant and ongoing that Minnesotans called it a season.

'Damnit!' Magozzi stood on the brakes and screeched to a halt about a millimeter away from the big bumper of the SUV in front of them. Smith felt the shoulder belt bite into his flesh and his heart jump to his throat. The bubble light strobed ineffectively, and there was no way to get around the congestion without taking out a few orange-and-white barrels. 'How much time, Gino?'

'Fifteen minutes, and there's goddamn construction all the way down Hiawatha. Shit, we're never going to make it. Next street, take a right, it switches back to . . .'

Magozzi veered the wheel hard to the right and stomped on the accelerator, pushing the Caddie down the shoulder, and through an obstacle course of cones and barrels, some of which died for the cause.

'Jesus, Leo! Half the pavement is gone . . .'

There was a sickening crunch as the Caddie bottomed out on a broken piece of pavement. Smith saw sparks fly out from the undercarriage like a swarm of fireflies, but Magozzi kept pushing.

'Time?'

Gino checked the Caddie's digital readout. God, he loved this car. 'Thirteen minutes.' He glanced to his right and saw the light-rail train keeping pace with them, heading for their intersection. 'You gotta beat that train to the intersection, Leo. If we stop, it's all over.'

'How fast do they go?'

'I don't know. Thirty, thirty-five. You're going thirty-six, Leo. That's cutting it a little close.'

'Yeah, well, I've got a thousand red taillights in front of me, and this fucking Cadillac is not a monster truck, so make a suggestion.'

Gino exhaled sharply.

*

Wild Jim scurried from the eighteenth green into the woodland border and found the tree he had selected before. It was old and broad, with soft bark to cradle an old man's rickety back. He sat down with his legs splayed and leaned against it, trying to make his heart slow down because, goddamn, it was beating so hard anyone could hear it. He laid the rifle with its night scope across his knee, emptied the chamber, and waited.

He'd told the man to come at ten; he'd told Magozzi to come ten minutes later. The timing was critical. Please, God, let this happen the way it should.

'Time, Gino!'

'Eight minutes! You gotta beat that train!'

The funny thing was that John Smith, sitting in the backseat of a stupid drug dealer's car racing a light rail to an intersection, was utterly ambivalent. Truly, this was so unexpected, and yet such a predictable outcome to the boring, faintly amusing, life he had lived. There would be a nicely framed picture of him on the wall in D.C., right next to one of the agent who had risked his life to save the child of a domestic terrorist last year, caught in the crossfire of justice. The man had been shot twenty-seven times in the act of saving a child. John, on the other hand, would die with a lamb kabob in his belly and the memory of a half-naked dancer in his brain, cut down by a light rail that could barely exceed the speed limit. Not exactly the heroic death he had envisioned. Still, he was afraid, because Magozzi had jerked the Caddie into the shallow ditch between the street and the tracks, was dodging poles and culverts and God knew what else, pushing the big car to a speed slightly faster than the train, but not fast enough. Even John could see that, because the intersection was just ahead, the wooden arms were coming down while the lights flashed and a bell clanged, and everything seemed to be going so fast, until suddenly, it slowed down.

I told you, John. I don't want you here for this.

Where else would I be? This is where I live.

And then he walked across the white hospital room to the white hospital bed and looked at the ever-so-white face of the first, and perhaps the last, woman he would ever love in such a way. The infinitesimal diamond was on her finger, clinging loosely to what little flesh was left, because the disease had been hungry. He had been twenty-nine, she had been twenty-seven on that day.

She managed a smile as he approached her bed, the first he had seen in many days.

That's funny, John.

What is?

Everything just slowed down, like in the movies. I like that. It gives you time to see things.

It was like that now as the Cadillac bumped over this and that as it raced the train in that grassy ditch so close to the tracks, because if he looked to the left, he could see the cars on the street next to them, the curious, startled eyes of the passengers in the cars. He saw a child with a circle for a mouth, and a woman whose mascara was running with tears, and then the car soared up and went airborne over the hillock that connected it to the intersection, and someone pushed fast-forward.

John felt the Cadillac bottom out on the tar, saw sparks and splinters from the crossing arms peck like demented crows at the windshield, and then Gino was bouncing up and down in his seat, pounding the dash with his fists, shouting, 'Fucking A, Leo! Fucking A! You beat the goddamned train!'

And then they were on a two-lane side street with lovely homes on either side, and John took a breath and watched the pretty houses slide by like a newlywed looking at real estate, and the world was very, very quiet.

Chapter Forty-one

'Okay. This is the way it's going to go down,' Magozzi said. The windows on the Caddie were closed, but still he whispered, as if there were ears in the parking lot near the eighteenth green, next to the polished SUV that Wild Jim had put there like a signpost. On the far side of the lot, behind the clubhouse and out of sight, they'd already checked out a low-slung Mercedes. They'd felt warmth still rising from the hood, careful not to touch the car itself. You never could tell what kind of alarm system these foreign models had as add-ons. 'Whoever this guy is, he's stalking Wild Jim. Obviously he's already on site, maybe checking the perimeter for people like us, maybe just waiting for a clean shot. If the judge walks into that, he's dead. If he's smart, and I think he is, he got here long before the meet he set up, and he's the one who's going to bring this bastard down.'

'So you're assuming they're both armed?' John was dismayed.

'The judge is always armed,' Gino said. 'But as far as we know, he's never shot anybody. He spent his whole career working for the law, not against it. I wouldn't put it past him to try to arrest the guy, though. I think he's trying to go out as a hero.'

Aren't we all, John thought, depressed by how small the 9mm looked in his hand.

Magozzi nodded at John's weapon. 'If we see anything, especially firepower, take a long breath before you pull the trigger. Make sure you home in on the bad guy.'

Ten minutes after he'd settled beneath the tree, his bottle of bourbon tucked between his thighs, Wild Jim's hunter's eyes saw the dark, hunched figure crab-walking along the sheltered margin of the woods surrounding the eighteenth green. Adrenaline burned through his heart like battery acid and his limbs went numb. Or maybe he was having a heart attack, which would actually be a wonderfully ironic outcome to this whole mess.

He looked up at the moon and the sky and decided there was little point in pondering God, destiny, and fate at this point, because he didn't believe in any of them. But the old saying that there were no atheists in foxholes finally resonated with him on a fundamental level – when your life was truly hanging in the balance, you instinctively thought about the bigger picture, whether you believed in one or not.

The glowing dial of his watch face read 9:55. 'You're a little early,' he said quietly in the general direction of his stalker.

The figure froze, then straightened slightly. 'If you move, you're dead,' the man replied, equally quietly.

The judge caught a glimpse of gun metal gleaming in the moonlight. 'I'm not moving.'

'No joke, I'm going to circle around behind you and if I see even one little flinch, your brains are going to be fertilizing the eighteenth green. Let me see your hands.'

Jim rolled his eyes and raised his hands. This asshole was just full of it. 'I know you've got a gun, so stop wasting time playing black ops. This is a business transaction, so let's get it over with before Christmas.' He heard a grunt and a rustling in the trees behind, and then the man materialized in front of him, his gun poised for a shot.

He didn't remotely resemble the person Jim had been expecting, and he suspected the feeling was mutual, because the man's eyes kept drifting from his human target to the Winchester in his lap and the bottle of bourbon between his legs. 'How stupid are you? You arrange to meet a killer and you aren't even holding your gun.'

'As I said, you're a bit early. Besides, I couldn't manage the cork while I was holding my weapon. Care for a splash?' Jim uncorked the bottle and took a swig. 'It is, without question, the greatest fermented mash my rather experienced palate has ever known.'

The man leaned forward and stretched his arm, moving the gun closer to Jim's temple. 'I told you not to move, goddamnit.'

'Yes, you did, but only because you were at a disadvantage at the time, and walking blindly into an uncertain situation. But since I am currently in plain view, you know that my movements have nothing to do with firearms or murder and everything to do with enjoying an innocent sip of fine spirits.'

The man's gun dropped a few inches, which was a great relief. 'So. You saw me with the faggot in the wedding dress.'

'That's imprecise. I saw you *kill* the faggot in the wedding dress. And for that, I thank you very much. I'd been trying to kill him for over a year. He killed my son, you see.'

'Whatever. How'd you find out who I was?'

Judge Jim sighed. 'I followed you up to where you parked your car. You have a very nice car, by the way, spectacularly clean, which makes it so much easier to read the license plate. And if you have any connections with the DMV, as I do, a phone number is quite easy to come by. My only surprise was that you actually used your own car. That is the kind of oversight that solves crimes, you know. So why did you come tonight?'

'Because you're fucking blackmailing me.'

Jim smiled. 'No, let's be perfectly honest. A man like yourself wouldn't pay off a blackmailer. You came here to kill me, which is sensible, and, ironically, my goal as well.'

The man grunted. 'Well, damn. That kind of takes all the fun out of it.'

'I'm sure it does, but the truth is you have no choice. I saw you murder a man. The question is, why haven't you killed me already? I know you have it in you.'

'Yes, I do. But I like to play with my food.' He smiled then, and Jim knew he was looking straight into the eyes of a sociopath. He'd seen them plenty of times before from the bench, and it chilled his blood and reversed all the heat the adrenaline had put into him earlier.

'So, did you kill them all?'

The man gave Jim a blank stare. 'What are you talking about?'

Jim settled back and drank some more bourbon while he contemplated the answer to that question. He took one more big swig before he answered. 'Did you kill all of the others on the list?'

'Who the hell *are* you, old man?'

'You know me as Hole in One.'

The man froze for a few moments, then started to chuckle, which eventually developed into a full-blown laugh. 'Are you kidding me? Are you KIDDING? You're Hole in One? From the chat room?'

'And you are Killer, right? That's your handle.'

Killer was having trouble believing what he was seeing and hearing. 'You put up the hit list? A useless old drunk? Oh, man, this is rich. Wait until the guys hear about this.'

So there are others, Jim thought miserably. *What have I done?* His eyes flicked to the other side of the green and saw man shapes hunched over, darting close to the trees while Killer's attention was diverted. *About time, Magozzi and Gino,* he thought, and then realized he had to act quickly.

'This is getting rather tedious,' he said. 'Either shoot me now, or I'm – '

Killer's gun fired before Jim could finish the sentence, but, truly, he was an appalling shot, at least in the dark. It was a miracle he'd ever managed to kill anyone.

'Idiot,' Jim muttered as he pulled the trigger on the .38 under his jacket. It made a dreadful mess of the man's knee, and that pleased Jim enormously. It was precisely what he had been aiming for. 'Come on over, Magozzi!' he called out, smiling a little as a howling Killer fell to one knee and tried to crawl away, his weapon forgotten on the grass behind him.

This is going to make a great movie, Jim thought, appreciating the cinematic perfection of moonlight on Killer's back as he crawled across the green in an absolutely senseless attempt at escape; the intensity in the faces of Magozzi and Gino as they rushed toward him; the rather frantic scramble of another man he didn't know racing to straddle the wounded villain, slapping on the cuffs while the eighteenth green's flag fluttered a little in the freshening breeze. He could almost hear the soundtrack.

He sighed happily, put down the .38, and popped the cork on the bourbon.

Magozzi stood over him, breathing hard, pale in the faint light of the moon, his facial features stretched taut.

'Good evening, Detectives. Perfect timing. Who's your friend?'

'Goddamnit, Judge, are you out of your fucking mind? What are you trying to do, commit suicide?' Gino screamed at him, punching numbers on his cell to call for a bus and backup.

Jim chuckled. 'I watched the man your friend is sitting on drown Alan Sommers in the river.'

The adrenaline rush leaked out of Magozzi's legs and put him on his knees. 'Bullshit. You were point-four-oh when they locked you up.'

'Point-four-oh when they locked me up the next morning. Not when I watched the murder, and not when I followed the killer to his car and memorized the plate number.'

Gino's mouth dropped open, then clicked shut when he dropped to a squat next to Jim and glared at him. It was surprising, really. Detective Rolseth had always seemed such a gentle sort to Jim, and yet in this moment he looked almost frightening.

'You old bastard,' he hissed. 'Are you telling me that all this time you knew who he was and didn't tell us?'

'I do apologize for deceiving you. Truly.'

'Well, big whoop, the man apologizes. What if he had killed somebody else the next day, or the next? What was all that crap about the law and justice being your life? And all the while you were giving us that load of bullshit in your condo, you were letting a known murderer run loose.'

Jim blinked rapidly, then closed his eyes. The sorry truth was he had never considered that. Too consistently drunk; too interminably focused on his own misery.

'This man is bleeding to death!' John called out as he wrapped his suitcoat sleeves around Killer's thigh in a crude tourniquet.

'Bus on the way!' Gino called back. 'I swear to God, Judge, you're going down hard for this one. I'll be the guy in the back of the room, applauding.'

'There were reasons . . .' he stumbled over his words.

'Don't bother, I've heard them all,' Gino's voice was shaking with contempt. 'Your son killed himself, you lost your job, you were abused as a child, whatever. Christ, I'm so sick of listening to excuses losers use for all the bad things they do.'

John ran over from the green and stopped, frowning down at Jim. 'How long for the ambulance?' he asked. 'That guy out there is really bleeding. Looks like the femoral artery got nicked. And this one doesn't look much better.'

'He's fine,' Gino snapped, pushing to his feet. 'Just contemplating his future in a state prison.'

Jim took a shallow breath. He wasn't feeling so good

anymore. 'Condo key in my pants pocket,' he whispered to Magozzi. 'Tape recorder in the jacket. I really wanted to do the right thing. I thought you could do something just a little wrong to make a lot of things right. But that was a misstep.'

'Slippery slope,' John murmured.

Jim looked up at the stranger. 'Yes. That's it precisely. I can't fix it. But tonight I tried. You've got your River Bride killer, and maybe a lot more.'

'Yeah, right,' Gino snorted. 'We've got nothing on this guy except the word of a drunk who just shot him. What the hell are we supposed to do with that?'

Jim smiled a little, and Magozzi thought the old man was just about done in, because the color was going out of his face. 'You have a little more than that,' Jim told Gino, pulling aside his sportcoat and showing the wet, soggy evidence of his reddened shirt. 'There's a bullet in this pathetic alcohol-saturated belly that will match the weapon that man dropped. Murder One, if dreams come true.'

'Jesus,' Magozzi whispered, ripping off his own jacket, wadding it up, pressing it against the flood of life that was seeping out of Wild Jim onto the grass around him.

Chapter Forty-two

Magozzi, Gino, and John Smith sat in the Cadillac in the golf course lot, watching the ambulances pull away. Siren and lights on one, the other dark and ominous.

Magozzi gave the quiet a minute and then turned to Gino. 'You okay?'

'Yeah. I'm okay.'

'Is that a lie?'

'I need to go home, Leo.'

'Then that's where you'll go. How about you, John?'

'Back to Harley Davidson's, please. I have to pick up the rental car to take to the airport tomorrow.'

Magozzi turned the key and pulled out of the lot.

John moved up to the front seat after they'd dropped off Gino and watched him walk up his front walk. Angela was out there in some kind of fuzzy pink bathrobe that sparkled in the porch light, opening her arms for Gino and leading him into the house.

'Nice,' John said.

'He's the luckiest man on the planet.'

'You ever think of going that route?'

'What? Marriage? Kids that puke all over you in the middle of the night? Christ, yes. I think of that all the time.'

John smiled and nodded. When he got into his rental he pulled out his cell and punched in a number. 'Harley. This is John. Could you stand some company?'

*

Magozzi called Grace from Judge Jim's condo. 'I've got a computer for you.'

'And I've got chicken piccata for you.'

He took a breath and let everything go when he heard her voice. He needed to be there. He needed someone waiting in a silly pink robe under a porch light. 'You heard about what went down tonight?'

'You made the news, Magozzi.'

'Do you have a pink robe?'

'Black.'

'That'll work.'

It took John two full glasses of wine and a large pizza to summarize the night's events for Harley. By the time he'd finished, the warmth of the burgundy had seeped into every cell, wrapping him in a cozy, fuzzy cocoon of contentment, and he wondered if he'd ever be able to extricate himself from the down-filled cushion of his chair.

Harley raised his glass. 'Well, here's to you, Special Agent John Smith, and your crazy, goddamned night. You got another one.'

'But not all of them. We're never going to catch the other murderers, and even if we do, another two will pop up for every one we put away.'

Harley shrugged. 'Oh, I don't know. Somebody somewhere will decide to go a little deeper into the dark side, and they'll find a way to slide into these foreign servers and anonymous networks all the dirtbags use. Then you'd be able to monitor the sites and servers undetected, and probably bust a whole lot of all kinds of cyber criminals, including our killers.'

'That's illegal. There are international agreements prohibiting it.'

Harley raised one bushy brow. 'Are there international agreements against spying? Because that's all this would be; just a simple matter of planting a little James Bond spy worm. He doesn't hurt anybody, he doesn't mess with the systems, he just keeps an eye on things and reports back. Now, if memory serves, you guys do quite a bit of spying yourselves.'

John was shaking his head. 'There is no way any government agency could be complicit in such an operation. We are signators to those agreements.'

Harley shrugged. 'Oh, hell, I know that. I'm just saying someday *somebody's* going to do it. And since you guys signed that silly agreement about not busting into foreign servers and anonymous networks, you're never going to be able to figure out who.'

John just stared at him, glass frozen on its way to his half-open mouth.

Harley smiled and reached into the humidor on his side table. 'I want you to know I make good on my promises. You got the belly dancers, and now you get the cigar.'

Smith ran the cigar under his nose like he saw people do in the movies and smelled chocolate.

'That's the real deal, Smith. Havana's finest. Enjoy.'

They smoked in comfortable silence for a few minutes, sipping burgundy and watching gray smoke curl up toward the pressed-tin ceiling of the study.

'You know, John, I still think this whole case is a damn fine way to close out a career. You know what's gonna happen now, don't you?' he slurred a little. 'You're gonna become an adrenaline junkie and start doing stupid stuff like base jumping and mountain climbing and deep sea scuba diving.'

'After tonight, I don't think I have any adrenaline left.'

'You can make more.'

Chapter Forty-three

Magozzi woke up the next morning in Grace's bed with Grace licking his face. She had a really big tongue. And it smelled like kibble.

He shoved Charlie the dog down into the crook of his arm and fell asleep again, trying to remember the details of what happened last night. He'd pulled up in front of Grace's fortress house and turned off the car. She was sitting on the front steps under the porch light in a fuzzy black robe, elbows on her knees, chin in her hands like a little girl. So daring, so brave, as if there weren't people in her quiet neighborhood who would jump out and kill her.

She fed him chicken piccata, whatever the hell that was, gave him a glass of wine, then tucked him into the big bed upstairs and held him until he fell asleep.

'Magozzi.' He heard her voice in his right ear, felt the movement of her breath stirring his hair. 'Ten minutes till breakfast.'

She had all his favorites at the kitchen table: orange juice, yogurt, and bran cereal. 'Gee, Grace, you shouldn't have.'

She made a cute little snorting sound. 'Eat it. It's good for you. Besides, I haven't been home long enough to shop this week. While you're eating, you can listen to the judge's tape.'

He eyed the little recorder she'd placed on the table

between them. 'I don't think I can take any of Wild Jim's monologues on an empty stomach.'

'He recorded his conversation with the murderer last night.'

By the time the tape clicked off, Magozzi had eaten half the yogurt, which was disgusting, two bites of bran cereal, which looked like bunny turds and probably tasted like them, and was gulping juice to wash it all down. 'Half of that tape is drunken bullshit. Alan Sommers didn't kill his son. His son committed suicide, probably because he knew his father better than we did and couldn't stand him.'

Grace studied him for a moment. 'Alan Sommers gave the judge's son the HIV virus. Jessie shot himself when he developed full-blown AIDS.'

Magozzi closed his eyes.

'Sommers was apparently golden on the meds, but seven other of his partners died, both before and after he passed on his little present to Jessie. The judge thought of him as a mass murderer, of sorts; one that couldn't be prosecuted.'

'Where are you getting this stuff?'

'He wrote a daily journal on his computer. He wasn't that bad a man, Magozzi. He sat down on the riverbank with his gun every night for a year, trying to kill Alan Sommers, but he couldn't make himself do it.'

Magozzi scraped back his chair and headed for the coffeemaker. 'So he put Alan on a hit list and had someone else do his dirty work. It's still murder. Don't fall for his poor-me crap, Grace. And don't forget there were six other people on that list.'

Grace held out her mug to give him something to do. 'He had no idea there were real killers on that site. He thought they were a bunch of twisted, juvenile blowhards pretending they were tough guys. In a way, he was making fun of them, holding up a mirror to what losers they were. So he taunted them with a list of people that he'd hated for years because they got light or no sentences for absolutely horrible crimes. He'd been either the prosecutor or the sitting judge on every case, and it almost killed him when the system he believed in failed.'

'Still murder,' Magozzi grumbled, refusing to look at her for almost a full second.

'It wasn't a hit list, Magozzi. It was a hate list posted by a despairing, ranting drunk.'

'We should have found that connection in the victim files.'

'Did you read the trial transcripts?'

'Trial transcripts are at the end of the files, and they're hundreds of pages. The box thing interrupted us before we got that far. We should have started with them. I should have known that, goddamnit.'

Grace started clearing the table. 'It wouldn't have made any difference, Magozzi. The murders had all happened by then.'

'Not quite.'

She stopped in mid-stride on her way to the sink, holding his cereal bowl in her hand. 'You liked him,' she said without turning around.

'No. I did not. What I liked was that cereal. Bring it back.'

Grace set the bowl in the sink and then did the weirdest thing. She walked over and bent to kiss his cheek. No passion, no pity, just a connection. It shouldn't have made Magozzi feel better, but it did. 'I have something to tell you, Magozzi.'

He stood on the front stoop of Grace's house, hands shoved in his pants pockets, thinking how strange it was that he wasn't reacting. Funny. You wait and wait for things to change; for people to change. You don't work at it, mind you; you just wish and wait and only tell yourself in secret that it will never happen. And then suddenly, right out of the blue, it does.

How about that.

Chapter Forty-four

John was standing in the doorway of the Big Boy's Room, thinking of what a comedown his own bedroom and tiny bathroom in D.C. were going to be tonight.

He could hear the soft murmur of voices and went downstairs after a final, longing look at the bedroom.

When he exited the elevator, Annie, Grace, and Roadrunner were standing in the foyer next to Harley.

Annie batted her eyelashes at him – he was certain of it this time around – and in her sweet sugary drawl bid him good morning. She was wearing a sunny yellow suit with an elaborate, veiled hat, like the kind women wore to the Kentucky Derby. In her hand she had a beautifully wrapped gift dressed up with a green satin ribbon.

'Good morning, everybody. What a wonderful surprise to see you all again.'

Roadrunner was grinning. 'We wouldn't let you go without a send-off, John.' He nudged Annie like an excited kid. 'Give it to him.'

Annie extended the gift. 'This is from all of us. And please don't say something stupid like "You shouldn't have" or I'll have to slap you silly.'

Smith cocked a brow at her. 'You shouldn't have.'

Harley laughed. 'You're getting a funny bone, Smith. Good for you.'

'Open it up, John,' Grace said with a smile.

He took his time unwrapping it, as if that would somehow delay his plane and his imminent departure.

'Jesus, John, you must be a nightmare on Christmas morning,' Harley gave him a good-natured needle. 'You're going to miss your flight if you don't kick it into gear.'

He chuckled and pulled the lid off the box. Inside was a stack of printed pages and a tiny cassette.

'Those are from Magozzi and Gino,' Grace told him. 'That's a copy of the judge's tape from the golf course, and all the entries from his computer journal.'

John smiled. 'Sharing information,' he murmured.

'That was the deal.'

'And what's this?' He pulled a single sheet of paper from the bottom of the box. John read a short list of names he didn't recognize.

'Oh, nothing much, really,' Annie said. 'Just the names of your other murderers, is all.'

John slid his eyes to look at Harley, who was rocking back on his heels, hands shoved deep in his pockets, like a little boy hiding frogs. 'Where did you get this, Harley?' he asked quietly.

The hands came out of the pockets and opened, frogless. 'It was the damnedest thing. We got an anonymous tip this morning, took a few minutes to check out the names, and it looks like it might be the real thing. Thought you might like to take them back to D.C. and follow up.'

'An anonymous tip.'

'That's right. An e-mail right out of the blue.'

'I suppose it was untraceable.'

'It was.'

Roadrunner said, 'Kind of a cool thing to hand over to your bosses if it turns out legit, huh?'

John looked from one face to another. No one was smiling. 'Very cool,' he said finally. 'Very cool indeed.'

Epilogue

It seemed that John Smith had fallen just a little bit short of every goal he'd ever set for himself. As a kid, he'd wanted to be a superhero with a cape; instead, he'd ended up a Fed with a blue suit. In college he'd wanted desperately to be one of those glorious golden young men who raced in the America's Cup and called out magical phrases like 'Hoist the mains'll!' and 'Man the helm!' or some such thing.

Surprisingly, he'd turned out to be a natural sailor, but never found a crew that would take him on because he couldn't remember all those pesky nautical terms. They'd always seemed a little silly to button-down John. Like 'hard a'starboard.' Who thought up such things? Why not just say 'Turn right'? Everybody knew what that meant. Which was, of course, the whole point. Every exclusive club had to have its own parlance.

How strange, then, that after so many near-misses, well into the second half of his time on earth, he was learning to excel at life – the one thing he'd never really aspired to.

Once a year for all the years he'd been with the Bureau, he'd taken the boat south to the Keys; sometimes all the way to the Caribbean. For two weeks he'd dance the boat through waters that had too many colors to claim one, watched sun and moon and ocean mingle like a trio of lovers, and felt his mind slow down and finally bob and drift like a piece of flotsam on the swells. He'd stop at any port where he liked to mingle with strange and interesting people who didn't know him, which gave him license to laugh and joke and be someone else. He ate bar food on rickety piers while his bare feet swung over the water, and sometimes drank with women whose names he couldn't remember. Two weeks a year. Less than eight percent of his adult life.

He closed his eyes and smelled salt, heard the ticking of the rigging against the mast and the ruffle of heavy cloth in the breeze, and then felt the wind in his hair for the first time in years. He hadn't had it cut for three weeks now, an all-time record. Maybe he'd let it grow long like Harley's and wear it in a ponytail, just another gray-haired man reverting to the wild.

He opened his eyes when he heard the familiar clicking up the three steps from the galley, then the soft padding of bare feet. He watched as Grace and Charlie crossed the teak deck to the bow. They both liked to stand up there where the wind was always strongest, whipping Grace's hair back, making her look like one of those figureheads the Vikings used to put on the prows of their ships. Charlie stood with his head poked through the rails, the wind blowing his tongue sideways out of his mouth.

John liked watching them.

P. J. TRACY

WANT TO PLAY?

Hide and Seek. And Kill.

Minneapolis, a brutally cold autumn. And a killer is at work. Two bodies are found, two slayings that the police treat as unrelated. But games-creator Grace MacBride knows different. The murders are exact copies of those in a game she is designing – one that already has hundreds of eager players. As the copycat killings mount up, Grace knows that she is both suspect and potential victim. And with the serial killers getting closer, she is drawn into a murderous game of cat and mouse …

Want to play?

'A thrilling page-turner with a nail-biting finish' *Sunday Telegraph*

'A fast-paced gripping read with thrills and devilish twists' *Guardian*

'A powerful thriller and an ingenious plot' *Observer Review*

P. J. TRACY

LIVE BAIT

Do you know evil when you see it?

Springtime in Minneapolis and with the thaw comes murder: an elderly man executed with a gunshot to the head and another literally frightened to death. But when Detective Magozzi calls on the analytical skills of Grace MacBride, it appears not only that the killings might be connected but also that the victims might be something other than they first seemed. As more deaths follow, Magozzi and Grace must quickly discover what secrets these men shared – and with whom – if they are to bait their trap and catch their killer...

'Impressive ... P. J. Tracy is about to become a household name'
Daily Mirror

'A winner. Don't forget to take it on holiday' *Time Out*

'A tense edge-of-your-seat thriller' *OK!*

'Brilliant ... *Live Bait* proves that the phenomenal *Want to Play?* was no fluke' *Amazon*

P. J. TRACY

DEAD RUN

If you go down to the woods today …

It should have been a simple journey – a drive from Minneapolis to Green Bay, Wisconsin. But a couple of unplanned detours lead Grace MacBride, Annie Belinsky and police deputy Sharon Mueller deep into the northern woods, far from civilization and a mobile phone signal. Then their car breaks down.

The nervous search for a landline and a mechanic leads the women to Four Corners, a sleepy crossroads town. And a place they soon wish they'd never stumbled upon.

Because something terrible happened in Four Corners.

Grace, her senses honed by a lifetime of paranoia, sees sinister stories in details that even Sharon misses. But it's Grace's instincts that might save the women's lives when they become witnesses to a chilling scene – and party to terrifying knowledge that they might never be allowed to leave with …

'A writer with all the credentials to sit firmly in the upper echelons of top crime novelists' *Amazon*

He just wanted a decent book to read ...

Not too much to ask, is it? It was in 1935 when Allen Lane, Managing Director of Bodley Head Publishers, stood on a platform at Exeter railway station looking for something good to read on his journey back to London. His choice was limited to popular magazines and poor-quality paperbacks – the same choice faced every day by the vast majority of readers, few of whom could afford hardbacks. Lane's disappointment and subsequent anger at the range of books generally available led him to found a company – and change the world.

'We believed in the existence in this country of a vast reading public for intelligent books at a low price, and staked everything on it'
Sir Allen Lane, 1902–1970, founder of Penguin Books

The quality paperback had arrived – and not just in bookshops. Lane was adamant that his Penguins should appear in chain stores and tobacconists, and should cost no more than a packet of cigarettes.

Reading habits (and cigarette prices) have changed since 1935, but Penguin still believes in publishing the best books for everybody to enjoy. We still believe that good design costs no more than bad design, and we still believe that quality books published passionately and responsibly make the world a better place.

So wherever you see the little bird – whether it's on a piece of prize-winning literary fiction or a celebrity autobiography, political tour de force or historical masterpiece, a serial-killer thriller, reference book, world classic or a piece of pure escapism – you can bet that it represents the very best that the genre has to offer.

Whatever you like to read – trust Penguin.